Ignighted

A Novel By
Bernard Bayede

ISBN: 978-0-620-91495-6

Tel: 076 636 7999

Email: khatidexxii@gmail.com

Produced and Printed by: Amazon KDP

Thanks to my family for supporting my dream,

always.

And thanks to Juliet for sharing it.

PREFACE

Max knew that sound anywhere. It was the sound of police sirens and they were getting louder by the second. On instinct alone, Max pressed down on the throttle. He'd been here before only so many times except this time he wasn't in a car... he was in a XF race car.

As Max's heart rate increased, he began to sweat inside his helmet. The sirens were getting closer but for the life of him his thoughts weren't on the Metro cops at all. Despite the clear and present danger, all Max could wonder was whether Shade was feeling the same way as him. Ahead of him, the *Tumbler* raced on, showing no signs of even noticing the sirens. It was almost easy to forget that they were in a race to decide their fate.

CHAPTER ONE
THE OTHER ISLAND

The city of Brisbane: known to its residents as a busy little town by day and quiet as the dead by night. Well at least it normally was. As Maximillian McKay sat on his motorcycle awaiting the green light, he couldn't help but smile. He looked to his left and eyed his opponent. When his opponent's eyes met his, Max closed his helmet visor. Max couldn't help but frown a little. He'd always seen them do that in the movies and they always made it look so badass – like the helmet equivalent of cocking a gun. In real life – not so much.

As Max continued to wait for the light, his phone rang. He clicked the button on his earphones which were already in his ears, inside his helmet to answer the call, not bothering to look at the caller I.D. "Yeah, it's Max."

"Is that how you answer your phone now? *Yeah, it's Max?* Well *Max*, it's your father speaking."

Max rolled his eyes. He knew why his father was calling him. Not a day went past without his father scolding him about one thing or the other. Max had become so numb to it all that he didn't even bother taking things seriously with him anymore. "Hey Dad, what's up."

"Well I'll tell you what's up. It's—" Max's father was cut off by Max's opponent revving his motorcycle. "What's that noise?"

"Oh, it's just my friend here. No big deal. Let me just tell him to keep it down." Max turned to his opponent. "Hey pal, could you just keep it down. I'm talking to my father." His opponent gave him the most confused of looks. Max realized that he didn't have a phone to signal that he was on a call. "On the phone. Yeah, I'm like, talking to my father so if you don't mind." His opponent gave him a middle finger. "So, I'll take that as a no. Yeah Dad, he's saying no. No, he's not gonna turn it down."

"Maximillian, so help me God. You better n—"

"Dad! Don't take the Lord's name in vain."

"Stop playing the fool with me. You better not be street racing, or this will be the end of you."

"What!?" said Max feigning his best 'shocked' tone. "Me street racing!? C'mon Dad."

"I'm serious."

"IT'S ALMOST GREEN, YOU ABORIGINAL ASSHOLE!"

Max glared at his opponent, who clearly wanted to face someone serious about what he was doing. Luckily for him, he managed to pick a sore point for Max. "Okay Dad, I have to go. This guy here is being a prick."

"Don't you DARE hang up on me!"

Max playfully gritted his teeth. "Okay, how about I put you on hold then. Okay, talk soon Dad."

"MAXIMILLIAN XOLANI MCKAY, don't you—"
As much as Max enjoyed hearing his last name

pronounced correctly as '*Ma-Kai*', he didn't have time for his father's scolding.

Having just put his father on hold, Max turned to his opponent. "Okay look pal, I think it's important that you know that I'm not aboriginal, okay. I'm not even Australian. I'm actually South African. I'm—" But before Max could finish giving the man his family ancestry, the light turned green and he was off. Max rolled his eyes. "Rude." He said before gunning his engine and taking off after him.

His take-off had left the few spectators who had been looking at him as curiously (but perhaps not as angrily) as his opponent during his phone call, in a puff of smoke from the screeching tyres. He was sure that, like his opponent, they thought he was a joke. After all, what kind of guy takes a phone call a minute before he's about to compete in a drag race? Unknown to all them, these were just the conditions that Max liked to race in: low expectations of winning and with an opponent who underestimated him.

His opponent didn't know anything about him (except that he liked to bet big) what with him being from Redcliffe and Max being from Brisbane City. Both locations had small racing scenes – so small in fact that it had brought Max here for a race. It had taken little convincing to get Redcliffe's best biker to race him.

The race itself was across Houghton Highway which ran between Redcliffe and Brisbane. The road was a two and a half kilometre straight shot which made sense with it being a bridge. Houghton Highway was known for its rush hour traffic which left drivers frustrated for hours on end. The same couldn't be said for the middle of the night which was when they had decided to race.

Max had noticed that his opponent was riding a Honda CBR900. It was definitely a magnificent motorcycle. Max on the other hand was riding a Honda Fireblade. Max knew that the Fireblade was the faster of the two assuming both bikes were still functioning on their factory parts. And while Max was sure his opponent hadn't tuned a damn thing on his bike, Max had. And Max had gone all out in an effort to make sure that his bike was less a motorcycle and more a rocket on two wheels.

So, when Max started closing the 20-metre gap he'd given the guy with his three second head start, he wasn't surprized at all. At 200 kilometres per hour, with lines blurring and only a rushing sound filling his ears, Max began to overtake his opponent. And just over a minute after the race had started, Max crossed the finish line in Brisbane screeching to a halt 100 metres away.

Max gave his opponent a smug look as he opened his visor – which definitely felt more badass now. And just like that he was two hundred dollars richer. But before he could collect his hard-earned cash, Max heard a very familiar sound: the sound of sirens. Max took a moment to look in the direction of the police who were definitely heading in their direction before turning back to his opponent who was starting to drive away.

"Hey, hey, hey. The money."

"Later aboriginal."

Max rolled not just his eyes but his whole head before hanging it at a loss. "I told you," he said mostly to himself, "I'm South African." With no more time to quip, Max gunned his engine and sped off. Using quick turns and his natural sense of direction, Max made quick work of losing sight of the police. But he knew better than to think that just because they couldn't see him that it was over.

As Max made his way through downtown Brisbane, swerving and dodging traffic at will, he realized that the sirens had all but disappeared. Just as Max smiled at his good fortune, ahead of him was a roadblock. Max surveyed his surroundings quickly and noticed a narrow wall that divided the street from the river to his right. Max increased his speed before lifting the bike off its wheels like it was a BMX and proceeded to drive atop the half a metre wall. He drove right past the roadblock and continued on his way.

*

An hour later, Max pulled into the driveway of his home and parked the motorbike under the carport. He took off his helmet finally letting loose his coily afro of black hair held neatly in place with a black band that did little to disguise itself as an alice band. As he unzipped his leather jacket, it hadn't occurred to him until just now that he had left his father on hold! As he fished out his phone, Max walked through the kitchen door only to find his father waiting for him.

"Hello Maximillian."

"Dad," said Max, acting surprized to find him up. "I was just about to call you," he said sarcastically.

"Oh? Before or after you took me off hold?" Max made a face. "Maximillian, I've had enough of you."

"Okay. What's that supposed to mean?"

"It means that it's time for a change." Max realized that a mic was about to be dropped. And true to Max's instinct, a uniformed police officer came into the room from the sitting room. "Consider this your reckoning for all your reckless behaviour."

"You're having me arrested?" Max decided to play dumb. "For what exactly?"

"Illegal drag racing for one thing," said the police officer.

"You can never prove that."

"Your father is willing to testify."

For once, Max was genuinely shocked. "You'd do that."

"It's a parent's duty to discipline their child."

Max thought for a moment and quickly reverted to his playful attitude. "That's all well and good but you forget there's two of you. What exactly would Ma think of you sending me to prison?" Max's heart sank when his father smiled. Max knew he'd somehow lost. He just didn't know how.

"I'm glad you brought that up because you're right. There are two of us which brings us to a choice, for you, Maximillian. You can stay here, under my supervision but serve whatever penance or punishment or whatever the law has in store for you. Or you can go to live with your mother, start with a blank slate."

Max studied his father's face to try and figure out if he was serious. When he saw that he was, he looked at the officer. "Can he," started Max unsure of himself, "is that a thing? Can you guys just decide when the law applies and when it doesn't?"

The officer took a breath before answering. "Well we're leaning into the lawyer's side of the law and order of things but we'd be making use of a technicality: we don't have the jurisdiction to prosecute you from South Africa especially when you were born there and have more rights as a citizen in that country than in ours."

Max thought that through. "So, you're basically deporting me."

"Well it's more of an exile," said the officer.

"Actually, I prefer the term deportation," added Max's father, coldly. "Albeit a voluntary one. Because remember, you can always choose to stay here." He looked at the officer as if to agree with him on his point. "I'm sure if you went with the officer willingly; confessed to your crimes; then you wouldn't be looking at actual jail time."

"He's right. You might only get community service."

Max stiffened his jaw. He knew that community service – while it looked like a cake walk to juvenile delinquents – was actually a trap that often did nothing for rehabilitation and actually did more to ensure they became the criminals they were convicted of being. No, this was a trick. There wasn't a choice here. It wasn't even an ultimatum. The decision had been made. The only thing left for him to do was agree to it.

Max sighed. "So, when does this banishment take place?"

*

Twenty-four hours later, Max was on a plane. "Here I come, South Africa."

CHAPTER TWO
HOMETOWN

Despite having not been to South Africa since primary school, Max didn't feel at all out of place when he stepped off the plane. But perhaps that was because he wasn't on the mainland, where the other nine provinces were. Perhaps it was because he was on Azania Island: the 10th province of South Africa and the shining example of what the rest of the country could be if it got its act together.

Azania Island was located far off the coast of the Northern Cape and was known as the "paradise that knows no colour" due to how all four major ethnicities in South Africa got along without any prejudices, at least none based on skin colour. In fact, the place was so celebrated for this distinction that it was the one place in South Africa where you were guaranteed to find Caucasians who spoke vernacular languages like Zulu and Xhosa and talking in one's home language in front of someone's face didn't work at all.

This was one of the reasons that Max hated being called aboriginal and was very proud of being South African. People like him of mixed race were some of the most celebrated but not for their unique ethnicity or rich complexion but rather because of what they represented. They were seen as a metaphor for many of what being a rainbow nation was really about. And with a Caucasian father and proud Zulu mother, it didn't get any more Azanian than him.

As Max walked through the baggage area, not bothering with the carousel since he'd brought everything he wanted to bring via hand luggage, he thought about his family and his heritage. He'd always wondered how a Zulu woman ended up with Caucasian man who ended up living in Australia. While they'd been reluctant to tell him when he was younger, his mother relented when he was

12 years old and told him that their careers brought them together and their careers pulled them apart. Max barely understood what that meant at the time as both of them were university professors, but he eventually got it once he understood what tenure meant for his mother and how moving to Australia furthered his father's career.

Growing up, Max learnt to deal with the fact that while his parents loved each other, they valued their careers enough to live on different continents. And while Max hated that he had to travel between those continents to see each of them, he also loved the change in scenery every holiday, that was until high school. Like a classic rebellious teenager, Max decided to put up a fuss about the fact that *he* was the one that always had to go to South Africa while his mother never came to Australia to visit him. When this blatant emotional blackmail didn't work, Max decided to forgo the annual visits to Azania and his mother decided to let him be and "come when he's ready."

Max wasn't surprised to hear that answer as his mother had always been able to value efficiency over her emotions. So, he figured that it had barely registered with her that years were going to go past before she saw her son again. When Max walked into the Domestic Arrivals area, he came face to face with his mother's efficiency-over-emotions tip when he saw a Xhosa man holding a sign with his name on it.

Not losing a step, Max walked up to him. "Hey, I'm John McClane, you must be Argyle."

The man was completely lost. "No. Joseph," said the man, ever serious. "I'm Joseph Sibusiso Mdluli."

Max realized that the joke was completely lost on the man. In fact, all his jokes would be lost on this ever-serious man. "Hello Joseph Sibusiso Mdluli. I'm Max McKay," said Max pointing at his sign.

"Makhaya," said Joseph, immediately mispronouncing Max's name. He then shocked Max by smiling. "I'm your taxi driver."

Max's smile was more understated as even he couldn't find his next joke funny. "My mom couldn't send an uber?"

*

15

As it turned out, Joseph Sibusiso Mdluli wasn't an ever-serious man at all as when they got talking during the ride from the airport, the man couldn't stop. "So, you see why maxi taxis are still the way to go my friend. They are still very good and as I've been saying since this whole uber thing got started, all we have to do is get with the times, make a phone app like they did and we'll be back on top. But eish, they don't listen to me."

After introducing himself, Joseph Sibusiso had started calling Max 'Shombela', which Max recognised as a clan name for the Zulu surname, Makhaya. It was then that Max had to correct Joseph Sibusiso and tell him his name was pronounced '*Ma-Kai*' not '*Makhaya*'. Since then, Joseph Sibusiso had just referred to him as 'my friend' while Max got the feeling that this would be happening a lot.

"Well you don't have to convince me. I was born in a maxi taxi, you know," said Max.

Joseph Sibusiso's eyes popped open. "Really?"

"Well technically not. I think my mom was just in labour with me in the taxi on the way to the hospital. But apparently the driver was quite the hero getting her there. Hence my name."

"You were named after the driver!?"

"No, I was named after the taxi. Maxi Taxi, Max" he said pointing at himself. The driver's smile widened. "Yeah, my dad made a point of telling me that one time I was in trouble. You see, he loves calling me by my full name when he's scolding me, and I once told him that I hate the name which was when he told me I could have easily been named Maxi."

"Ya, Maxi does not sound like a very good name, my friend." They both laughed at the driver's joke. As they continued further and further away from Azania International Airport, Joseph Sibusiso regaled him on the interesting history of the Island Province. "I liked the old airport because it was so much closer to the city, but we had to move with the times, neh. Everything needs to be bigger and more complicated."

As they travelled past the rural outback and closer to the bustling city, Joseph Sibusiso told him about how despite Azania being very different to the mainland and ahead of its time, it hadn't kept poverty from existing. Luckily for the city, it had one of the most efficient municipalities in the country which was making great strides in providing homes for the less fortunate and that the unused land that stretched from where the airport was to where the city was located, was going to be used for them.

They eventually travelled past the township of Noresto which Joseph Sibusiso said had evolved so much that he didn't believe it should be called a township at all. "Egypsia is a township. Unlike Noresto, people still have to hustle there to make a living."

Egypsia was an iconic township on Azania as the place had become the trailer park centre of South Africa. It all started when the Department of Housing decided to be innovative in their approach to housing the less fortunate and decided that instead of RDP houses, they were going to provide caravans. The idea was the same: to get rid of all shacks. And unlike on the mainland where people had no qualms getting an RDP house and then having a shack regardless, the 'travel-trailer initiative' worked as there was no longer a single shack in Egypsia. Unfortunately, there was a resounding side-effect.

Where caravans were specifically used because of their versatility and their ability to be placed anywhere, the people of Egypsia decided to use them for *everything* including houses, saloons, taverns and tuckshops. And thus, the trailer park township was born. While extremely unique in South Africa, it was an epic backhand to the Department of Housing.

Egypsia was located about an hour's drive east of the city, according to Joseph Sibusiso, meaning that they weren't going to go near it. Instead, they continued on the M3 before clearing a hill to the sight of the city. "Welcome to the City of Ngelosi."

Max smiled just as he did when he first remembered seeing the city as a kid. Meaning "angel" in Zulu, the city lived up to its name as it could very well rival Los Angeles as a city. And while people from elsewhere did in fact compare it to the likes of Los Angeles, South Africans preferred to compare it favourably to their own beloved cities as they claimed it had the paradise-feel of Cape

Town; business-hub busyness of Johannesburg and the laidback nature of Durban.

Max remembered his father telling him that the city's call to fame was its freeways which ran around the city expertly guiding traffic in and out of the city in one of the most efficient ways he'd ever seen in his life. Apparently, the key to the island's success at handling traffic came from the main freeway on the island – the M3 – employing a right-hand traffic policy, completely unique in South Africa.

It was the only freeway in the country where people drove on the wrong side of the road. The genius was in the complex interchanges with the other freeways that brought the traffic back to the proper side of the road which somehow *reduced* congestion. In less complex freeway exits, one-way roads were used where onramps and offramps joined the M3 to normal streets.

Just as Max was appreciating being back in Ngelosi, Joseph Sibusiso took an offramp and headed west from the city. His mother didn't live in the city but rather in a suburb just on the outskirts. In fact, it was between the city and the beachfront making it one of the most lucrative suburbs on Azania if not South Africa.

As Joseph Sibusiso drove down the familiar dead-end street of Scully Road, Max watched as his mother's home came into view. It was built on a hill: a double storey house with a front door upstairs and a back-door downstairs and a steep driveway that ended behind the house. Max remembered being scared as a kid every time they drove down the driveway. He spared Joseph Sibusiso getting that same fear and told him to drop him off outside.

"Are you sure you'll be fine out here, my friend?"

Max gave him a smile as he stepped outside the taxi. "Don't worry about me. I'm home now." As Max looked at his home now, Joseph Sibusiso drove away leaving him to contemplate his future here. Max almost had to laugh at the fact that he was now living on a dead-end road because for Max, this definitely felt like the end of the road.

*

Max had found that the house was locked leaving him to wait on the veranda like a vagrant looking for a handout. All Max could think was that this was typical of his mother: organise a driver to pick him up from the airport only to not be home when he got there. As he waited, watching the sun go down, he wondered what it would be like staying here permanently.

For one thing, he'd be the new kid in school. *Great*, he thought. *The new Grade 11 student. Because there's nothing as embarrassing as starting out at a new school in the middle of high school.* Before Max could bum himself out anymore, he was momentarily blinded by a pair of headlights that then swiftly travelled down the length of the driveway as the familiar BMW X3 drove into its parking spot under the carport in the backyard. Max wondered if his mother even saw him.

A few minutes later, she came up the outer stairs towards the veranda where Max was now standing, bag in hand. Max heard her speaking to someone. "Yeah, he's here safe." His dad on the phone. "Yeah, I know Geoff. I know. I'll do the best I can. Good day to you too." She ended the call just as she reached Max.

"Good day?" said Max. "That's how you end a call with the former love of your life?" Max raised his eyebrows dramatically. "Wow."

"Oh, so are those the first words you're going to say to your mother?" said Nosipho McKay, opening the front door to her house.

Max shrugged. "Well technically my first words were 'good' and 'day' so," he said watching her jiggle the key.

Max's mother continued into the dark house, systematically turning off the alarm and on the lights. Max looked at his mother for the first time in 3 years. She hadn't changed a bit. With the natural chocolate complexion of a Zulu woman and a youthfulness about her, she didn't look at all like a woman in her forties. She was also thin which was a result of her not eating as much as she should – a constant complaint of her father's back in the day. And, as always, she was dressed smartly.

She continued. "First of all, what do *you* know about love?" Max had had his fair share of entanglements with girls, but he wasn't going to share that with her. Besides, she had a point: he'd never been in love with any of them. "And second of all, I'll have you know that your father was telling me to keep you out of trouble."

"Oh, I see," said Max sarcastically. "And did he tell you that he basically deported me?"

Max's mother took off her coat and heels before giving him a cold look. "Don't disrespect your father in this house; *his* house."

Max immediately shut up. But it wasn't the fact that this was technically his father's house, since he'd bought it way back when, that shut Max down. It was seeing his mother take off her high heel. Max had a lot of not-so-fond memories of getting smacked as a child and it was his mother who got the most mileage in the discipline section. Her and that damned high heel.

Max nodded. "Anything else I should know now, Ma, since I'm going to be here a while?" With no wasted motion, his mother went over where everything was in the house including the alarm code and where she kept the spare key. She told him that she'd enrolled him into Harbour High School and that he started tomorrow, 7a.m. sharp. She also told him that there would be NO STREET RACING whatsoever and that she expected him back home after school with the exception of extracurricular activities.

Max contemplated this rule as he made his way to his room – the only bedroom upstairs, with his mother's downstairs. The room looked the same as it did the last time he was here: bare of most childish things. No posters and no toys with the idea being that he didn't spend enough time there to play with them. It had only taken a minute to unpack his stuff. In fact, when his mother saw that he only had one bag, she gave him her Mr. Price card to go buy new clothes. Max had been amused by this: she knew that he hated Mr. Price and their lack of designer labels. But functional everyday clothing had its benefits.

As Max stripped down to his boxers and prepared to sleep, he continued thinking about his mother's rule about street racing. Was there even a street racing scene in

Ngelosi, let alone a motorbike racing scene? Max settled into bed with a pit in his stomach. He was now stuck in a city that was probably as boring as his mother's phone conversations.

Just when Max had resigned himself to his fate, he heard it: that very distinctive sound that he'd recognise no matter what continent he was on. It was distant, probably back on the freeway but Max knew exactly what it was. It was the sound of cars racing. Max smiled like all was suddenly right with the world.

CHAPTER THREE
MOAN-A-LISA

Lisa Visser had never liked how beautiful she was. It wasn't that she didn't appreciate being a blonde, blue-eyed bombshell even for a 16-year-old. She just didn't like the unwanted attention she got from boys. That was why she refrained from makeup and liked that the school rules prohibited girls from wearing any.

Unfortunately for Lisa, she sometimes needed those good looks to get her out of trouble as was the case when she and Angela arrived at school late and faced break time detention unless they could smile their way out of the prefect's little black book. Lucky for Lisa, Angela was very good at using her looks.

Angela Mabasa was polar opposite to Lisa in that while she was just as good looking, she relished her looks. Pushing the boundaries of the school uniform by wearing makeup whenever she could, Angela loved being a hottie. Lisa sometimes wondered why she bothered with the makeup. Her dark, earthy, Zulu complexion was flawless, and her full lips made her smile that much better. Her only weakness was also her one true joy: male companionship.

Angela had dated many boys in school all in the pursuit of some epic romance that only existed in the movies. She wanted to be swept off her feet. Instead, what she usually got was either a plate of Streetwise Two or two hours in a dark room watching a movie. It was all futile but that didn't stop Angela from trying.

When it came to her own looks though, sometimes Lisa wondered if she was lying to herself about not liking them. After all, one had to have good looks to complain about them. That was the reason she didn't voice her complaints to anyone, *ever*, least of all Angela. But that was also the reason that made her friendship with Angela interesting. With Angela being all about her looks and

Lisa not being about them at all, they seemed to fill out the spectrum of the friendship rather well, occupying both sides of it.

"Thank you, Lew," said Angela to the prefect, smiling her sexiest smile.

As they walked away, Lisa barely managing to hold her own smile, she leaned into Angela. "Lew?"

"Yeah, Lewellyn. Coolest prefect in school." She then looked over her shoulder as they continued towards the school. "And also, my James Bond fantasy."

Lisa rolled her eyes. While this was typical of Angela, Lisa couldn't help but get it: muscular, blonde *and* ruggedly handsome... he was definitely James Bond-like. "Your fantasy but not mine."

"I'm shocked."

"What's that supposed to mean?"

"Lisa, when's the last time you even kissed a boy?"

"You know I don't value myself based on that stuff."

29

"Oh, how noble." Lisa could feel the speech coming from a mile away. "Lisa, I know you like this whole tomboy thing you've got going on—"

"I am not a tomboy." Lisa used to be offended by hearing Angela saying this but after three years of high school, she'd gotten used to Angela's unfiltered nature. "Just because I like using my hands for a living and don't wear lipsticks, it doesn't mean I'm not into boys." Neither did being a tomboy but today wasn't the day to explain that to Angela.

"Okay, so who was the last boy you kissed?"

"That would be Dean."

"Your ex-boyfriend? The first team rugby player. Damn Lisa, that was a year ago." Angela looked at her best friend. "We need to get you a man." Lisa simply scoffed as they continued on to their first class.

*

Their first class was with Miss Riley. Miss Riley was their English teacher and librarian. She was young for a teacher but took pains to make herself look older by wearing the most-old fashioned spectacles ever. The class filled up quickly with everyone taking their usual seats even though there was no seating arrangement.

Lisa sat next to Angela as usual, listening to her go on with her plan to get Lisa a boyfriend. "I mean, there's so many to choose from." Indeed, there were many boys to choose from, but none that she was interested in. That was when *he* walked in. "And then there's *him*," said Angela in that voice she only used when she was flirting.

Lisa followed Angela's eyeline and saw him too. He'd walked in side by side with Thompson Mashaba. Lisa had never seen him before, so he was clearly a new transfer. As Lisa looked at him, she couldn't help but like what she saw: a 16-year-old boy who was tall for his age and clearly worked out but wasn't heavily muscled, with a caramel complexion. He was also quite handsome but what got Lisa's attention the most was his hair. The way his coily locks fell over his face, there was just something sexy about it. Lisa had to look away to avoid staring.

While looking away, Lisa managed to actually overhear useful information including the fact that his name was Max McKay – which Max had corrected to something that sounded oddly like Makhaya – and that he was from Australia. But judging from those beautiful locks, there was no way he was aboriginal. No, he was one of South Africa's own; Azania's own.

As the two boys took their seats, Angela noticed Lisa making a point not to look at them. The smirk on her face said it all. "It looks like someone has called dibs."

"Shut up, Angie," said Lisa, playfully.

When Angela continued to tease her, Miss Riley noticed and put a stop to it. "So, for your next assignment you'll be working in pairs. You," said Miss Riley pointing at Lisa, "will be working with Christina Langa. Maybe some separation from your friend will produce less gossip and more work."

"We weren't gossiping, ma'am." While Angela rebelled against Miss Riley as she always did, Lisa looked behind her in an effort to see Christina who was one of the smartest students in her class but favoured sitting in the back rather than in the front row. However, as Lisa looked towards the back of the class, she caught sight of Max pulling his beautiful locks into a hair band that bunched it up neatly at the back of his head. Lisa refocused and caught sight of Christina sitting at the back who looked back at her.

Christina Langa was a curious person who sometimes came off as unlikable. As an intelligent young South African, the world was her oyster and she knew it. Christina was as interesting as they came in Azania with her lighter skin tone and blonde streaks in her plaited hair extensions. She was also the clear-cut contender for Head Girl next year although she'd yet to say anything about it. Christina broke the eye contact by turning to look out the window. This was clearly going to be a very long assignment.

*

The rest of the day had been pretty much average. Thankfully, she'd managed to avoid looking at Max for the rest of the day although that did not stop Angela from going on and on about him. At some point, Lisa had to ask her to stop, at which point Angela pointed out how much Lisa moaned about things like this. This caught Lisa off guard and when the last bell rang soon after, she departed to go to the "Shop".

When Lisa arrived at Vince Visser's Workshop twenty minutes later, she didn't waste time and went straight to the back to change. As she took her school uniform off and put her blue overalls on, she smiled. *This* was her element, not talking about boys all day. This was where Lisa was at her most comfortable.

Since the beginning of high school three years ago, Lisa had been working at her father's garage. But she'd been going there all her life. While her mother hated how much interest she took in cars, she'd persisted in learning all there was. And her father had been by her side the whole time, showing her the ropes. He'd eventually agreed to giving her a job there since she was willing to work for half the price thus giving him half a salary less to pay and more quality time with his daughter.

Every school night for the past three years, Lisa and her father closed the "Shop" at 6pm and got home by 6:30 in time for supper at 7pm. There was nothing that Lisa loved more than working on an engine. However, when she walked into the workshop and saw the only car there, she clenched her jaw. It was a beautiful white Mercedes SLK and Lisa knew *exactly* who it belonged to.

Lisa looked around the shop, expecting to see her through the glass by the front counter or in the waiting room but to no avail. However, when she turned around, she saw her, deeper in the workshop looking at a bare engine. "How much for this?"

Shaan Moodley, what a woman. Everything about her screamed power and success. From the way she spoke – commanding respect, to the way she dressed – impeccably perfect. She was currently dressed in an all-white designer ensemble that looked like it should be worn by the managing partner of a law firm on the TV show *Suits*. But the woman's stunningness didn't end there as she was also naturally beautiful too – an almost flawless Indian lady. She also somehow made her short hair work for her. While Lisa had once assumed that all short hair on women made them look somewhat less feminine, Shaan proved otherwise. Perhaps it was to do with whatever kind of hair product she put in it that made the short strands spike in all different directions.

Lisa approached her. "It's not for sale. But I thought you were only interested in buying my *services*. Now you want my stuff too."

Shaan turned to face her. "Your stuff?" Shaan gestured to the engine. "That's yours?" She raised an eyebrow when Lisa affirmed. "I didn't know you took part on the scene."

Lisa scoffed. "I don't." Lisa continued when Shaan gave her a curious look. "I've got better things to do with my nights."

"So that's not an ex—"

"No," said Lisa simply, before she could call it what it was.

"Interesting. And here I thought I could recognise an engine for one of those machines anywhere."

"Lost your touch, perhaps." said Lisa playfully.

"Clearly I have, otherwise you would have accepted my job offer by now."

"I told you, Miss Moodley, I'm not currently looking for a job."

"And I told you, Lisa, to call me Shaan. Please, I insist."

"Like I said, Shaan. I'm pretty comfortable where I am, right here."

Shaan simply smirked and Lisa knew why. While Shaan's job offer seemed all sweet and perfect – like her – on the outside: an opportunity to work at one of the most successful car dealerships in Ngelosi as a mechanic, Lisa knew that that wasn't the reason Shaan wanted her. Shaan wanted her to boost the image of her business. A young girl working as a mechanic was an inspirational story and if Shaan could claim that story for herself, she would.

"You wouldn't even have to come on full time. What if I offered you a part time gig or a holiday job? Don't kids love holiday jobs?"

"I'm still not interested." This time it was Lisa who was smirking, and it was Shaan who knew why. She knew that Lisa had all the cards and the more she pushed; the more power Lisa got in making the decision.

"Well I'm just going to take that as a 'let-me-think-about-it' which would have been the smartest thing to say. Then again, someone who's involved with this," she said pointing at the engine again, "might not be the smartest person in the world."

"I told you, I'm not on the scene."

"Well you wouldn't be the first person I knew to lie to me about that."

Lisa's jaw stiffened again. "If you're interested in winning today, I can take you to your car. It's ready."

Shaan smiled, gesturing for Lisa to lead the way. While Shaan may have been a formidable businesswoman, she also respected gusto and it had definitely taken some for Lisa to say no three times. When Lisa took Shaan to the front counter, Shaan surprized Lisa and her father by ordering some more work done – clearly looking for another opportunity to talk to Lisa – to which Vince gladly accepted, relishing the job. He also asked Lisa to give Shaan a lift to wherever she needed to go which made Lisa clench her jaw again.

After getting changed into more regular clothes, Lisa jumped behind the wheel of the convertible at Shaan's insistence and started towards her destination: downtown Ngelosi City.

CHAPTER FOUR
IGNITED

When Max first heard Thompson Mashaba – his tour guide and closest thing to a friend since arriving in Ngelosi – tell him that he was taking him to a place called "The Dive", Max thought for sure that he was taking him to some dodgy looking bar. Instead, Thompson drove him to a local beach where a double decker eating establishment stood as the centre of attention.

"My friend, I give you: The Dive." From the moment Max met Thompson, he knew that he was going to like him. From managing to make him feel at ease on his first day by introducing him to the right people – including his 'inside girl' at the tuckshop who let him cut lines when it was busy, to him explaining things that weren't even a part of the school syllabus but definitely a part of the Azania lifestyle. "There are certain things that you just have to try simply because you're in South Africa," Thompson had told him. "Now they're some things you'll enjoy like bunny chow and vetkoek. Other things you won't like such as amasi and tripe. But you have to try them all."

Thompson also had a likable personality, sometimes making him come across as animated, so it was easy to like him. He'd also gotten his surname right, noting that the pronunciation of '*Ma-Kai*' and not '*MacKay*' was how the Scottish pronounced it. But the one thing that made Max *know* that he was going to be fast friends with him was when he saw his car. It was a beautiful red 1990 BMW 320i. Complete with low profile tires and big spoiler on the boot, it was an old-fashioned beauty. Max smiled when he offered to show him a few places in it. And it wasn't just for show as the car growled like something evil when he turned it over, making Max almost fall in love with it right then.

41

After giving him the abridged tour of North Ngelosi–
the borough just outside of the city where they stayed –
Thompson had pulled into the parking lot of The Dive.
Max looked around and saw all the similarly aged kids,
half of whom were in their bathing suits, on the beach.
"So, this is where the kids hangout after school, huh?"

"Pfft, you say that like you're not a kid yourself.
C'mon." But before Thompson got out of the car to take
him inside, he placed something he hadn't seen in a long
time on the steering wheel and locked it.

"Is that a steering wheel lock?"

"Yep," said Thompson, proudly.

"Isn't that a bit old fashioned?"

"That's the point. When car technology changed so did
the criminals. Now they're just as hip as the rest of us,
able to hack alarms and what have you. But, in all their
effort to upgrade, they left some basic skills behind: like
how to deal with a steering wheel lock or a gear lock.
Now, suddenly, the old ways have become the best. It
ain't impenetrable but it does give car thieves who weren't

expecting it a spectacularly hard time." He then lifted both eyebrows like a man full of himself and started for the restaurant.

When they got inside, Max realized that he would have to rethink calling the place a restaurant. With a bar and open planned eating area downstairs that opened up straight to the beach and a more closed in eating section upstairs, the place was something of a cross between a bar, a restaurant and a diner. Max loved it.

"Thompson!" A man standing behind the bar gave his friend a shout. "Come to try your luck again at getting me in trouble?"

"How's it going, Tar?" said Thompson. The man Thompson called Tar was a Coloured man who had a mesmerising look about him. While he had the light brown complexion that Max had, he had his black hair cropped short and had a beard to match it giving him that elsewhere look. But what made him truly exotic was his eyes. His eyes were very light brown making them a powerful feature on his face. And as Max could see by the way the women walking past the bar looked at him, he was a hit with the ladies.

The man was wearing a white vest with a sleeveless shirt over top of it making the tribal-like tattoos on his shoulders visible. While he wasn't heavily muscled, he was still fit. If Max hadn't pegged him as a local, then he could have easily mistaken Tar for being from Hawaii or some such other exotic place.

Thompson tapped Max on the arm. "Max, meet the owner of this fine establishment."

"Flattery still isn't going to make me give alcohol to a minor, Thompson." Tar extended his hand. "Pieter Stevens. But everyone, and I do mean everyone, calls me Tar."

"Max McKay."

"Makhaya. A Zulu man, I see. Nice."

"Actually the name is Scottish, father's side. But my mother *is* Zulu."

Tar smiled, understanding. "Still. Very cool name."

"So is yours. Tar?"

Tar explained the name as he continued working the bar, multitasking. He told him that "tar" was an expression that referred to a Navy man and that since he's been talking about joining the Navy since he was a kid, people got to calling him Tar.

"I'm telling you now, man," added Thompson, "if you're ever in a jam near water, he's the man to call. He's been a nipper, a lifeguard, a diving instructor, you name it."

"No, I think that pretty much covers it," joked Tar. "Now get your asses upstairs or out on the deck before I kick you out."

Thompson noticed Max's raised eyebrows. "His amazing hospitality is something you get used to. But he just wants us away from the bar."

As they made their way upstairs, Tar shouted, "I'll send Stevie over to take your orders so you better start thinking about what to eat otherwise you'll eat after dark."

When Max wondered about menus, Thompson told him
he knew them off by heart.

When a young 15-year-old girl with the name "Stevie"
embroidered on her golf shirt came to wait their table,
Max knew immediately that this was Tar's younger sister.
While they weren't as a powerful a feature as Tar's, Stevie
also had light brown eyes. The most striking difference
between her and Tar was Stevie's complexion which was
chocolate brown like most Africans. But her facial
features were the giveaway along with her mouthy smile.
She was definitely Tar's sister.

"Hey Thompson. And you must be the new guy. Max,
right?" Max's eyebrows rose again. "We go to the same
school. I'm one year behind you guys: Grade Ten."

"Well it must be a really small world if you know my
name."

"Just a small school," added Thompson.

"Besides, with a name like McKay," she said
pronouncing it correctly, "you were bound to be

memorable." Stevie smiled before moving on to her job. "So, what can I get you guys?"

"We'll have two specials, thanks." Before Max could complain, Thompson just gave him a wink. "Trust me, Max. The special is what you want." Stevie took down their orders and went on her way. "By the way, don't read too much into Stevie remembering your name. She's not into you."

"I didn't say anything," said Max, almost laughing.

"Not like someone else who couldn't keep her eyes off of you." Max played dumb. "Back at school?" Max's poker face was the stuff of legend. "When we first got to class?" When Max continued to act like he didn't know what he was talking about, Thompson began to become bewildered only for Max to laugh, letting him know that he knew exactly what he meant.

As Max and Thompson waited, Max looked around at the folks in the place. They were sitting in a booth by the railing so that they could see right down to the bar below while also sitting by the window so they could see out to the parking lot. Max saw that the place really was frequented by teenagers mostly with the few adults around the bar being beach bums looking to offload. With North Ngelosi being perfectly wedged between the beach and the city, it was no shock that this place was popular with the teens.

Just as Stevie brought their meals, Max heard the sound of loud engines outside. He looked out the window to see three bikers pulling up. They were all dressed in leather but the lead biker – who had ridden a Honda CBR1100XX, also known as the Super Black Bird – was wearing a bright red leather jacket with black sleeves. He was an Indian man who took off his helmet to reveal stylish hair complete with bangs. He was good looking with youthful features. He had a clean shaven face that seemed to suit him. He looked like one of those guys whose good looks would only be defeated by his bad aging. The other two guys were more average-looking both with similar short-cropped hair.

Max felt like he'd waited enough. "Thompson, tell me something, is there any street racing around here?"

The question caught Thompson off-guard. But the next thing that happened caught Max off-guard as well. Thompson had given Stevie, of all people a quick look before answering. "What makes you ask that?"

Max was curious about the evasive answer. "Well because I heard them, last night. There were cars racing somewhere and I was curious as to whether there's any street racing around here."

"Why, are you a street racer or something?" The question had come from Stevie of all people who was now fully engrossed by the conversation, clearly knowing something that Max didn't.

"Or something," said Max, deciding to be a little evasive himself. "But it was motorcycles back in Australia. Is it the same here?" said Max pointing outside to the bikes.

Stevie almost laughed. "Ironic that you point out *his* bike out of all people when asking that question."

"Stevie," said Thompson, clearly warning her about saying too much.

However, Max had understood her quip. "Why, who is that guy?" Max's question was answered by the greetings exchanged downstairs, which Max looked down to witness.

"Well if it isn't our favourite would-be sailor," said the Indian biker. "How are you doing, *Tar*?" Clearly, by the way the man greeted Tar, they clearly had history. And not pleasant history.

"What can I get you Moodswing?"

Max looked back at Stevie and then Thompson. "Moodswing?" They still didn't answer. "Guys," said Max almost smiling now, "I can always go downstairs and just ask the man. Do you think that will be more secretive or less secretive?"

"It's not about being secretive," said Thompson. "It's about being inclusive. And you're not on the *in*side." There was a moment that passed before one of them finally relented.

"His name is Terrance Moodley. But everyone calls him Moodswing," explained Stevie.

"Stevie," said Thompson, warning her again. "Your brother's gonna kill you."

"He's always *gonna kill me*," said Stevie, rolling her eyes.

"What, whoa," said Max, "Tar is in on this too?"

"No," said Thompson. "None of us are and that's the whole point. That's why we shouldn't be speaking about it. We're not part of the scene."

"At least not yet," said Stevie, clearly with an element of hope in her voice. Thompson scoffed loudly before rolling his eyes at her comment. Clearly, she wanted to be on this scene and Thompson was tired of hearing it.

"Okay guys, and what's the scene?"

Thompson slouched back in his chair, defeated and looked between Stevie and Max before shrugging as if to say, "screw it" and dove back into the conversation. "Since we've said so much already," started Thompson.

"You guys haven't said anything," complained Max.

"Yeah well here's the low down. There is a racing scene and I'm telling you right now that it's like nothing you've ever seen."

"What, it's on two wheels," guessed Max.

"No, it's on four."

"So, cars. You guys use cars."

"Yes and no."

"What?" Max was confused.

"*Thompson.*" Now it was Stevie who was complaining about his roundabout way of explaining. Max shared the sentiment.

"Well if I said yes, you'd assume sedans and hatchbacks. If I said no, you'd assume trucks or something."

"So, what do you race around in, quad bikes?" Max was beginning to become unsure of whether there was racing here at all.

"Nope."

"Perhaps it would be easier if you showed him, Thompson." Stevie spoke the words as if it were the simplest thing in the world.

Thompson sat back again, surprised. "That's suicide, taking him down there."

"I'm not talking about taking him down *there*. I'm talking about taking him to your hiding spot."

Thompson narrowed his eyes. He thought about denying he had a hiding spot but realized quickly that it was futile. "How do you know about that?"

"I know a lot about the scene," said Stevie looking at her feet as if what she was about to admit was a crime. "I kinda discovered it myself when I wanted a place to watch the races from but then I saw you there, so I had to find another spot."

"Okay seriously, your brother is going to *kill you*," he said again.

Max had had enough. "Okay guys," he said ending their argument, "Thompson, take me to this spot of yours so that I can see what you're talking about with my own eyes."

Thompson thought about it for a moment before shrugging. "Okay." He looked at Stevie. "We'll be taking these to go."

Stevie gave Thompson a frustrated look before picking up the plates again. "I wish you'd take me to go," she said under her breath.

*

As the sun went down, Thompson drove them to another borough also on the outskirts of Ngelosi named Empiko. However, where North Ngelosi bridged the beach to the city, Empiko overlooked the city as it was located on a hill that rose and rose and rose forming a natural border to the city. And lucky for Thompson, it also overlooked North Ngelosi. And at a very particular point – that point being an old abandoned plant that had a beautiful view overlooking a main road and what was across that road – they could see something quite breath-taking.

On the way through the plant, Thompson made sure to give Max a proper introduction to what he was about to see, hyping it up like a main event prize fight. "Now you see, Max, what you should know is that this city of ours, it doesn't sleep at night. If anything, it comes alive when the sun goes down. While everyone else says *good* night, we say *ig*nite. Because that's what we do: we ignite the fuel that burns inside us, and we let it out on the blacktop."

Max had looked at him at this point. "You talk like you wish you were down there."

"A part of me does. But another part knows that I'd have to be part-crazy to take part in *that*."

"Why, you've got a fast-enough car?"

"Not for what *they* do." Sitting in the car, Thompson took out his binoculars and looked through them. Having found what he was looking for he started to hand them to Max but then hesitated. "You're about to enter a world of which you've never seen the likes of. Are you ready?"

With enough hype for an entire lifetime, Max took the binoculars and looked through them towards the direction

Thompson had been looking, now dying of anticipation. There, across the main road, was a parking garage. Judging from the lights being out, the parking lot clearly wasn't supposed to be used anymore. But that certainly wasn't the case. As Max looked more closely, Max's jaw suddenly dropped when he saw what vehicles were parked in the lot.

"Are those Formula One cars!?"

CHAPTER FIVE
SPEEDMONGERS

Moodswing didn't care how much of a racket he was making when he rode his bike up the rampway and into the Lot. There was a reason he always made such a big entrance: he needed everyone to know that he was there. He needed everyone to know that he'd arrived on the scene!

Terrance Moodley was a 21-year-old rich kid who loved a thrill. At least that's what everyone else thought. And that's what he wanted them to think. It's what gave him an edge: them underestimating him. But that wasn't what he was all about at all. He was a racer through and through. It was what he always wanted to be. And not a street racer like every punk on every street corner wanted to be since *The Fast and the Furious* debuted but rather the only kind of racers that seems to truly be in tune with their vehicles: an open-wheel racer.

Moodswing remembered as a kid, watching the races on TV. Whether it was Formula One, IndyCar or the now defunct A1 Grand Prix and everything in between, Moodswing wanted nothing more than to do what they did. Unfortunately, opportunities to get into one of those vehicles was far and few between for a South African so Moodswing and a group of his rich kid friends had made a plan.

After secretly purchasing the old A1 race cars, Moodswing and his friends started racing them around the freeways of Ngelosi like kids at an amusement park. Their races were also unique for being mano-e-mano: no pack racing. Eventually their racing scene evolved with competition becoming stiffer. Most of his rich friends wanted to taste success – particularly since they raced for money often times – and would ask their poorer friends to drive for them. Eventually, racing for the cars themselves became popular which culminated in almost anyone who could drive entering the scene.

While Moodswing had fond memories of the past when it was just him and his friends, he still loved coming down here because the one thing that had remained consistent was the spirit of competition. True to the nature of Azania itself, the scene hadn't degraded to wars of hatred or pushing of agendas. It was still just purely about the cars. Although, occasionally, aggression did play a part.

While Moodswing was considered a relic of a past long forgotten by some, he was considered the godfather of the scene by others. He had been one of the fastest when it was just the rich kids and he was one of the fastest now that it was all speedmongers. And while he wasn't specifically in charge, his word carried a lot of weight. While they had designated race organisers – the people who also ensured that the winners got paid and disruptors got beaten up – Moodswing was still able to get his way just with his reputation alone.

Another way that the scene managed to retain its order despite evolving radically from what it once was, was due to the establishment of the titles. There were only three but three was enough to keep all the racers behaving as one did not want to get taken off the list of contenders and dropped to the back of the line.

There was the "Duke of Drag" championship for all the speed freaks who raced from one mark to another, no turns, no complex strategies. There were the "Relay Baron" championships for those that preferred working with a partner as they alternated laps. And then there was the big one: the "King" championship. That was the only title that tickled Moodswing's fancy and was also currently held by him. Being King meant you were the best, period.

The championships themselves were represented by shiny gold helmets with the Relay titles simply having gold-plated accents, the Duke title being plain, polished gold and the King title being gold plated *and* embossed with fancy designs. They were holdovers from the rich-kid days. Another holdover from those days was the lie that the race cars were ex-formula three cars from a previous era hence their name for them: XF race cars.

Just as Moodswing approached his waiting race car, one of the race organizers approached him. "Hey King, interested in racing tonight?"

Moodswing shrugged. "Depends on the opponent." This was always Moodswing's M.O. He made a point to act like a King as well.

"It's Bomba, Moodswing."

Moodswing pretended to think. "Who's that again?"

"Bomba? C'mon, you know Bomba." But Moodswing feigned ignorance so the Organiser continued. "Former Relay Baron, former Duke of Drag. Bomba."

Moodswing suddenly 'remembered'. "Oh *Bomba*. He's not at the top of the list of contenders," said Moodswing as if confused. "Is he even on the list?"

"I wouldn't really be asking if he was."

"Then who does he think he is asking the King for a race?"

The organiser shrugged. "I think he's at the end of his rope and maybe he's taking one last grasp at a chance at glory."

That annoyed Moodswing. Holding this title wasn't a joke to him so he wasn't just going to defend his title against any old dumbass. But if this one wanted one last grasp, then he was going to give him one last grasp. "I guess I could use a tune up race. But if this loser wants a shot at a blaze of glory on his way out, then he's going to get one and I'm going to make sure he *stays* out."

"What are you talking about?"

"Title on the line but loser leaves town. Tell him: take it or leave it."

The organiser nodded. "Okay. I'll tell him to get ready."

"Whoa, whoa, whoa," said Moodswing stopping the man in his tracks. "We're not doing this *now*. I'm the King. My race goes *last*."

The organizer hesitated sheepishly for a moment before recovering. "Okay. I'll think of something else to

put on before—" The organiser was suddenly distracted
by a scuffle nearby.

Moodswing also noticed and looked up to see the Jele
brothers – who went by Longitude and Latitude – shoving
and pushing another duo of racers. "It looks like you have
your opening race, Admin." Admin was a nickname they
gave the organizer that went all the way back to the
beginning which was short for administrator. They were
usually meant to be stubborn and resistant but Moodswing
had a way of turning these guys into butter.

*

Moodswing watched through the opening on the side
of the parking lot as Longitude and Latitude moved to the
start line on the main road. They were swiftly joined by
Jay and Kay, two racers that Moodswing barely knew.
The four of them were facing the direction that led to
where the main road met the freeway and that's where the
fun began.

The main road separated North Ngelosi from Empiko.
Moodswing looked across to the old plant which hadn't
been in use in over a decade. It was strange though,

because looking across at it, Moodswing swore that he could feel someone watching him. But maybe it was all in his head because he couldn't see anything. Besides, all the good stuff was on the road, three stories below.

As Admin sent a pretty girl out to the start line to start the race, Moodswing looked around at the other racers. While Moodswing stood and watched the race the old-fashioned way, the others were using their phones, tablets and laptops to watch the race on the secret streaming service on the deep web. Using the traffic surveillance, which one of these clever numb nuts managed to hack, the rest of them could watch the race in its entirety from the comfort of the parking lot. It was one of the few things that Moodswing completely adored about the evolution of the scene: now they had at least a few nerds that could make the whole thing an even better experience. Yet, despite that, Moodswing sometimes preferred doing things the old-fashioned way and watching with his own eyes like he was tonight, even if it meant he only saw parts of the race. But he wasn't the only one.

As the race kicked off, Moodswing smiled at the sound of the engines deafening anyone who could hear them. There was nothing like the rumble of an XF engine. He watched as Longitude led the relay against Jay while their partners waited on the start line for them to return.

Moodswing had known Longitude and Latitude for a long time, since high school in fact where they went by the names Long John and Luthando. They'd always been popular with tales of their extreme sports adventures, so they fit in quite neatly at the scene in the fast-paced world of underground racing.

There was a reason that Moodswing wasn't watching the race on his tablet and that was because he wanted to use the time to prepare for his own race. He went back to his own vehicle where his two 'colleagues', Mook and Goone who served as his 'support team' as well as fellow bike riders were waiting for him to tell him everything he wanted to know about his race car tonight.

However just before he could make his way down to the start line, rumblings began amongst the racers which eventually reached Moodswing: there was another race set to happen before his. And it was a race that everyone had been waiting to see for weeks. Leonidas vs. Shade. While Leonidas was the up and coming XF racer from out of town, Shade was something else entirely.

Shade was the mysterious lone wolf of the scene, a complete enigma that Moodswing was convinced either had watched too many pro wrestling matches of The Undertaker and Sting or read too many Batman comic books. The man's taste for theatricality was on another level. While all of the other XF racers including Moodswing occupied the second and third levels of the four-storey abandoned parking lot – with the first level having a flooding problem and the fourth level, a space problem – Shade hung out on the roof, all by himself.

And while Moodswing didn't admit it out loud and hated that he liked it, he kind of thought that Shade was as cool as hell. There was something about this lone dark figure all dressed in black (black racing suit, black gloves, black boots, black helmet), perched on the roof, looking down upon the other racers racing that had a larger than life feel. Only adding to the wrestling/comic book feel of it all was when Shade got the call, he could be heard racing down the parking lot ramp ways and making his way to the start line.

When Longitude and Latitude successfully retained their Relay Baron titles, that was exactly what everyone heard as Leonidas prepared himself for the most important race of his underground racing career. As Moodswing watched the ever-silent Shade take to the start line, Moodswing couldn't help but wonder just who the hell was under that helmet. This was one thing that no one knew as Shade never took his helmet off. Even the one time that he had been forced to take it off due to a fire safety incident, he had been clever enough to wear a protective mask under his helmet which conveniently protected his identity.

Shade's race intrigued many as Moodswing watched everyone "oh" and "ah" as they watched on their phones and tablets. While Moodswing wanted nothing more than to do the same, he had to put his game face on, literally as he put his helmet... his *crown* on his head, but not before polishing it. Moodswing slid into the tight space that formed the seat of his vehicle.

Just like all the other XF race cars, his vehicle had a name. This was another holdover from the rich boy days as they'd wanted each vehicle to have a distinctive identity akin to racehorses. And thus, a trend that never died was born. Every race car had a name and no name could be retired or repeated. His vehicle: The *Dracula*.

The *Dracula* was a black vehicular beast with red vinyl stickers in the shape of dripping blood. It was intimidating to look at and that was the point: to intimidate all his opponents. While the other vehicles had changed drivers over the course of the history of the scene, the *Dracula* had been his baby since the beginning. Moodswing remembered everything about the vehicle. From the first time he sat in it and was intimidated by being so close to the ground, to being surprised that he was basically lying down while inside it rather than sitting, conventional wisdom be damned.

As Moodswing calmed his nerves, tuning everything else out, he found an inner peace: exactly the headspace he needed to win. By the time he heard Admin call his name for his race, Moodswing was ready. He drove the *Dracula* down to the start line passing the victorious Shade in his vehicle, the *Tumbler* on his way back up to the roof.

As Moodswing stood on the start line across from Bomba, Moodswing couldn't help but smile. He hadn't had a race that felt like it was going to be this easy since the good old days. When the girl lowered the red cloth signalling the start of the race, Moodswing took off, holding on tightly to the steering wheel as the vehicle vibrated with the movement of the road beneath him.

As he took the onramp on to the freeway, Moodswing thought about everything he'd been through in the past few years: graduating high school, surviving varsity and during all that time, managing to be at the top of his game on the scene. Of course, not everyone was happy with his choice of night-time activities as his father, and later, his sister, made sure to mention, repeatedly, all the time.

While his father had eventually given up on getting him to take over the dealership and passed the mantle onto

69

his sister, his sister had also picked up the mantle of being on his case to leave the scene behind and join the family business. But Moodswing had no intention of leaving the scene. Not while he was still at the top of his game.

Moodswing had been right about the race being a cake walk. He was nearing the end and Bomba hadn't even managed once to come within centimetres of overtaking him. With the finish line in sight, Moodswing couldn't help but *not* feel sorry that this guy would be leaving them forever. Honestly, Moodswing didn't need or want racers like him taking up space on the scene.

Moodswing came to a sliding stop after crossing the finish line. While he, Mook and Goone celebrated Moodswing's win with him, Moodswing looked back to the frustrated Bomba and couldn't help but smile as he realized that he'd just been banished from town. But while Moodswing celebrated, he couldn't help but feel like he was being watched. On instinct, Moodswing looked up to the roof of the parking lot and saw Shade, or a silhouette of Shade as he watched from his perch.

When it came to Shade, no words were needed to form a conversation. Moodswing knew exactly why Shade was looking at him. He looked under his arm at his helmet, his beloved and cherished golden crown and just knew that it wasn't *him* that Shade was looking at. Suddenly Moodswing felt that he was about to have a whole other set of problems on his hands in the near future.

CHAPTER SIX
RECOIL

When Max woke up the next morning, he still couldn't believe what he'd seen last night. He'd gone to sleep smiling and woke up smiling. It was the most amazing thing that he had ever seen. Racing ex-Formula Three vehicles, in the middle of the night. It was unbelievable. But Thompson had let him in on the secret: that they weren't actually ex-formula vehicles at all but rather former A1 vehicles, at least that was the rumour. Although that did not take anything away from what he saw last night. Hell, even if Thompson had told him that the cars were built from scratch from the ground up, nothing could take away from what he saw last night.

When Max took off for school, his mother had already left. She had told Max that with her being as busy as hell at the university, there was little chance that he would see her as he'd be asleep when he got home which suited Max just fine. Of course, she claimed that she would be checking when the alarm is switched on and off and expected it to be switched off when he got home from school and back on when he went to bed, by the time she arrived home. But Max doubted she was going to be checking the alarm like that every single day.

Max's second day of school was something of a bore although no one else would know it from looking at Max as he seemed to have a smile permanently etched onto his face. Not a minute would go by without Max daydreaming about the sound of those engines crackling in the night like they were trying to break the sound barrier.

Thompson had explained the scene to him from the titles they raced for all the way to the names of each of the vehicles, although he failed to explain how he knew all of this considering that he'd never set foot in that parking lot. By far, the most fascinating vehicle to Max had been the

Tumbler. There was something about the all-black race car and the way it moved like a shadow in the dark that made it alluring. It was clearly the perfect metaphor for its driver, Shade. A mystery man to say the least.

Max remembered watching from the plant as the race organizer called Shade by shouting "Mthunzi" out loud and on the roof, Shade – who had been perched on the roof, arms crossed watching the race below – turned swiftly around, jumped in the *Tumbler* and sped off down to the ground floor and came speeding to the start line like a bat out of hell. Max found this amusing because all of this made Max think of Batman right down to the "Mthunzi" call being like his bat-signal.

Thompson had explained Shade's backstory, or rather lack of one, as Shade being this racer that had shown up one night from out of nowhere. It had been a notable appearance because almost all the other racers on the scene had either won, inherited or simply borrowed their vehicles from the rich kids who had once dominated the scene while Shade had been the first to come with his own race car. Absolutely no one knew where he had gotten it from.

While the idea of racers coming from all over – including some from the mainland – seemed to be the beginning of a trend starting with Shade, it turned out not to be because most of them got sent packing. Most of them, courtesy of Shade himself including the latest one, Leonidas. Despite the exclusivity of it all, the scene seemed to welcome new racers as long as they were really, really fast and they could keep a secret. Above all else, they had to be able to keep their mouths shut about the scene.

This is what made what Max and Thompson did last night extremely dangerous. The only people who should know about the scene were the XF racers and those invited by XF racers to look after their vehicles. Perhaps the only thing more dangerous than being behind the wheel of an XF race car, was being the guy watching all this from an abandoned plant across the way.

When school ended that day, Max found himself excited to get back to the plant and watch the racing again.

Unfortunately, Thompson pointed out that there was nothing to watch until the sun went down which was still 4 hours away so they agreed to meet at The Dive at 5:30PM. Thompson had suggested that he take a taxi to meet him by The Dive.

"I've been in one of your taxis," he'd said. "And let me say, I've never experienced something more uncomfortable in my life." So instead, Max opted for walking. He walked to school every day, so he had no qualms walking down to the beach. It took half an hour, but it was refreshing and just the breath of fresh air he needed to prepare him for the adrenaline rush to come.

*

On his way there, Max found himself walking past a place called Vince Visser's Workshop which was a garage. He recognized the last name as belonging to a girl in his class. As Max walked past, he noticed the cars inside, one of them a beautiful white Mercedes SLK. But what caught Max's attention was something in the corner: an exposed engine.

There was something about the shape of it that caught Max's attention as it was too small to be a car engine. That's when it hit him. It was the size of a race car engine. Not caring that he didn't belong there, Max walked into the workshop and went right to it. It was beautiful.

From what he could tell about engines, it was a masterpiece. Spanning roughly 6 meters by 6 meters, it was a heavy looking thing. No way that it weighed less than 150 kilograms. This thing was a V8 engine, no doubt capable of no less than 500 horsepower. Max wondered if it was at all possible that this was Shade's engine. But before Max could inspect it further, he was immediately joined by an angry blonde girl.

"What the hell do you think you're doing?"

Max turned around to find Lisa looking at him – more like scowling at him – with another pretty girl standing behind her. They were both wearing the same school uniform that he was: the distinctive sky-blue shirt with a badge on it. Of course, where he wore the grey pants, they wore the dark blue skirts, although Lisa's friend wore hers notably shorter than Lisa. "I was just admiring this piece of artwork."

"This area is off limits, completely." said Lisa, not caring.

Max smirked, ignoring her anger and gestured to the engine. "What is this doing here anyway?"

"You don't listen very well, do you? Off. Limits."

Max continued to ignore her. "Do you know the owner? I'd very much like to speak to him."

"There is no him. Now get out."

"It doesn't have an owner? Well then I'd very much like to know how much it costs."

"It's not for sale."

"Are you sure about that?"

"Yes."

"Well if it's not for sale and it doesn't have an owner then what is it doing here?"

"It's still being built." It was Angela who had spoken. Although she regretted it. Judging by the smile on her face, she was very much enjoying watching her best friend and the new guy bantering. Lisa gave her a hard look to which Angela apologetically raised her hands.

Max didn't miss a beat. "Being built by who?"

"Whom," said Angela, channelling her inner grammar-Nazi.

"Angie," said Lisa, trying to shut her up.

Max noticed the way that Lisa was eyeing Angela; the way she got defensive when she revealed something about the engine and then it hit him. "Wait, *you're* the one that built it?"

"And what's it to you?" said Lisa, still defensive.

"Hey, no, I believe it. I'm all for girls working on cars. I'm just impressed that you *built* this baby from the ground up."

"It's her little pet project," added Angela, earning another disapproving scowl from Lisa.

Lisa turned back to Max, having had quite enough. She stepped towards him, raising a hand as if about to shove him, but Max began to move backwards towards the door as she advanced, her hand inches from his chest. "Now I've told you already that this place is off limits. If you don't leave, I'm going to have to throw you out."

Max feigned thinking about that for a second. "I'd kind of like that, actually."

"You're a bit of a jackass, you know that."

"You're a bit rude, did you know that?"

"Oh, she knows," said Angela, again, chipping in unnecessarily.

Max hadn't lost his smirk throughout their argument, sort of enjoying the feisty side of this girl. "It don't matter though. I like a girl who knows her way around an engine."

"Oh, then you're going to love me because I can tear one apart and put it back together. And if you don't leave now, that's exactly what I'll do to you." Lisa picked up a monkey wrench.

While Max knew that she had absolutely no intention of using it, he raised his hands in surrender and began backing away until he was outside, all the while, not losing his smirk. "My name's Max by the way. Max McKay."

"Well *Macks Mac-Kai*, it was good meeting you," she said sarcastically. "Now scram."

Max's smirk widened, impressed that she pronounced his name correctly. While she hid it well, Max could tell that there was a hint of flirtation in her voice. It was faint but it was there. "And your name is?"

Lisa didn't answer but Angela did. "Her name is Lisa," said Angela, earning one final hard look.

"It's good to meet you, Lisa." said Max, finally turning around to leave. But just before he was out of earshot, he heard Angela point out to Lisa that she so has a crush. As if Lisa needed to be told that.

*

After picking him up from The Dive, Thompson and Max headed over to their hiding spot at the plant. As they parked in the spot facing the scene, Max couldn't help but compare the experience to the one and only time he went to the Drive-in to watch a movie on the mainland in Durban. He had marvelled at the idea of watching a movie on a big screen like you were in a cinema but from the comfort of your own car.

Thompson currently had the binoculars. Max had resigned himself to getting a pair of his own soon but for now, they were going to have to share. "Okay, cool. Max, you're going to love this one."

"Why? Who is it? Is it Shade?"

"No. Shade isn't the only badass racer around here." Thompson handed him the binoculars. "You see the guy in the black vehicle with the white skull vinyl stickers? That's Solo Magubane." The racer that Thompson had pointed out was a young man, undoubtedly in his mid-twenties, with a rugby backline's build. He was a Zulu man, with short hair and a confident look. "He's one of the first from the second generation of XF racers. The first to win his vehicle in a race and thus the first XF racer who *wasn't* a rich kid."

82

While Thompson had been explaining, Max hadn't taken his eyes off of Solo's vehicle. "What's the name of his car?"

"That beauty?" said Thompson, smiling. "That's the *Abominable Seduction*."

Wow, thought Max, *what a hell of a name.* In fact, Max loved all the names of the vehicles. From Latitude and Longitude driving the complimentary *Heads* and *Tails*, respectively to Shade and the Batmobile-inspired name of the *Tumbler* to Moodswing's reigning *Dracula*. They were all just so cool. "And the guy he's racing?"

Thompson took the binoculars back and checked him out. "I think that's a chick. And I think she's from out of town."

"They're girls on the scene?"

"Oh yeah. In true Azanian spirit, there's no discrimination to be found here." Thompson heard Max express how cool that was. He was still using the binoculars so he couldn't have seen Max make the fatal mistake of taking his smart phone out and pointing it at the race. Thompson had just lowered the binoculars in time to see Max take the photo. "No, don't take any—"

What happened next happened fast. While the flash hadn't been on when Max set up to take the picture, when Thompson grabbed for it to stop him, he must have touched the flash button on the screen because a moment later, a flash emitted from the camera. Everything stopped as Max and Thompson froze, the phone now on the floor, having been dropped.

As they held their breaths to see if anything happened, a thousand thoughts went through Max's mind. *Did they see it? They couldn't have, could they? No, the light reflected off the windscreen, they wouldn't have seen anything. But it was so bright! No, nothing is happening, they didn't see it. But the windscreen is transparent, fool, of course they saw it.*

With things still quiet 10 seconds after the flash, Max was about to breathe a sigh of relief when all of a sudden, they heard engines firing up in the parking lot. A few seconds later, three motorcycles came speeding out of the building and onto the main road, turning away from the freeway.

"Oh crap!" said Thompson. "We've got to go."

As Thompson fired up the car and screeched his tires, reversing, Max watched across the parking lot and saw that no other vehicles were leaving. "Are you sure? Only three of them came out of there."

"It's enough, trust me," said Thompson now speeding his way out of the plant. "If that's who I think it is, then the three of them are enough."

Max felt the jerk of the car as Thompson power drifted onto the road and started towards the city. "Who do you think it is?"

"Moodswing, Mook and Goone."

Max didn't recognise the two other names, but it didn't take a detective to know that Mook and Goone were the two guys Max had seen with Mooswing at The Dive yesterday. "Well why only three guys? Why wouldn't they send the world after us?"

"They're still trying to keep a low profile. Which is *exactly* why they're after us in the first place! The scene is a secret and us knowing about it compromises that secret!" Thompson was speaking very loud and very fast as he swerved between cars, finally making it onto the freeway.

Max finally saw the three bikes behind them, watching as they began gaining on them. "What the hell are they going to do to us if they catch up!?"

"I don't know but I'm imagining our kneecaps hurting if they do!" As the bikes got closer, Thompson tried to trick them by taking the next off ramp at the last possible second only for two of the bikes to anticipate it and follow while the other doubled back like Thompson had wanted. Thompson continued down another road before turning onto a road that ran along the shoreline. "Dammit!"

"What!?" said Max.

"We're running on empty. We're out of fuel."

"Huh, that doesn't happen in the movies." Max knew that he was worried as he always found his sense of humour in moments of distress.

"We're gonna have to try and lose them on foot. Hold on." Thompson turned down another road heading towards the beach and then swerved onto another more familiar road. They were heading towards The Dive. Thompson drifted into the parking and came to a stop before immediately making a break for the beach. "C'mon. Maybe we can lose them in the crowd."

Max didn't need to be told twice as he followed Thompson onto the promenade which was still surprisingly full of people despite being night-time. By the looks of it, they were mostly teenagers which was good as it would allow them to blend in better. Max was glad that he wore his cargo shorts instead of his favourite old blue jeans as they fitted in naturally on the beach. Thompson was also dressed in shorts having changed some time after school like him.

As they continued walking, further and further away from The Dive, Max began to breathe more lightly. "I think we lost them."

However, just as Thompson turned around to confirm, he tapped Max. "I don't think so."

Max looked back to see one biker who had ridden right onto the promenade. While he was still by The Dive, the brick paving that formed the promenade was a straight shot to where they were standing. Then the worst happened as one of the bikers pointed right at them and started driving right down the paving followed swiftly by both his friends.

Thompson answered the next question Max was going to ask. "They must have recognised my car. Dammit." Thompson looked at Max. "Hide. We need a place to hide." Thompson then spotted the pier. "C'mon."

Max and Thompson broke into a sprint for the pier which was about a hundred meters away. The pier was bridged right from the promenade and built on concrete stilts meaning you could walk on the beach right underneath it. As they approached it Thompson led Max on to the pier before immediately jumping off on the other side, onto the sand not a metre below. Max realized the brilliance of Thompson's plan. He wanted to give the riders the impression that they were on the pier only to hide underneath it. The plan also seemed to work as the two of them heard the bikers turn onto the pier, bikes and all from the paving.

Thompson and Max waited for a minute before deciding to make a break for it. However, when they came out from under the pier, the third biker who had waited at the beginning on the pier, where it met the promenade, spotted them and immediately jumped on Thompson. Max, in turn, jumped on him and pulled him off. When the biker continued trying to punch him, Max pulled off his helmet to reveal Moodswing.

Moodswing answered him with a punch to the face. The right-cross didn't hurt as much as Max would have thought due to him still wearing his riding gloves. Not to be outdone, Max threw a haymaker of his own which landed but when he tried to follow up with another, Moodswing ducked.

Max could tell that Moodswing didn't grow up fighting. While the same was true for Max, he at least had been in enough fights to know how to handle himself. While he didn't know martial arts, he knew how to block, duck and punch. But he was a brawler when it came to fighting, meaning his environment came in handy when he fought. Unfortunately, they were on a beach with not much to use to strike with.

Matters got worse as, just as Thompson got back up to try and help, he was jumped by Goone and Mook who proceeded to double-team him. When Max tried to help him out, Moodswing hit him from behind and started kicking him while he was down. The beating was as unpleasant as anything that Max had experienced in his life. But it came to a pause when Moodswing decided to play his role as the bad guy to its full potential.

"So," he said, lifting Max by the scruff of his shirt, "who the hell are you!?"

"He's no one," said Thompson, speaking through a swollen lip. "Just a friend I was giving a lift to. Leave him alone!"

"Shut up, Thompson. I always knew you were a loser. I didn't think you were stupid too. Spying on us; taking photos of us."

"We weren't taking photos, promise."

"I said shut up!"

"We need to teach them a lesson," said Mook in a thick Afrikaans accent.

"We can't just let them walk out of here," said Goone.

Moodswing smiled. "Oh, they won't be walking for a while. Goone, hold out Thompson's leg."

"What!? Wait, wait, wait! You're going to break his leg!? Are you guys crazy!?"

"Don't worry, mister mystery guest. You're next." Goone did as he was told while Mook held on tightly to Max. Moodswing climbed back onto the pier and prepared to jump onto Thompson's extended leg. Max could barely breathe. But just before Moodswing could launch himself, he was suddenly pulled backwards. A moment later, another figure came flying from the pier and landed right on Goone. Mook let go to try and help his friend only to be tripped by Max and then kicked by the mystery man.

However, as it turned out, the mystery man hadn't needed Max's help as his kick had been some kind of karate spin kick. The man then began beating up Mook and Goone expertly, having clearly been trained in some kind of martial arts. And as if Max and Thompson weren't impressed enough, Moodswing had managed to recover and finally launched himself at the mystery man only for the man to nail Moodswing in the gut.

"Get out of here, Moodswing." The person that spoke finally showed his face, stepping out of the shadows. It was Tar Stevens.

"Tar," said Moodswing. "You're going to pay for this."

"Not as dearly as you if you don't get back on your bikes and leave." Moodswing and his friends didn't need to be told twice as they got back on their bikes and left. Tar turned to Max and Thompson. "Are you guys okay? Do you need the hospital or something?" They both shook their heads, having been humiliated enough for one night.

"Good. Then you should get out of here too. No telling if they'll go looking for backup so better safe than sorry."

Before either Max or Thompson could say anything else, Tar started back towards The Dive. Max didn't know what to make of what just happened. All he knew was that they had just gotten their asses handed to them and a man Max had met just yesterday had saved their asses. It looked like he had been wrong. There was nothing boring about Ngelosi at all.

CHAPTER SEVEN
THE CONFRONTATION

Max had had wounds on his body before, and they were all the same. They healed after a while. But the wounds that didn't heal were the ones on his ego. He never liked it when someone got the better of him. That's why he always *needed* to win when he was in a race. That idea that someone out there got to say they were better than him ate at him. Max knew that this was a flaw in his DNA.

However, the one thing that wasn't a flaw; the one thing that Max knew how to do very well when it came to his pride was swallow it and thank someone when they did him a solid. For once, Max was thankful that his mother was as distant as she was as this allowed him to avoid explaining his injuries altogether. The good news was that he'd be all healed up in days and the anti-inflammatory and pain medication he'd found in the cabinets would ensure he didn't feel a thing.

Max decided to skip school for the day, in part to avoid questions about his face but also because there was someone he wanted to speak to. While he'd only been in school two days, it already felt weird to be dressed in a t-shirt and jeans this early in the day. He arrived at The Dive and was amused to find the place almost completely empty. Although this didn't surprise him as the regular clientele was currently walking the hallways between school bells. In fact, when Max walked in, Tar noticed him and called him out on not being at school immediately.

"I wasn't in the mood for school."

Tar, who was moving chairs off tables as he was still opening the place up, smiled at him, amused. "Don't teach my sister this sort of thing otherwise *I'll* be the one kicking your ass." It was clear that Tar was determined to keep his sister on the clear and righteous path.

"I'll be sure not to but that's what I came to speak to you about, actually. The ass-kicking."

"Hmm." Tar looked at him as if for the first time. "Are you sure that you're alright, man?"

Max dodged the question. "Where did you learn to do all that? The martial arts, I mean."

Tar smiled again. "I was taught by this rogue karate instructor who started an underground fighting ring on the other side of the island."

"What!?" Max then saw Tar's smile widen and he knew that Tar was messing with him. "That's funny."

"So, you didn't skip school to ask me where I learnt to fight. What did you come here for?"

"To thank you. Last night, Thompson and I got in over our heads about something, trouble found us, and you bailed us out, so I came here to thank you for that."

However, Tar was interested in only one detail of what he just said. "You got in over your heads about something?"

Max knew where this was going. He couldn't make things worse by exposing more secrets, so Max simply nodded.

"Hmm," he said again. "You two wouldn't happen to have been spying on the scene, would you?"

On instinct, Max wanted to deny this but then something occurred to him. How would he even know to ask that question unless... "You know about the scene?"

Tar thought a moment, clearly having the same dilemma that Max had just a moment ago. But, as Max did, he also relented. "I used to be a part of it."

I knew it, thought Max, remembering Thompson and Stevie's shady reactions two days ago. So that meant that Tar used to be a racer. But before Max could ask him about it, the two of them heard an all too familiar sound come from outside. It was the sound of three motorcycles. It was Moodswing and his thugs.

Tar rolled his eyes. "I'll handle this," he said before simply stepping behind the bar. While Max initially found this odd, he noticed that Tar was obscuring his hands. He was clearly hiding some kind of concealed weapon. However, the fact that he hadn't brought it out yet suggested that Tar was at least hoping to resolve this without another fight.

When Moodswing walked in, he did a double take upon seeing Max and then smiled. "Well, well, well. I came here to have a word with *you*, Tar but it looks I'm going to get twice my money's worth."

Tar scoffed. "It's just like you to talk about getting your money's worth. I thought the scene would be rid of you trust fund babies by now. But lo and behold: the last jedi."

Moodswing actually laughed at the joke, genuinely finding it funny being called the last jedi. "Tar, you put a beating on me and my boys. So why shouldn't I do the same to you?"

"Oh, you can try," said Tar, not backing down an inch.

Moodswing realized the futile nature of his threat and turned his attention to Max. "I never actually got your name."

"What's it to you?" said Max, defiantly.

Moodswing shrugged sarcastically. "Oh, I don't know," he continued in the same vain. "You spy on me; you hit me in the face, and you don't even want to introduce yourself?"

There was this air of authority that Moodswing carried that Max didn't like. The man actually believed he was all that. But he was also basically calling him a coward which Max wouldn't tolerate. "Max McKay."

"*Macks Ma-Kai*" said Moodswing, pronouncing it properly. "So, tell me, *Makhaya*," he said now deliberately pronouncing it wrong, "why were you and your friend spying on me?"

There he went again, believing that he was all that. It was like he *genuinely* believed that Thompson and him were there to spy on *him*. "We weren't spying on *you*. We were just there to watch the races."

"*Just* there to watch the races," he repeated like a school principal would when interrogating a discipline case. "Hmm, and the camera flash? You were *just* taking photos too?"

This one Max had to deny. "My phone rang and the screen, it's very bright."

Moodswing rolled his eyes. "Oh c'mon, you're going to have to do better than that."

"Na-ah," said Max, now smirking. "I don't *have to* explain myself to you."

"Oh really?"

"Yes really." It was Tar that spoke. "Now, Max has explained himself and I'm sure he won't be doing anything so stupid again so, you can leave now."

However, Moodswing didn't move, remaining silent for a second. "No, I don't think so. I'm not going anywhere until I do what I said I was going to do last night and that's teach this jackass a lesson."

"There's only one jackass in this room," said Max, now ready for a fight, "and it's not me."

"Why you—"

But before Moodswing could jump him, Tar leaped over the bar counter and landed in front of Max and shoved what looked like a broomstick cut in half into Moodswing's face. Max looked in Tar's other hand and saw an identical stick. Both had white cloth wrapped around one end forming something of a handle on them. It was clear that Tar knew how to handle himself with these too. "How the mighty fall," said Tar.

Tar continued. "Terrance 'Moodswing' Moodley: rich kid, trust fund baby turned common thug. What happened to the old way, Moodswing? What happened to the old *you*? The guy who took all his frustrations, all his raging issues and turned them into fuel, unleashing them where they belonged, on the blacktop?"

Moodswing just looked at Tar, stared at Tar. "What the hell are you suggesting?"

"A race, between you and Max."

A moment passed before Moodswing burst out laughing. "You want me to race this nobody? What the hell would I do that for? I'm *King*!"

"Then this should be no sweat for you," said Tar with authority. But while Tar was sure, Max certainly wasn't.

Feeling like he was about to melt into a puddle of water right there on the floor, Max struggled to find his voice to tell Tar a glaring truth he might have overlooked. "Tar, that's all well and good; was a nice speech but I don't have a race car."

Tar didn't even flinch, still looking Moodswing dead in the eye. "I'm sure Moodswing here can arrange something for you to drive in. If memory serves me, you relieved some of your friends of their vehicles back in the day."

Moodswing stiffened his jaw. Clearly, he didn't like being cornered or worse: being told what to do. "Oh, I can arrange whatever I want, it doesn't really mean I'm going to."

"Really?" said Tar, pestering on. "So, you would rather *willingly* let one of those glorious machines sit in a garage somewhere gathering dust than use it to show this guy what makes you King?"

Moodswing thought for a moment and there was a clear sign that he was willing to give in when his expression changed, but then his ego kicked back in and he lifted his chin. "Even if I do have something that I'm willing to lend him for the race, what the hell is in the race for me?"

"Oh please," said Tar.

Max furrowed his brow. "You get to kick my ass in a race, remember?"

Moodswing shook his head. "Not good enough. If I have to lend you a vehicle to do it, then not good enough."

"Then what do you want?" asked an exasperated Max.

"You're in high school right. Well you look like you're still in school so let's go with something juvenile but scary all the same. I win, you have to do whatever I say for a week."

Max immediately realized why he'd called this juvenile. He suddenly saw himself wearing a dress, drinking from the toilet, rolling around in a pig sty or worse. Max wanted to just walk away from this whole ordeal. But then he realized what was right in front of him: a chance to race in one of those beautiful machines. Max was now primed to say yes, but if he was going to risk that kind of embarrassment, he was going to need some incentive of his own.

"I'll accept that but only if you accept one of my terms in return."

"Me and my guys *not* kicking your ass is the only thing you're getting out of this, McKay."

"No, it's not. If I win, I get to keep the vehicle I race."

While Moodswing wore an expression of shock on his face, Tar smiled, proudly. "The kid knows how to play. Now seal the deal, Moodswing." Moodswing's silence showed that he was resistant, but Tar pushed it. "Moodswing, you *know* you don't *need* more than one vehicle. They're just trophies that no one sees anyway now say okay and get this race set."

"Okay," said a reluctant Moodswing, "but you don't get to choose. You get the vehicle I give to you."

"Is it fast?" said Max, smirking.

"All XF race cars are fast, jackass."

"Then deal."

*

Max felt like he was existing on autopilot, not really being in control of what he was doing. After the dramatic confrontation with Moodswing, Max had been given an address on a piece of paper where he was told that he needed to pick up the vehicle from. Not knowing who else to call, Max called Thompson who got so excited after hearing about everything that happened this morning that he cut school two hours early to come help him move the vehicle.

As Max waited for Thompson at the address – which was a storage unit, downtown – Max couldn't help but wonder if he was in over his head. After all, it had been Thompson who thought things through about organizing an old unmarked delivery truck and a small ramp to drive it onto the truck. It was Thompson that said he knew where he could practise in relative privacy. But it took Thompson himself to point out, when he arrived, that it was Max that had the balls to stand up to Moodswing and negotiate the use of this baby.

"I still can't believe you managed to pull this off," said Thompson as he helped him open the trolley door of the storage unit. "I mean, I feel like I've been slowing you down all this time. When you're without me, you get things *done*."

Max corrected him. "*Tar* got things done. I was just there for the ride." Once the door was open, Thompson got the light, revealing a tarp on a very low vehicle. It was Max who took the tarp off to reveal the vehicle that, hopefully, had his destiny written all over it. When Max first saw it, he did a double take. He wasn't sure what to think.

While the vehicle was a beautiful machine, just as stunning as all the others structurally; aesthetically, it couldn't have been blander. In front of Max and Thompson was a bright yellow XF race car with absolutely no vinyl stickers or markings of any kind. "Is this factory-made? Why does it look so—"

"You're not complaining about it already, are you?" Max bit his tongue. But then Thompson smiled, showing that he was just pulling his leg. "Relax. There's a good chance Moodswing lent you this vehicle specifically for this reason, among others," he said trailing off.

Max looked at him. "What other reason is there?"

"This vehicle doesn't have a good history on the scene. In fact, I can't remember any race that this bad boy won."

Max was now almost staring at Thompson. "You're kidding me, right?" *Dammit*, thought Max. *I asked him if it was fast when I should have asked him if it had ever won a race in its existence.*

Thompson picked up on Max's distress. "I wouldn't worry too much about it though. The last guy who owned it before you was a rich kid who struggled to drive his *regular* car so there's a good chance that it was *him* and not the vehicle that was the problem in the equation."

"Mmhmm," said Max, not sold on Thompson's reassurance. Even if Thompson was right about the rich kid being a failure of a driver, there was still a reason that Moodswing gave him *this* vehicle to race in. And unless Moodswing truly believed that Max was as bad a driver as the previous guy, then it had to mean that Moodswing believed in curses or something or was just stupid. "Well it's silly to dwell on the alternative which means we'll just have to hope that I'm a better racer than that other guy."

"Oh, I have little doubt. If everything you told me about your street racing days in Australia were anything to go by then you should take to this bad boy just fine."

This time Max was reassured, and they shared a warm smile. "Just one more thing before we get going. Do you know what the vehicle's name is?"

Thompson grinned, indicating that this wasn't going to be something Max was going to like. "It's called *Baby Cradle*."

CHAPTER EIGHT
BABY CRADLE AND THE DRACULA

Who said that people who named cars didn't have a sense of humour? Well it certainly wasn't Max as he had smiled when he heard the name of his XF race car. *Baby Cradle.* He had to admit, while it was the least intimidating vehicle name he'd heard so far, there was definitely something about it that made him *want* to drive it.

After using most of what was left of yesterday to move *Baby Cradle* across town to an abandoned harbour, they had stored her away for the night and returned the next morning for their practise run. This time, Thompson had skipped school with Max and driven him to the vacant container port where they were currently preparing.

With most of the flat surfaces around the place completely empty, it was perfect. When Max asked why a place that was so vast in space was empty, Thompson explained that it used to be where storage containers were stored. There were literally kilometres of asphalt to play with.

"Okay," said Thompson after they'd made their way to the biggest terminal, "we're going to use this one." They lowered the *Baby Cradle* out of the truck. Thompson then gestured for Max to wait before getting in the vehicle. "This is an important moment so let's do it right. For all intents and purposes, I will be your tech support."

"Tech support?"

"It basically means your guy in the chair. Tips on how to drive; fuel consumption; distance of the straight..."

"You're going to be able to tell me all that while I'm driving?"

Thompson then showed Max his tablet. On the screen was a black interface with a lot of red diagrams including dials, levels and digits that wouldn't be out of place on a racing video game. "Don't you know? There's an app for everything."

"You're kidding me."

Thompson shook his head. "The Information Age is a beautiful thing. It's finally putting the resources of experts in the hands of ordinary people."

"Okay expert," joked Max, "so, if you're in the chair, what exactly am I doing?"

Thompson looked at him. "You. Drive. The car."

"And here I thought you drove it with the tablet. I guess technology is not that advanced."

Thompson rolled his eyes. "Just get in the vehicle."

Max did as he was told. The first thing that he realized was that he wasn't sitting upright in the vehicle. In fact, he was almost lying down inside it. Oddly enough, Max found himself feeling perfectly comfortable to drive. The steering wheel was a perfect distance from him, and the pedals were perfectly in reach, but Max wasn't concerned with the things that worked. He was more concerned by how close he was to the ground. He was, however, glad to see that the back wheels were further back than he'd imagined as he expected them to be by his head for some reason.

"Okay, fire it up," said Thompson. Max once again did as he was told as Thompson continued. "Now the steering wheel is one of the most important gizmos here and also one of the most complicated, but we will get you well acquainted with that by tonight. Now, one important note, the gear shift is automatic which means you don't have to—"

"Uuuuhhh," said Max, "Thompson, we have a problem." Max turned the vehicle off as Thompson followed his eyes and saw it. "There's a manual gearbox in here."

"Crap, this vehicle is analogue."

"What does that mean?"

"It means it's obsolete." Thompson then looked to the heavens. "Dammit, I always knew that those rich bastards were lying about these being ex-formula cars."

"Not necessarily." Max pointed out that it would be a lie if *they'd* said all the cars were ex-A1 GP vehicles because those never had manual gear shift levers. But older Formula One cars – particularly those before 1991 – *did* have manual gear shift levers. However, Max did point out that the outside of the car definitely looked like the other more modern XF racer cars, But Thompson dismissed this as simply them putting a new carbon fibre shell on an old car.

"All this still doesn't help our current problem," said Thompson. "All this computer stuff, the app, it won't work. Not unless we get a geek to do some magic under the hood—"

"We don't have time for that."

"Then it means you'll have to rely on good old-fashioned badass driving."

Max nodded. "Well at least now we know why Moodswing gave me *this* car."

"But he also made a mistake. This might surprise you, but all the vehicles have to be built and designed the same way: same chassis, same engine, same technical specs—"

"Oh c'mon. How the hell can they regulate that?"

"Easy: cheaters get knee-capped. But my point is this: technically, this car is as fast as his, obsolete or not, so you definitely have a shot of winning."

Well that's good to know, thought Max. However, he was still trying to figure out just how in the hell the racers on the scene managed to control the specifications of each driver's vehicle. The idea was ludicrous. He understood what Thompson said about kneecaps but could fear of bodily harm really keep all of them in line?

Before Thompson told Max to fire it up again, he remembered that he left something in the truck. While he fetched it, Max quietly spoke to the car. "Okay, *Baby Cradle,* I know Thompson thinks you're obsolete, but I don't. *I* think that you and I are going to get along just fine. If you look after me tonight, then I'll look after you from tomorrow. Deal?" Not a moment later, Thompson came back with a helmet. "Where the hell did you get that?"

"It's memorabilia. In a town like this with an underground as *powerful* as this, getting your hands on this stuff, especially if it's already used, is not that hard. Don't worry, the guy who sold it to me said that it had only been used once so it shouldn't stink." They both laughed. With his helmet firmly on his head, Max turned on the ignition and thus, beginning a relationship that hopefully would last beyond the night.

*

When Max and Thompson got to the parking lot, awe overtook them. They'd managed to do all they could during their training session to prepare for the race, but nothing could have prepared the pair for what they were about to experience. The first thing they realized was just how organized the scene was.

It all started at the gate that was the entrance of the parking lot. The man standing at the gate gave them a hard look as if staring into their souls before handing them a ticket and waving them through. As they went into the building, they saw that the ground floor was flooded and ascended up to the first floor. That was when they saw them: dozens of people standing around beautiful XF racers. Thompson quickly pointed out that this wasn't all of them which was when they saw the barrier blocking off the ramp to the second-floor lot.

"Upstairs is for the big shots." The words came from a man who'd approached them. When Thompson saw who it was, he fell silent as if starstruck. Max also didn't know what to say. "You must be the new guys. I'm Solomon Magubane. Everyone calls me Solo."

Max saw that Thompson was still a bit star struck so he extended his own hand. "Max McKay."

"Max *Makhaya*," said Solo, genuinely impressed. "Huh, never thought I'd meet a guy with a name cooler than mine." This one time, Max didn't bother correcting the name.

As they laughed, Thompson got over his moment of shock. "Sorry," he said, extending his own hand. "It's just I'm a big fan." Solo took the hand. "Thompson Mashaba."

116

"Yeah, I've heard how much of a fan you are. Watching us from across the road."

"I can explain that," said Thompson.

"Moodswing already did," said Solo.

Max rolled his eyes, imagining what Moodswing must have said. "Where is Moodswing?"

"Oh, the King. He's upstairs on the second floor. Like I said, big shots," he said pointing up towards the heavens.

"Then why aren't *you* upstairs? You're one of the best on the scene."

Solo laughed in grateful amusement. "Wow, you really are a fan. But I'm not going to count my eggs on that until I make it in Auto 1." At that moment, Solo's name was called. "That's my cue. It's racing time." Solo was already dressed in his racing attire: a black protective suit that had a logo on the back that consisted of a pair of watchful skull eyes.

Max himself was also dressed in a race suit. But unlike Solo and almost all of the other racers, Max's suit didn't have a personalized logo or insignia but instead was as

117

bland as his XF race car: plain dark blue. Max had wondered at first why he couldn't just wear his biker leathers, but Thompson had told him that he needed something that would protect him if his car caught fire.

Left to their own devices temporarily, Max and Thompson unloaded *Baby Cradle* from the delivery truck, and it took a moment for others to notice the newest member of the scene. But eventually the whispers began, and it wasn't long before they were joined by one of the other XF racers. "You know, I thought I recognised this machine."

Thompson recognised the person speaking. "You're Touch Mkhize."

"Since I was born." Touch looked from Thompson to Max, also moving his finger from one to the other. "I take it, you're the driver," he said pointing to Max to which Max nodded. "And how did you get your hands on *Baby Cradle*?"

"I made a bet with a King," said Max, with a smirk on his face.

Touch smiled. "My kind of guy." Touch looked behind them. "So, good luck with that." Touch turned to leave just as someone else approached them from behind.

"Ah, you made it." Moodswing's voice boomed above the bustle of the other racers. He walked over to them with women under each arm as if he was a baller. "I'm glad you could find the place. Then again, you have been spying on it."

"You really need new material, Moodswing." said Max.

"It's Your Majesty to you, McKay." Moodswing gestured for someone to come closer. "Admin, do your job and make sure *Baby Cradle* here," said Moodswing, a little too smug at the sound of the name, "is up to spec."

Max watched as Admin and a man who at least looked like a mechanic inspected *Baby Cradle*. When he was done, he gave Admin a nod who in turn gave Moodswing a nod. It was clear to Max that Admin was a little bit scared of Moodswing which Moodswing clearly used to give the perception that he was in charge. But Max could tell he wasn't.

Moodswing smiled. "Alright then." Moodswing suddenly raised his voice so everyone could hear him. "Ladies and gentlemen, it's official: we now have our feature race and main event of the evening: the *Dracula* vs. the *Baby Cradle*!"

While Max truly did hate Moodswing, he had to admit that the man did have a flair for putting on a show. Even Max had to admit that he was excited about the race. Now all he had to do was win.

*

This was the second time that Max was sitting in *Baby Cradle* yet everything about the moment felt like it was an all-time first experience. Upon hearing his name being called out, Max was directed to the start line. It felt just as awesome to hear *Baby Cradle* come to life now as it had been during the training session. Max reached the start line only to find Moodswing already there and the man couldn't have been fuller of himself even if he tried.

Max had been told about the route of the race by Thompson an hour ago which was easy enough to remember. It was simply taking off on the main road which bent North as if heading out of the city which was where it met the M3 – the freeway that Max had arrived on with Joseph Sibusiso. However, where the M3 ascended up the hill, the route had them go onto the interchange and join the M1 which travelled East in generally the opposite direction to which they started on the main road. After one hell of a straight stretch there, the journey back to where they started began as they took the offramp back on to the main road much further east than they'd started and simply followed the road along the shoreline until they got back to the finish line.

Max hadn't bothered asking Thompson this, but he really wanted to know how he knew all this considering that he hadn't set foot on the scene in person before tonight. But Max didn't have any more time to ponder the question as a pretty girl walked in front of his car and stopped in front of both of them. Moodswing, who still hadn't put his helmet on, gave the young woman – who could have easily been a teenager – a wolf whistle.

"Hey girl. Aren't you looking fine tonight."

As Moodswing took this moment to flirt with the lady, Max took the moment to once again speak to *Baby Cradle*. "Okay *Baby Cradle*, I know he's the King but he's also overconfident which means we can get him. I have experience in street racing, and he doesn't know that. We have a destiny you and I, so let's fulfil it." The helmet had muffled out his words, so no one had heard him. Now done flirting, the woman lifted her red cloth in the air before lowering it and on cue, their tires spun as the race began.

The first thing that registered was the sheer amount of noise of the engines. But lucky enough, his earphones, which were firmly tucked in his ears, were drowning it out. Max had timed his first gear shift perfectly as they continued down the main road for about half a kilometre before curving north. Up ahead, he saw the M3 onramp that inclined onto the freeway.

"Okay Max," said Thompson's voice, speaking as if inside his head, "you're coming up on the freeway." He was speaking to him through his earphones.

"Yeah I can see that, mister mission control," said Max sarcastically.

"Hey, just doing my part, man."

Thompson was right so Max couldn't really be upset. "How can you see this if you're not wired into the car with the app?"

"I'm streaming the race like everyone else here. Remember what I told you about the traffic surveillance cameras?"

Oh right. As Max sped onto the freeway, he looked up and right there, high on a pole, was a round camera which was capturing their every move right now. Max remembered Thompson telling him something about how when the scene took over the cameras for their races, they looped another image for the official surveillance system so that authorities looking at it would be none the wiser to the race. Of course, that didn't help with the civilians currently on the freeway as Max made his first swerve to avoid a civilian car.

"Damn."

"Yeah," said Thompson, having seen what happened – or didn't happen, "that was close. In other news, Moodswing is just ahead of you."

Max darted his eyes a few metres ahead to his right and saw the black and red vehicle speeding on, in the emergency lane. "Yeah, I can see him. He's in the yellow lane."

"Which is where you should be because the offramp you're going to take is on the right-hand side of the road."

"But that's in a kilometre, am I right? So, I've still got time to get that side."

Thompson made a sound that was clearly negative. "I don't know, man. These cars are fast. You'll be there in no time."

However, that didn't matter as Max made up his mind to cross the lanes when he saw Moodswing turn to look at him and blatantly stuck his hand up to wave at him. "Jackass," said Max. Max then moved into the slow lane after passing another car which hooted at him. He waited to pass another car in the middle lane before joining it. But before Max could join the fast lane on his right, he quickly understood just what Thompson meant about how fast these cars were.

Ahead of him was a car in the middle lane which was just ahead of a car in the fast lane which looked to be overtaking the other. Realizing that he was coming entirely too fast to fit between the gap between the cars, Max swerved back into the slow lane before crossing all three lanes ahead of the two cars to finally end up in the fast lane.

Max looked up ahead at Moodswing now just a couple of meters ahead of him as he raised his hand again, this time pointing his index finger straight up. Max looked at him, confused for a moment before Moodswing rotated his wrist so that his index finger was now pointing to the right. Max understood what he was saying immediately when Moodswing suddenly swerved onto the offramp and Max followed him, nearly hitting the barricade having almost missed it.

Thompson made another sound effect. "Jeez, that was close. Eyes on the road, buddy."

"Next time, a little warning would be good."

"Right. I just assumed you knew the route."

"Oh yeah, from the dozens of times I've done this before," said Max, sarcastically again. "I'm driving pretty fast here, Thompson. Even if I do know the route, just tell me when the next turn is coming up." Max tried not to be too hard on Thompson. After all, *Max* was the one driving.

"I got you, man. It's just a bit of a learning curve over here too, man. Well the good news is that the Mike One is quieter this time of night. It's not very busy."

"Right, and the bad news?" said Max shifting gears again following the interchange.

"Isn't it obvious? You're still behind Moodswing."

Well that's about to change, thought Max, defiantly. Max began to start gaining on Moodswing but when he got close enough, he saw Moodswing wave again and it was clear that Moodswing was playing with him. To prove it, Moodswing accelerated. The M1 was as Thompson had predicted, without much traffic so much so that both

126

Moodswing and Max were driving on the oncoming side of the road: the right-hand side. While not as brightly lit as the M3, Max could see clearly ahead of him. He was currently doing 220 kilometres per hour but judging from Moodswing who was pulling away, *he* was doing something closer to 240.

The road itself was definitely a longer stretch of straight road than the M3. It didn't have any inclines or downhills making it the perfect place to contest who was a better driver. In fact, Thompson had mentioned that this was where the scene had their drag races with plenty of asphalt to determine the Duke of Drag.

Suddenly, Thompson's voice came alive in his ear. "What is he doing? Doesn't he see it?"

"What's going on, Thompson?" But Max didn't need any explanation as he saw it right in front of him. Continuing to show off, Moodswing once again pointed out the offramp straight ahead however instead of going right, he swerved past one of the only cars on the freeway ahead of him onto the fast lane before crossing back across both lanes now ahead of the car before power drifting right onto the offramp (technically the *on*ramp in truth) in an clockwise direction, counteracting his swerve.

While Max admitted that his move was beautiful, stunning to behold especially in an open wheel car like theirs, he'd had about enough of Moodswing's showing off. Lucky enough, it seemed the universe, lady luck or whatever power that be had also had enough as Moodswing suddenly came across a problem which was marked by Thompson's gasp.

On the 'offramp', Moodswing had come across a car entering the freeway. And while it would have been easy to dodge, Moodswing was still in a drift, counteracting his earlier swerve. With it being impossible to straighten up in time to pass the car, Moodswing was forced to slow down. This gave Max the perfect opportunity to pass him as he'd driven onto the 'offramp' without swerving and simply passed the car on the right and left Moodswing in his rear view.

Max smiled as he continued on, now back on the main road and officially in the home stretch. "Tell me you saw that."

"Yeah I saw it," said Thompson, clearly smiling. "Now don't get cocky, kid."

"Are you quoting Han Solo?"

"Just live up to your name and punch it to the max."

Max didn't need to be told twice as he knew why they called Moodswing, King: he was currently the best on the scene. He also didn't want to make Moodswing's mistake of getting overconfident. He had an opportunity and he needed to capitalize on it. As Max sped on, travelling down the much darker road at 240 kilometres per hour, he couldn't help but take in the view to his left. The way in which the full moon sat looming in the sky, hiding behind the clouds with what little light was coming from it bouncing off the ocean's surface, it felt like one of those epic moments. This suited Max perfectly as he realized – with the finish line coming up – that he was about to realize something of an epic moment himself.

As Max looked in his rear-view mirror, he had to give it to Moodswing as the man had managed to catch up and was now just a few feet behind him. But it was too little too late as Max crossed the finish line first, converting his lead into a victory. Despite winning, Max realized in those final moments just how formidable Moodswing was... or would have been if he hadn't been showing off.

As Max re-entered the parking lot area, he was given a hero's welcome with Thompson giving him one hell of a manly hug, almost in tears while the other XF racers and their companions gave him handshakes and pats on the back. Max knew he must have done something quite monumental when he saw Shade of all people give him a long look as he glimpsed him leaving down the rampway having been on his usual perch the whole time.

While everyone else officially welcomed him to the scene, all smiles, there was one person not smiling which was the King himself. Scowling at him from across the lot, Max realized that he may have just gained an enemy for life. But that didn't matter. Max felt like he was floating on cloud nine. After all, he never felt better than when he was moving at high speed. And now, because of this race, because of *Baby Cradle*, he had a future filled with high speed moments.

CHAPTER NINE
DETAINED

Lisa wasn't new to the break time punishment of prefects. She'd been here before. However, all the previous times had been for silly things like wearing her uniform incorrectly or being caught in the school passages during class. This was the first time she'd been to break time detention where she felt she deserved it. After all, she had *antagonized* poor "Lew" into giving it to her when she'd arrived late to school again.

Angela hadn't been with her this time, but Lisa knew what she had to do: smile, blush, be generally cute. But, for the life of her, Lisa couldn't stomach it. She just couldn't stand the idea of getting out of punishment

131

because of her looks. Those same looks she said that she didn't like having. While she might be stuck with her looks, she sure as hell didn't have to use them to get away with murder. So, she'd promptly decided to ignore Lewellyn and walk away, forcing his hand. Break time detention was the result.

Unfortunately, the one thing she couldn't have counted on, in getting break time detention, was meeting *him* again. *Oh great,* thought Lisa upon seeing him. *Now I'm going to have to deal with this too.* The first thought she had upon seeing Max sitting there was just how sexy his hair made him. She hated that there was a part of her that was attracted to this guy. But Angela had seen it and so had he two days ago in the Shop. While Lisa had been arguing with him, trying to get him to leave, she had also been beside herself at being that close to him. And now he was here and sitting at the desk right next to the one she'd been directed to.

Prefect's break time detention wasn't like normal detention. For one thing, it was held in a small quad behind the prefect's room. In the quad, old desks – the types you could flip open and store stuff in – were lined against the walls under what little cover there was in what was supposed to be the veranda that ran the edges of the quad. Unfortunately for the punished, this meant they got no sunlight which came in from the void above and the detention didn't get cancelled when it rained because they were technically under cover.

Lisa took her seat next to Max and made a point not to give in to her emotions about being that close to him. Upon seeing *her*, Max smiled, first surprised and then amused. Lisa was not in the mood. "We missed you in school the last two days."

Max gave a slight nod of approval. "Yeah, that's why I'm in here right now. Break time detention now and teacher's detention after school."

Lisa made a face as if to say "ouch". "Well there goes your Friday afternoon. I hope whatever you were doing was worth it."

"Oh," said Max smiling rather proudly, "it was worth it."

Lisa wondered just what the hell could make him proud of having to spend his Friday afternoon here, in school instead of on the beach. Indeed, it was Friday which almost made Lisa second guess her plan of getting herself punished when she realized it. But she'd went along with it, anyway, figuring that at least it wasn't afternoon detention.

To Lisa's utter relief, the two of them were joined by Darcy Stevens who preferred to go by the nickname "Stevie". She remembered that Stevie was Tar's sister who worked in Tar's beachfront diner every day after school the same way she herself worked at the Shop. Stevie sat herself down on Lisa's right so that Lisa now sat between Max and Stevie. If Lisa had arrived just two minutes later, she could have strategically had Stevie sitting piggy in the middle.

"Hey Max," said Stevie, enthusiastically.

"Hey Stevie."

Lisa looked from Max, who was still grinning like an idiot about whatever the hell he was doing these past two days to Stevie who was also grinning for reasons unknown. "You two know each other?"

"We've met," said Max simply.

Lisa looked at Stevie who nodded in agreement. Lisa accepted it and moved on. "So, Stevie, what are you in for?"

"Bunking class."

Lisa rolled her eyes. This wasn't the first time that Stevie had done this. "Your brother is going to kill you."

Max almost laughed. "Everyone keeps saying that."

"I had to," said the ever-excited Stevie. "I didn't have any data, so I asked a friend of mine to download the video of the race."

"You're still into *that*?" said Lisa in an exasperated tone.

"Ssshhh," said Max just as the prefect came closer. The prefect quickly dispatched their detention work to them – writing lines – and told them that she would be in the prefect room and could hear everything and that there would be no talking. All three of them dismissed this idea believing that there was no way she could hear them whispering from a room all the way on the other side of the quad. So, they swiftly continued talking.

"So, who was racing in this race you just *had* to download?" asked Lisa. She was well aware that half the school was into the underground racing that happened almost every night. While only a dozen or two of them took part in the scene, almost everyone else streamed it live. The fanbase was extraordinary. But Lisa was one of the very few that wasn't interested.

When Stevie didn't answer her question, Lisa gave her a look and saw that Stevie was looking at Max who was smiling prouder than ever. Then it hit Lisa like a hammer. "You!? You've," said Lisa whispering very loudly, "you've been here three days! You're racing already!?"

Stevie interjected before he could answer for himself. "And he's very good at it too. He beat Moodswing."

"How—" Lisa cut herself off, not sure what to say. She recovered quickly. "How the hell did you get a vehicle in *two days*!?" The last they spoke, the guy wanted to buy *her* engine.

"I'm resourceful." This time, Max's smile was more flirtatious.

Stevie bumped her. "Hey, check it out." Lisa glanced at Stevie's smart phone and saw the high-angled surveillance footage of Moodswing counter-steering on a drift onto an offramp, narrowly missing a car and another bright yellow XF race car passing him onto the main road."

"That yellow one, was *you*?" said Lisa referring to Max.

Max nodded. "It's called *Baby Cradle*."

"How badass," said Lisa teasing him. "But you didn't answer my question: how did you get it?"

Once again, Stevie interjected. "Rumour has it that he and Moodswing made a bet: the car versus Max doing anything Moodswing wanted for a week."

"How juvenile." *Speaking of juvenile*, thought Lisa... "Stevie, you're only fifteen. You shouldn't be involved in any of this stuff, even knowing about it."

Stevie's eyes popped open. "The whole school knows about it, Lisa. Even the Grade Eights. Why does everyone insist on treating me with kid gloves?"

"Maybe because you're a kid." The words came from Max. Lisa was stunned by them. In that moment, she felt like she was seeing another side of Max. Not the daredevil side, but the side that knew right from wrong. "Your brother is just trying to look out for you, Stevie." Stevie waved him off and got to work with her lines.

Meanwhile Lisa gave Max a thoughtful look. "That would be sweet and all if it wasn't so hypocritical. You're also a kid, you know. *You* shouldn't be doing this stuff either."

Max gave her a long look, as amused as ever. "You're Mother Teresa now?"

However, Lisa wasn't one to whimper into a ball at the sound of one insult and retaliated. "That depends. How often are you this flirty with nuns?" While the quip was meant to undercut Max's flirtation, she realized that she'd said it with way too much flirtation in her *own* voice to be effective. If anything, he was probably more attracted to her now.

Lisa also found herself locked in a stare with him, which she realized had been a mistake. How the hell was she going to pull away from this when he had such pretty eyes? Lucky for Lisa, she had back up she didn't ask for. And unlike Angela's words, Stevie's words were a welcome distraction from the romantically tense moment.

"Hey, are either of you guys going to the beach party tonight?"

*

For the third time this week, a motorcycle pulled into the parking lot in front of the beach. This time Moodswing was alone when he climbed off, took off his helmet and looked at the diner in front of him. He sighed. *I can't believe I used to like coming here as a kid*, he thought. As Moodswing walked to The Dive, he thought about his teenage years which weren't that far behind him.

139

A lot had changed in the past 7 years and not just on the scene. Even in his life. Back when he used to hang out with his rich friends, Moodswing was just another face in the crowd. It was the older kids that were popular back then. Even when they did the unthinkable and procured what they would come to call the XF race cars, Moodswing still wasn't the talk of the town. No, that came later when he started winning races.

That was when his other friends started to take him seriously. While they had tried to buy him out of his popularity, Moodswing had relented and forced the issue to be handled on the asphalt. Nowadays, they called that the old way, even though that was still the way they handled it to this day. He'd watched as his rich friends dwindled to be replaced by better competition which forced Moodswing himself to become a better racer. But even though he was the best now, there were still some old ghosts that he never got the better of, such as Pieter "Tar" Stevens.

"What the hell are you doing here, Moodswing?" Those were the words that greeted Moodswing when he walked into The Dive.

Moodswing held out his hands as if suggesting that it was obvious. "I heard you were throwing a party here tonight."

Tar gave him a hard look. "Yeah well, you're not invited."

Moodswing feigned confusion. "It's a public beach." Moodswing started forward, slowly. "C'mon Tar, what happened to your shining hospitality?"

"You wore it out," said Tar, defiantly, "around the time you started beating up teenagers on the beach."

"Oh, c'mon now. I did as you said: handled it the old way. Your boy even beat me; has the keys to the car and everything. You *won*."

Tar smiled. "Is that why you're here," he said as he continued in cleaning the tables as he had been when Moodswing walked in, "to tell me I won."

"This time," added Moodswing, sombrely. "You won *this time*. But you never beat me when it counted."

"And when was that?" said Tar, pretending to be confused.

"On the scene; on the blacktop."

"We never faced each other on the blacktop."

"That's because you left." Moodswing was now right in front of Tar. "You just quit and scurried off, like a coward."

Tar's face had darkened before something dawned on him and he smirked. "So that's what's bugging you. It's the idea that I was better than you and you never got a chance to disprove it." Tar had hit the nail on the head judging from Moodswing's stiffened jaw. "Well that's too bad because I'm never going to get back on the scene. I'm retired and honestly, you should too. Let the new blood take the reins. Our time is done." Tar circled round to another table and started cleaning it.

Moodswing shook his head. "No, only *you*'re done. And you're right, once upon a time I did resent you taking away my opportunity to beat you, but not anymore. No, I'm glad you retired because you didn't belong."

While Moodswing thought he had him with his insult, Tar's smile only widened to his chagrin. "But I know someone who does. Max McKay. He was here all of two days and he beat your ass all over the street. The *King's* ass. How did that feel, Moodswing? How did that feel?"

Moodswing's stiffened jaw twitched as silence overcame him momentarily. "I hear you applied to the Navy again. How's *that* going? What is this, your third time now?" This time Moodswing's insult landed perfectly as Tar clenched his own jaw... along with his fists.

"Get out," he said pointing to the door. "Get out!"

Moodswing smiled and turned around. However, on his way out, he issued a warning. "Don't ever get involved in my business again, Tar. Or you'll regret it."

Moodswing didn't care if he could never face Tar in a race. If he couldn't beat him on the streets, then he'd settle for beating him out here in the real world. He vowed a long time ago that he'd never let anyone get the better of him again. He was never going to play second fiddle to anyone again. Not Tar and certainly not Max McKay. If they were going to cross him then he was just going to have to cross them right back.

CHAPTER TEN
PARTY AT THE BEACH

"Don't you just love beach parties?"

As they got out of the car, Lisa wanted to roll her eyes at her best friend's words. Angela knew very well that she didn't like parties in general. But Lisa knew why Angela loved them. It was because she got to show off her body shamelessly. Even earlier in the car, Angela's silver BMW 120d, Angela was already wearing her bikini. Then again, when you were as much of a bombshell as Angela was, it was a shame to come to the beach and *not* wear a bright white, revealing bikini like hers.

Lisa herself had settled for wearing her red bikini *under* her clothes which was a simple Mickey Mouse vest and a pair of short shorts. Lisa had actually settled for a lot of things today including coming here in the first place. But while she would much rather be working in the Shop again, she decided to accept Angela's invitation knowing that her father would still want her to live a normal teenage girl's life at least *once* in a while. Angela had been shocked when she only had to ask once.

"Wow," Angela had said earlier. "And here I thought I was going to have to guilt you into coming by telling you how lonely I was during break when you abandoned me." Indeed, Angela was all set to tell her how stupid it was of her to get into detention. Lucky enough, Lisa mentioned that Max was there which was enough for Angela to completely change her tune about her being in detention. Of course, Angela being Angela, she then asked if he's a frequent detention attendee. "Because if he is, then you might want to sharpen your delinquency skills."

Lisa had enjoyed that joke. Even as they locked up the car and headed for the beach, Lisa smiled, remembering Angela's words. When Angela suddenly broke out into a run towards the beach, she called back to Lisa to come with. "No, you go ahead. I think I'll hang back here at The Dive."

As much as Lisa was all for *coming* to the party, she had no intention of *partying*. No, she planned on just sitting in one of the booths in The Dive and relaxing. As she made her way into the beachfront diner, she looked out onto the beach at the party set up. Most of the action was a short walk down the beach where a small amphitheatre was located next to the promenade. In the centre of the amphitheatre was a local band, performing one of the current favourites in school. All one hundred of the teenagers at the amphitheatre were jamming to the song at that very moment.

On the beach itself was a sea of people – young people – either swimming or lounging on the beach with a collection of gazebos lined alongside the promenade from the amphitheatre to The Dive. *Wow,* thought Lisa. *Tar didn't spare a cent on this one.* Of course, he was going to benefit the most as all those excited little teenagers would be coming to his diner to get something to eat.

When Lisa walked inside, she greeted Tar and then headed upstairs. It had been a while since she'd been a regular at The Dive. In fact, she hadn't been back here since she dated her ex-boyfriend. If there was one thing that he loved other than rugby, it was coming to the beach. But all of that was behind Lisa now. When she got upstairs, she found none other than Stevie, sitting in the corner booth wedged between the window overlooking the parking lot and the railing overlooking the ground floor.

Lisa approached her. "On a busy night like this, I thought you'd be working the tables."

Stevie had been watching something on her phone but looked up when Lisa spoke. "Tar gave me the night off. He heard about my detention and is punishing me."

Lisa laughed. "Giving you the night off is *punishing* you?"

Stevie raised her eyebrows to say "yes". "Hey, that's one pay-check out the window and a crapload of tips down the toilet too." Lisa conceded that she had a point. "You haven't been back here in a while. What gives?"

Lisa shrugged. "Change of scene, I guess."

"Huh," said Stevie going back to her video, "and here I thought it would be because a certain good-looking racer asked you on a date."

Lisa knew that she was talking about Max. How could she not, considering that she was sitting right there when she accidentally flirted with him? Although, as the day went by, Lisa started to wonder if it had been an accident at all. *It had to come from somewhere, didn't it?* But, upon seeing the amused smile on Stevie's face, Lisa decided to change the subject.

"What are you watching anyway? Is it still that race?"

Stevie's grin widened. It clearly was. "You should really watch the whole thing. Your boyfriend is very good."

"He's *not* my boyfriend."

"Aha. Anyway, you should watch it."

"And you should stop. Seriously Stevie, why are you so into this?"

"Why? Are you saying that I shouldn't be because I'm a girl?"

"I'm the last person to tell you *not* to like cars because you're a girl. I'm talking about this," she said pointing to the phone. "That, what they're doing right there is absurd. Racing that fast in live traffic. Someone's going to get hurt one day."

Stevie fought off rolling her eyes, clearly having heard all this before. "You know, where were you guys to tell my brother all this when *he* was the one wearing the helmet, sitting behind that wheel? Lisa, of course there's a risk in doing this but there's also a purpose."

Lisa looked at Stevie as if for the first time. She'd never heard her speak like this before. "What purpose are you talking about?"

Stevie tried to speak but struggled to find the words. "Lisa, when you find something that drives you, something that gives you the fuel to go as far as you possibly can, you can't tell me the thing you should do is ignore it."

While Lisa listened to what Stevie was saying, all she could think of was that she didn't sound like a *fan* of the scene. She sounded like a racer. "Stevie," said Lisa, her concern now raised, "you haven't been trying to—" Lisa was suddenly cut off when some excited whispering downstairs turned into a small cheer and a round of applause. Lisa looked over the railing to see Max walking into The Dive.

Lisa wasn't at all surprised by this reaction. It wasn't much of a secret that the young regulars of The Dive also made up the fan population of the XF racing scene. In fact, when the sun set at The Dive, that was when the cell phones, tablets and laptops were brought out as the patrons glued their eyes to the underground races. Unfortunately, that was not Lisa's concern right now.

While Lisa's eyes were still on Max, he looked up and his eyes met hers. Lisa turned away. "Oh crap." Suddenly, for some insane reason, Lisa wondered what she looked like. She quickly shook her head. *No, no, no. Don't do that. Don't do that thing all girls do when they like a guy. Lisa, he's a bad boy. He's a racer for Heaven's sake.*

151

Unfortunately, this time, Stevie's words were *not* the welcome distraction they were last time.

"Don't worry," she said, once again smirking, amused. "You look hot." Before Lisa could rip her a new one, Stevie was back into her video, eyes down.

"Well, well, well. Fancy meeting you here." There was no doubting it this time. Max was definitely flirting with her.

Lisa searched for the words but couldn't think of a good retort. "Yeah, fancy." Lisa fought hard against the urge to smack her palm to her face. *That's it, Lisa? That's the best you can say?* He must have thought she was a chump.

Max leaned in expertly: not so close as to invade her personal space but also close enough that Lisa understood that what he was about to say was for her ears only. "You know, if I knew you wanted to come here, I would have asked you out on a date."

Lisa's eyes widened ever so slightly, and her cheeks seemed to automatically twitch. *Dammit Lisa! Don't blush. Don't blush. Don't blush!* Lisa refrained from blushing. *Good, now say something clever, dammit.* "Maybe it's better you didn't. What if I'd said no?" *Argh no, that was... pretty good.* But there was no taking it back now: she was flirting. Max smiled. *Oh great, now his smile is irresistible.*

There definitely was something about the way his mouth went crooked so perfectly. Had it always been this way when he smirked? Had she just not noticed? Because she was noticing it now. Lisa looked back at Stevie who was now trying to hide behind her phone. Max noticed her too.

"I'm sorry, was I interrupting something?"

"Oh no," said Stevie, sliding out of her seat. "I was just leaving." She nodded at Max as she left. "Nice seeing you again, Max."

"See you, Stevie."

Lisa didn't know whether to be grateful that Stevie was gone and now she didn't have an audience or to be upset that she was gone because now she was left alone with her crush. *Damn, being a girl is complicated sometimes.*

"So, what's good here?" asked Max. When Lisa simply looked at him, as if disappointed that *that* was the best he could do, Max continued. "That's a sincere question. The one-time Thompson brought me here, he decided not to bother with the menus, so I literally don't know what they serve here."

Dammit, don't laugh. Don't laugh. Lisa laughed. She hated to admit it, but Max's sense of humour was delightful. At the very least, it was going to be an enjoyable evening, one way or the other.

*

After the food they ordered arrived, the two of them got to talking. "So, shouldn't you be racing or something, what with it being night-time and all?"

"Nah, I wanted to give the *Cradle* a night off."

Lisa tried not to laugh. "*The Cradle.* You've already nick-named it."

Max shrugged. "Why not? It's mine now."

154

Lisa remembered what Stevie said about their juvenile wager. "And how does it drive?"

Max narrowed his eyes and leaned forward. "You know, for someone who doesn't like this underground racing scene, you sure are interested in how I race."

"Because I asked one question?" But Lisa wasn't afraid of explaining herself. "For your information, I'm interested in the engine, *not* your racing."

"Aha. What, looking for tips?" said Max, clearly referring to the engine in the Shop.

"Ha, oh please. I'm already building the greatest engine of all time."

"Is that right?" Max smiled when Lisa nodded. "Okay, tell me about it."

Lisa dodged the question. "Excuse me. We were talking about your engine, not mine."

Max shrugged nonchalantly. "You show me yours, I'll show you mine."

Lisa pretended to think but wore a playful smile on her face. "What do you want to know?"

"Let's start simple: what's its name?"

"The *Yellow Prancer*." Lisa lost her smile when Max laughed. "Something funny over there?"

"Well it's not exactly a badass name."

"This coming from the driver of *Baby Cradle*?" This time Max lost his smile, so Lisa went on. "I mean, it's cute I'll give you that. As cute as your hair but it's not badass."

"Well let's just say the *Cradle* leaves all the badass on the blacktop."

Lisa laughed. "The blacktop? You're calling it that already?"

Max ignored the jab and continued. "What about the name of your engine: The *Yellow Prancer*. What's that about?"

"I told you it was the greatest engine of all time, right? Well, I gave it a name that mirrored the greatest car engine of all time." Lisa thought she was going to have to explain the name but to his credit, Max got it.

"Oh, I see. It's named after the Ferrari logo, the badge. A prancing stallion on a yellow background." Max smiled. "I actually like that. It's also not so on the nose since technically—"

"—the stallion that's prancing is black, not yellow," she said, completing his thought. "Now, your turn. Tell me about *Baby Cradle*.

After bantering more about whose turn it was to say what, they ended up telling each other all about each other's engines. Lisa explained why she was building the *Yellow Prancer*: as a metaphor for what dedication and hard work can bring you. Max didn't fully buy it and explained that why he loved racing was that he found the most peace when he was travelling at 200 kilometres an hour.

"What about you?" said Max after they'd said all there was to say about racing. "Tell me about you."

This time, Lisa didn't know what to say? "What do you want to know?"

"Anything. Anything about you, your life. What do you like, what do you not like? You know: the stuff that makes you who you are."

I'll tell you what I don't like, thought Lisa, *questions about what I do and don't like.* But Lisa knew she couldn't say that. It was going too well to go there. Lisa thought. "Why don't you tell me who you think I am?"

"You want *me* to read *you*?" After Lisa nodded, he made a face. "I don't know. I'm very perspective."

"I'll be the judge of that," said Lisa, smugly.

"Okay." Max leaned forward again and looked at her as if in deep thought. "You grew up well off. We're not talking a lot of money, just enough that you tend to always get what you asked for. It was enough for you to know what it looks like overseas but not so much that you won't have to work when you're older otherwise you'd be in private school or some such.

"You're highly intelligent but about the practical stuff, not the theoretical stuff. You hate studying. You prefer to be using your hands. I wouldn't be surprised if you intentionally enrol at a Technikon over a university as you have a high respect for trade work. You're probably friends with your plumber."

"Isn't everyone?" said Lisa, impressed with what she was hearing so far.

Max smiled before sighing, as if the next part was going to be hard. "You hate the fact that you are ridiculously beautiful. It's not just that you're hot. It's the fact that you *know* that you're hot. You're self-aware of just how much you can get away with because you're beautiful and you loathe that."

Holy crap! How did he know that!? Lisa was beside herself in awe. She had read him like an open book. And to top it off, he'd said it in such a way that it came off as a total turn on. *How the hell did he do that?* And he wasn't even finished yet!

"But at the same time, you know well enough *not* to complain about your looks because beautiful people—"

159

"—don't get to complain about being too beautiful."
He totally gets me. But Lisa knew she couldn't get smitten
just yet. "Well," she said trying her damnedest not to
sound impressed, "that was excellent. But can you tell me
what my favourite colour is?" They both laughed. After
finishing their meals, Max – ever the gentlemen – stood
up and asked her if "she would mind too badly if he could
take her on a walk?" She'd said she wouldn't mind at all.

*

As they walked along the promenade, further and
further away from the party, Max had continued to read
her, now delving into her favourite foods and drinks.
While he admitted that he himself was an open book – as
he had eaten his favourite meal tonight: burger and coke –
he struggled a bit figuring out what Lisa liked.

"Sea food?" he said, upon hearing her tell him after
failing to guess. "Really, you're that girl?"

"What's wrong with seafood?"

"Girl, the ocean is for swimming, not eating out of."

"Hey, I'll have you know that I know the greatest fish and chips joint on the island." Lisa made a face. "Don't tell Tar I said that."

"Well I'm all for some hake with a side of chips but I still firmly believe what I said." Max then looked down the beach at the ocean. "In fact," he said before taking off his t-shirt, "I say we put my theory to the test."

"What?" While Lisa's response worked perfectly well for what Max had said, she had in fact, been reacting to the sight of him without his shirt. *Lord, tell me I'm not melting.* The man was stunning, even more so when he finally let his beautiful locks out from his hair band. What fascinated Lisa the most wasn't his full chest, tight stomach or the way his pants held him around his waist, but rather that he wasn't perfect.

While he had abs, he only had four to speak of and while his coily hair was sexy as hell on his head, the few curly hairs he had on his chest seemed out of place on his stunning physique. And now that he was without his top, he appeared to be slouching ever so slightly. But dammit, these were the things that she found truly attractive about

161

him as she believed those perfect types belonged exclusively in the movies, not in real life. She turned back to his face just as he spoke.

"So, what do you say? Night swim?"

"That's not exactly the safest thing in the world."

Max pointed up to the heavens. "It's still a full moon. Which means we've got plenty of light to see anything unsafe."

Lisa was running out of excuses, but she did suspect an ulterior motive. She narrowed her eyes. "You just want to see me in my bikini, don't you?"

He leaned in close. "Yes," he said simply.

Good Lord. There was something so attractive about his confidence right now which only became more so when he took two steps back and extended his hand. Lisa didn't waste any more time and took off her Mickey Mouse vest and her short shorts to reveal her red two-piece bathing suit. Ever the gentleman, Max made a point not to oversexualize her once she was in her swimsuit and instead took her hand and they quickly made their way into the water.

The water was freezing cold, but it didn't matter. The chemistry between them seemed to be warming them up quite nicely. She marvelled at how graceful he looked in the water. She had expected his hair to misbehave in the ocean but instead it looked like it was born to be in water. But that got her curious.

"Can I ask you something?" she said as they treaded water. "It's about your hair."

"Shoot."

"What the hell do you do with it when you're racing? Does it fit into the helmet?"

Max laughed. She was glad he wasn't offended by the question. "It's interesting that you ask me that while we're swimming. I wear a swimming cap to keep it down."

This time it was Lisa who laughed. "And don't you worry that you're going to look hella stupid wearing a swimming cap when you're nowhere near a swimming pool?"

"I wear a bandana over it."

Lisa gave him a look. "Why the hell do you do that?"

"Well it kinda looks stupid wearing a swimming cap when I'm nowhere near a swimming pool, don't you think?" Upon hearing her own words thrown back at her, Lisa burst out laughing and Max joined her. They continued laughing until Max made a face and not a good one. He said that he wasn't feeling too good before he immediately became drowsy.

Lisa immediately knew something was wrong and they began for the shore, but Max didn't make it two metres before his head went under. Lisa grabbed for him and brought him back up before she screamed for help. While Lisa expected to be screaming forever, help quickly came in the form of Tar.

Tar quickly got Max out of the water and began administering CPR. Lisa expected many minutes to pass with Tar trying to revive Max but not ten seconds after Tar started did Max cough up a mouthful of water and start coughing.

"Max, are you okay!?" said Lisa.

"Yeah," he said, hoarsely. "Although I'm still a bit drowsy."

"Drowsy?" said Tar. "Sounds like you ingested something that was trying to put you to sleep. What, did you take sleeping pills with your meal earlier?"

"What?" said Max. "No," he said, or more like coughed.

Tar looked at him thoughtfully before dismissing his thought and helping Max up. "Well, whatever it was, it's all the same: no more night-time swimming, hey?"

Lisa watched Max give Tar a thumbs up before giving her – or at least tried to give her – a reassuring look. "C'mon," she said. "Let's find Angela and get you home." Lisa was thankful that Max didn't argue. As Lisa helped Max walk, focusing on that task instead of thinking about what could have happened, she looked up and saw someone she hadn't seen in a while but could never mistake for anyone else: Moodswing. But what got her attention about Moodswing was the look on his face: he was staring intensely at Max. And in that moment, Lisa had an unthinkable thought and wondered if what happened could have been foul play.

CHAPTER ELEVEN
THE ORIGINALS

Max had always hated Saturdays as a kid. While every other kid in Brisbane cherished Saturdays because the weekend meant no school, Max hated them because it meant chores: around the house and in the garden. As it turned out, not having a mother about the place somehow meant double the amount of housework since – between him and his father – they had to take care of everything. And with one of them having school and the other having work, the weekend was the only real time they had to do them.

This was what led directly to Max's school day, night-time activities back when he used to be a street racer on his bike. Ironically, school nights were the only time he was free to have some fun. While his mother had made no mention of chores here and he didn't seem as restricted here as in Australia, Max still didn't have any joy for Saturdays.

He was currently standing outside The Dive, looking at the mess from the party. What was it with kids and making a point not to throw trash in the perfectly reachable bins?

"Are you here to help clean up," said Tar coming out with a roll of black bags. "Because I'd really appreciate the hand."

"Well considering that you saved my life last night," Max rolled his eyes, "*again*, it seems like the least I can do."

Tar smiled. "Good." He then tore a bag off and handed it to him. "Take this."

*

As the two worked their way across the beach, Max couldn't stop thinking about earlier in the week, when Tar

168

came to his rescue the day after Moodswing and his thugs tried to beat him up. "Hey Tar, can I ask you a question?"

"Shoot."

"The other day, why did you stand up for me against Moodswing?"

"Isn't that obvious? He'd just beaten you up the day before. What was I supposed to do, side with him?"

"That's not what I—" Max rethought his question. "When Moodswing came for more of me and you jumped between us, you suggested a race between us. Why? You didn't know me. You didn't know whether I could drive or not."

"I did that because it was the fastest way to get you out of that jam in a hurry. If I goaded him into a race, then he wouldn't hurt you."

"But you had no way of knowing whether I could drive."

"Well I assumed you knew how to drive."

"That's not the same thing."

"I'm not sure what you want me to tell you here?"

Max was also struggling with what to ask. "I guess I just want to know what you saw in me that made you think that I could even stand a chance against Moodswing."

Tar thought before he answered and smiled. "I saw your guts. It reminded me of myself back in the day."

"You mean, back when *you* were on the scene?"

Tar froze for a moment before continuing, the memory troubling him. "Yeah."

"You know, I could have used some tips though, on how to drive."

"You seemed to have managed well on your own."

Max smiled, feeling smug. "It wouldn't have hurt. It could have been a big help actually."

Tar stopped picking up litter, now quite serious. "Max, I'm going to stop you right there. I'm going to say to you the same thing I told Moodswing yesterday: I'm never going back onto the XF racing scene. Not to race and certainly not to coach. So, if you're looking for your Yoda, sorry pal, but I'm not it."

The tension in the air was thick. Max almost found it ironic that tense moments like this would usually have one find a beach to walk on, yet they were already there. Max decided to cut that tension. "Well I was thinking more along the lines of Bodhi from *Point Break,* but I guess Yoda is a good analogy too." It worked as Tar found himself unable to resist laughing. "So now that we've established that you have no interest in rehashing the past, do you mind if we do something?"

"And what's that?"

"Rehash the past." Once again, Max's sense of humour hit the spot as Tar couldn't help but laugh. Max then asked him what the scene was like back when *he* was a part of it.

The tension had completely fallen away as Tar proceeded. "The scene back when the rich guys were in charge was a different animal altogether. From the get-go, the scene was designed to be a place of fun. And that's why the rich boys were so important: because they provided the resources for us to have fun."

"Wait, you were part of the *first* generation? I thought only rich guys were on the scene back then?"

Tar laughed. "That's a bit of a myth, actually. Understand something: not all of the trust fund babies could drive so some of them," Tar searched for the word, "contracted out. So not-so-rich guys like me, Solo, Touch, the Jele brothers, we ended up racing. But the cars didn't belong to any of us back then. We were simply the hired help. But man, were we good. And the better we were, the more that the trust fund babies were willing to pay us for our services."

"Wow. Thompson definitely left this part out of the stories."

"That's because, contrary to popular belief, history isn't written by the victors. It's written by the guys with the biggest wallets. And that's why the history of the first generation will have you believe that only rich kids were racing. But after the second generation came along, we were more than happy to let that history remain like that because you see, the second generation had us *owning* our vehicles which meant our victories were our own."

"It sounds like the second generation was much better than the first."

"In many ways but we still owed a debt to the first. You see, it was the trust fund babies that created the concept. They were the ones that were crazy enough to take professional wrestling and put it together with *The Fast and the Furious.* Clearly those guys had watched too many movies and too much wrestling as children but without them and that crazy way of thinking, there wouldn't be a scene for you to be competing on."

Max raised his hand for Tar to stop, having gotten lost. "Hold up, hold up, hold, hold. Professional wrestling? How does anything that goes on down there have to do with wrestling?"

Tar smiled. "Someone clearly hasn't been to the second floor yet. That's where the truly crazy congregate before they race."

This certainly explained why Shade was on the roof. "I thought it was where the hot shots congregated?"

"It's also where the racers with the craziest personalities congregate. When you see them, you'll understand. Straight up gimmick land." Tar saw the fascinated look on Max's face. "Pee-ess: when you see Siren, *don't* stare."

"Why would I stare?"

"Trust me. Anyway, that's the history of the first generation of the XF racing scene."

That put a thought in his head. "So then what generation does that make me?"

"They try to keep it uncomplicated so you would be third generation simply because you've almost never interacted at all with the first generation."

This was interesting to Max. But there was still so much he wanted to know. "Another thing, how the hell do they keep order down there?"

"Everything is handled by majority vote and popular decision. But don't overthink it. Remember, the scene was started so these guys could have fun. So, don't start thinking that it's run like a social club or something.

When it comes to keeping the peace, Admin and his crew are picked like teams in a friendly soccer match: people need to agree."

"But then how can you be sure that Admin isn't going to be biased?"

"Has Thompson told you how they hold people accountable down there yet?" Max looked at Tar, unsure how to answer that. "Cricket bats to kneecaps. The moment a decision is made that stinks to high heaven..." Tar made a popping sound with his mouth.

Max's eyes widened at the confirmation of what Thompson had said. "That sounds far more violent than I anticipated."

Tar laughed. "Well you can relax. While those were definitely the old ways of doing things, I hear that times have changed. Now, exile is the more popular choice. They just eighty-six the culprit and he's banned for life."

Max breathed a sigh of relief. While he had no intention of doing anything to earn the other racers' err, he certainly didn't want to risk bodily injury on the off chance that something he did didn't sit well with them. Exile was definitely the healthier choice in his opinion.

Despite all this new knowledge being thrown his way, there was one thing that Max desperately wanted to hear about. "What made you leave the scene?"

This question got Tar's attention and not in a particularly good way judging from the change of expression on his face. His face now had a sadness to it, and it was clear that this was not a topic he wanted to discuss at all. However, there must have been something about Max that made Tar willing to open up about it because Tar began to spill.

"As I said earlier, I was one of the very few involved in the first generation that wasn't rich. I was hired by one of the rich kids in school called Jeremiah Smyth. But over and above being the guy who hired me to drive for him, he was also my friend."

Max saw the way Tar had said that. He really meant it. Admittedly, Max was surprized to hear that he was friends with people he'd been calling trust fund babies since he met him. Clearly, there was more than meets the eye when it came to the history of the XF racing scene.

Tar continued. "Jeremiah couldn't drive for jack." Tar smiled at a memory he was recalling. "I remember the first time I met him; he drove through the front glass window of this local shop. Scared the crap out of me. After paying the lady off – way too much money, I might add – he turned to me, a stranger on the street, and said: 'how would you like to earn a couple of hundred bucks?' Not minding the easy money, I said 'sure' and he asked me to drive his truck. Little did I know that, in the back of that truck was his XF race car.

"You see, Jeremiah had just procured it. That's why he paid that lady so much money for the damage to her shop because he needed to handle that immediately and not call any more attention to the incident than he already had. I drove him to the parking lot which, back then, hadn't been used in years. Now, Jeremiah could talk. Oh man, could the guy talk. On the way over, he told me all about the big secret of the underground racing scene they were about to create. Of course, I ribbed him about not being very good at keeping a secret.

"After arriving, Jeremiah revealed the car to me: this big navy-blue formula one car. At least at the time I thought it was a formula one car. I remember him proudly christening it *Queen Elizabeth's Revenge*. Or *Queen Diana's Revenge*. Or some English queen I'd never heard of's *Revenge*. He told me that it was meant to be a nod to Blackbeard's pirate ship: the *Queen Anne's Revenge*. Of course, I rolled my eyes at the idea and asked him: if he was insistent on naming it after a Queen, then why not name it after a South African queen? He liked the idea but like a typical non-black mainlander, he had no clue about the proud lineage of queens we had. So, I helped him out. And thus, the *Queen Nandi's Revenge* was born."

"*Queen Nandi's Revenge*," said Max, in awe of the name. He almost had tears in his eyes listening to Tar recall what must have been a beautiful race car. "And how did it drive?" Naturally, this was the first question on Max's mind after hearing the name.

Tar smiled, smugly. "Well at first, I wasn't going to find out as Jeremiah had every intention of being the first guy to race that night. I ribbed him about whether he could handle that thing after the way I saw him drive. He ribbed me back by saying that I got to drive the truck, now he gets to drive the race car."

"And?"

"He was as bad at driving that as he was driving the truck. It was a miracle he didn't hurt himself, the other driver or worse, civilians on the street. After getting back and bragging that he would have the car repaired by the end of the week, he said 'new plan: next time, you drive.'" Tar nodded at Max's surprised reaction. "And mind you, this was still day one. I was still a stranger to him. But not after that day.

"After getting to know each other that week, Jeremiah managed to get me 'authorized to race'," said Tar using quotation marks, "and just like that, I had my first race. From then on, I played the role of the driver while Jeremiah played the role of the ever-fussy race car owner and, I guess, team manager. Even though we were a team of two." Tar sighed. "We had a good run, Jeremiah and me. A good run."

"So, what happened?"

"Competition began to get stiff. Around the time Solo won the *Abominable Seduction*, the rich kids were beginning to get restless about the increase in competitiveness and all of them wanted to prove themselves. Jeremiah was no exception. So, one night, he insisted on racing *Queen Nandi's Revenge* against this other guy named Tyger and his vehicle: The *Bronze Bruizer*. I guess the name wasn't a dead giveaway that he should stay away. Long story short, Jeremiah crashed."

At this point, Tar breathed heavily as he recalled the dark memory, tears beginning to well in his eyes. "It was bad. Jeremiah ended up paralysed from the neck down." Tar noticed a frightened look on Max's face. "The good news is his parents managed to find the best doctors in the world or whatever and word has it that he's regained feeling in his arms and torso. But the damage was done to his legs. He'll never walk again, regardless of what any doctor does. There's just way too much damage done to that part of the spine."

While Max felt completely miserable about hearing about the accident, he couldn't help but feel relieved that at least *something* could be done about his paralysis. It was the kind of miracle one only heard about in soap operas. "I'm sorry to hear that, Tar."

"Not as sorry as I was. I hated myself for ever letting him near that car that day. I still do." Tar's guilt was written all over his face. "I was responsible for that vehicle and I let it hurt him."

Max wanted to tell him that it wasn't his fault, but he knew that Tar had heard all that before, so he kept his mouth shut. Tar saw the look on his face and gave him an expression suggesting that it was okay.

Tar went on. "Jeremiah, of course, was a champ about the whole thing, at least in letting me off the hook. As you can imagine, he was traumatized by not being able to move his body, but he blamed himself for getting in the car, *not* me." Tar laughed a kind of laugh of despair. "He even had the nerve to give the car to me telling me he had

181

no more use for it." Tar had to wipe away the tears this time, as they seemed to be free falling. But he managed to recompose himself. "It didn't matter though because on that day, I decided that I'd never get in another XF race car ever again."

Max understood. In fact, he now felt like he understood Tar completely. That was how he was so knowledgeable about the scene yet was not at all a part of it. "So that's why you hate the scene, so much?"

This time Tar's laugh wasn't of despair but of genuine amusement. "I don't hate the scene. Not at all. I loved that place. At the end of the day, that one bad memory does *not* erase all the fun times we had down there. Besides the fact, it's a testament to all the good drivers down there, like yourself, now, that more accidents haven't happened. I just believe that all the racers need to understand the risk and accept the consequences. When you can do that, then by all means, have a joll of a good time."

Max couldn't help but be relieved to hear that as he half expected Tar to suddenly disapprove of his racing on the scene. But he did nothing of the sort. He even said that when Jeremiah contacted him to tell him that the paralysis on the top half of his body was gone, he had encouraged Tar to go back to racing because he was *far* less accident prone. But Tar had declined, unwaveringly.

However, Tar did make one thing clear in regard to what he *did* disapprove of. "My sister can have no part of the scene. After seeing first-hand what can happen to someone who's not a natural street racer, I don't want to risk her neck down there." Tar explained that ever since Stevie found out that he was a racer, she's been obsessed with the scene. He even once caught her researching unofficial racing lessons and admitted that he can't be sure she didn't find what she was looking for. "With our mom gone and our father in prison, I'm the only thing she has left."

Tar explained that his mother had died of cancer when they were younger and while they didn't know it at the time, their father had turned to crime to keep them in school and put food on the table. Luckily, by the time he went to prison, Tar had managed to get The Dive up and running and their father had made enough legitimate money to get Stevie to the end of Matric.

"My Dad is also one of the reasons I'm obsessed with getting into the Navy. I feel like the Stevens' have stolen enough from the good people of Azania. Now it's time for one of them to give back. So, like clockwork, at the beginning of every year, I apply." But Tar explained that they have yet to accept him, so he spends his days running The Dive.

While Max had simply been in awe of Tar's history on the scene before, he was now in awe of the man himself. "Wow, you really are Bhodi."

Tar laughed at the comment, clearly now back in the pre-tension frame of mind and looked up to a group of men approaching the beach. "I might not be able to be your Bhodi, but I think I know a couple of guys who might be."

Max turned around to see Solo Magubane, Touch Mkhize and another Caucasian racer he'd seen on the scene but hadn't actually met. They were dressed very casually which automatically made Max compare them favourably to Moodswing, remembering how both times he'd seen him by the beach, he was dressed head-to-toe in leather. But these guys clearly weren't here for the wrong reasons as Solo lifted a similar roll of plastic bags to Tar's except Solo's roll was orange: for recycling. Yes, there was clearly more than meets the eye with these guys.

CHAPTER TWELVE
THE APPRENTICE

It had been over four years since Moodswing had set foot at Harbour High. And even though it had been that long, it felt like it hadn't been long enough. He hated this place. One of the reasons that he and his friends started the scene was because they needed some way of creating good memories of their high school days lest they became wasted here. But, unfortunately, Moodswing had to come here if he was going to kick-start his plan.

Twice now, Moodswing had had his plans for Max McKay disrupted by Tar. Twice now, he had been owned, conversationally, by Tar. Tar was becoming a bane of his existence and he needed to get rid of him. He needed to get Tar out of the picture of the scene. Tar's ability to command any kind of respect was supposed to have ended the day he decided to leave. Yet, last week, Tar was able to get an entire race set – a feature race, no less – and a race *he lost*.

While Moodswing knew that Max McKay was the immediate threat to his reign as King, the truth was that Tar was the linchpin that held that threat together. After all, Tar was the one that saved McKay from the beating on the beach. Tar was the one that got McKay the opportunity to win *Baby Cradle*. And Tar was the one that ticked him off, royally, when he suggested that he was always better than him. So, if he was going to take down McKay and reaffirm the credibility of his reign, then he was going to have to get rid of the linchpin and make Tar's words mean nothing on the scene. And Moodswing knew just how to do it.

It had been two days since the beach party which had given Moodswing plenty of time to think. And all that thinking had led him here: sitting on his bike outside Harbour High at 7 o'clock in the morning. Fortunately, he didn't have to wait much longer as the person he was waiting for soon showed up. He honked his hooter which also got the attention of people he had no interest in seeing right now, namely one person.

Across the small parking lot of the school stood McKay who was with a blonde girl whose name he'd never bothered to remember. Standing next to the blonde was a girl who'd just approached her: a light-skinned African girl with blonde streaks in her plaited hair. But the one Moodswing was interested in was the one on the far right, watching a video on her phone: Darcy Stevens. Moodswing pointed his finger at her and when she asked "me?", Moodswing smoothly used the same finger to call her like a father calling a child when they were in trouble.

Naturally McKay and his blonde girlfriend tried to stop her from coming to him, but Tar's younger sister was too curious for her own good. Even if she didn't know who he was, the idea of a man dressed in leather from head to toe, complete with riding gloves and a biker's helmet hiding his whole identity calling her without saying a word, would have been enough to scare any other girl away.

When she got to him, still clutching her phone in one hand and the strap of her school bag in her other, Moodswing lifted his visor to show her who he was. "Do you know who I am?"

She nodded. "Moodswing," she said. "King of the XF racing scene."

"And you're Darcy Stevens, right?"

She got notably excited from hearing him say her name. "Everyone calls me Stevie."

"Right, Stevie." Moodswing took off his helmet so that he could have a proper conversation with the girl. "I hear that you're interested in racing." She nodded. "Specifically, being in the race." This time, she didn't respond. "Is my information wrong?"

Stevie evaded the question. "Why are you asking me that?"

Moodswing smiled. "Good, you cut straight to the chase. So, let me do the same. I wanna make a proposition to you. A racing proposition," he added quickly, so as to make sure he understood his intentions, perfectly.

"What proposition?"

"I teach you how to race." This got Stevie's attention right away. Before she could express her surprise, Moodswing continued. "I teach you how to race and you debut on the scene with your own race car."

Stevie's excitement reached an all-time high before completely dropping as she gave him a look. "Wait, why?"

"Well I could tell you that it's because I'm interested in nurturing young talent; mentoring an apprentice who could someday soon take my place as I retire from the scene. But that wouldn't, strictly speaking, be true. Honestly, this is about your brother."

"My brother?" This confused her. "What does this have to do with Tar?" While Stevie fully expected him to admit to having a beef with Tar, Moodswing decided to spare her the truth of the matter.

"Well, I don't know if he told you this, but your brother was very good in his day, down on the scene. One of the best. In fact, one of the biggest regrets I had about him retiring was that I never got to face him. Anyway, he's made it abundantly clear that he's never coming back. But I think we don't need him back. Because there's another Stevens who's just as good as he was. Except that she hasn't been given the chance to show her stuff. I'm willing to give you that chance."

It was clear that Stevie was beginning to think that this was too good to be true. "So, just because of that, you're willing to give me lessons and just," she struggled to tame her excitement, "give me a car?"

"I gave one to him, didn't I?" said Moodswing, pointing to McKay who clenched his jaw, notably. "Granted he won it in a race the same way you'll have to but if you're as natural-born a racer as your brother, I think that will be a walk in the park for you."

Moodswing could see that Stevie was contemplating it. He saw her look back at McKay who, along with his girlfriend, gestured for Stevie to go back. But Moodswing knew that she wouldn't. The hook had been laid and this was one of those once in a life-time opportunities.

"What do you say?"

Stevie was still looking at her friends. "I say my brother is *so* going to kill me."

"For doing the same thing he did? Maybe Tar needs to jump off his high horse." But Moodswing could see that he was going to lose the pitch to Stevie's integrity if he didn't sweeten the deal. "How about this: just a few lessons in driving a race car. When you see how good you are, maybe then you'll see that you were kinda destined for this."

After a moment, Stevie finally turned back to him and surprised Moodswing by actually smiling. But it was what she said next that absolutely astonished the racing King. "Actually, since we're being so honest and all, I've already been taking racing lessons." On Moodswing's look, Stevie answered his next, and quite obvious, question. "In a city now notorious for its underground racing scene, it wasn't that hard to find someone who offers racing lessons in 'ex-formula' race cars."

Upon hearing this news, Moodswing adjusted his negotiation and went for the close. "Then what are you waiting for? Get on the bike and let's go see your new XF race car." Moodswing had managed to regain the role of the astonisher in the conversation as Stevie looked at him wide-eyed.

"What, right now? But I've got school."

Hook, line and sinker. She was now no longer talking like someone who was on the fence or going to refuse. Moodswing continued. "School can wait. But this offer can't." Moodswing darted his eyes over her shoulder. "It expires once your friends manage to rescue you."

Stevie turned around to see that Thompson had joined McKay and the others. And he seemed more proactive than the rest. "What the hell is this!?" he said to the others.

"It's Moodswing trying to get to Tar, I bet." said McKay.

His girlfriend shook her head disapprovingly. "C'mon, he *knows* that he doesn't want Stevie to have anything to do with the scene."

"Then we need to do something," said Thompson, starting towards them.

When Stevie turned back around to Moodswing, he was already holding out his helmet for her and putting on a pair of black sunglasses. Moodswing was so sure that she was going to come with him that he was already kick-starting his bike. Not two seconds later, Stevie had the helmet on and was climbing onto the bike, straddling it while holding onto Moodswing. Moodswing smiled as he took off just moments before Thompson and McKay tried to grab for her. But it was too late. The beginning of Moodswing's plan was on the way.

*

It had been a couple of days since Moodswing had made Stevie the offer she couldn't refuse. The first two days had been hard for her as she had to deal with the consequences of riding off into the sunset with him. In fact, after setting eyes on her new XF vehicle, she had burst into tears saying that there was no way her brother would let her keep it. But luckily, Moodswing had a plan.

"You're going to have to lie to him," he'd said. "When you get back to him and he asks you about today, you tell him the pitch I made to you, but you leave out the part where you agreed to it. You tell him, once I tried to change your mind by letting you test drive the *Dracula*, you said no and that you couldn't possibly betray him."

"But I *am* betraying him," she'd said. "And it's not like I'll be able to get away with that lie after I have my first race—"

"Oh, by that point it will be too late. Once you're one of us, popularity and majority will do the rest. As long as the rest of us want to see you race, there's nothing that Tar can do."

"You seem so sure of that."

"Your brother was one of us. He knows that once you're on the in, only *you* can say when you want out."

It had worked as Stevie came back the following day after school, and the next day and the next. Together, they had practised driving with one another on a racetrack just outside the city, hidden away from the world. It was a racetrack that his father had built in order to satisfy those customers of his that hated that they couldn't let loose on the cars they had just purchased from him.

Now it was Friday night: Stevie's first night as a racer on the scene. Moodswing had been sure to tell Stevie to keep her helmet on until after the race. Until then, she'd hang out on the second floor with the other big shots on the scene. It was perfect too as the likes of McKay and Thompson were on the first floor which meant there was little chance of them putting two and two together until it was too late. Or course that didn't stop some of the other XF racers here on the third storey of the four-storey parking lot from sticking their noses where they didn't belong.

"Hey Moodswing," said Solo, "who's the babe?"

Stevie, who was already sitting in her vehicle, having found it to be the perfect way to avoid talking to anyone, jerked her head up at being called 'the babe'. But Moodswing hushed her.

"What makes you so sure she's a female?"

Solo raised his eyes and gestured to the ride. Solo had a point. The vehicle Stevie was currently hiding in was bright pink, passion pink, and forewent vinyl stickers for fancy paint patterns that looked like waves of darker pink flames. Stevie's helmet was also coloured pink. Inside this bright pink vehicle, was a frustrated Stevie as pink happened to be the one colour she hated in the entire world. Moodswing had found amusement in this.

Solo gave Stevie a closer look, clearly not able to tell it was her with the helmet on. But when he leaned closer, she shut the visor. "Have we met before?" She kept her mouth shut to which Solo simply shrugged. "So, she doesn't talk but does she have a name?"

"You'll find out her name when you find out the vehicle's name."

But Solo maintained his smile. "So, it *is* a woman. Interesting."

"Why's that so interesting?" The person who spoke was a woman herself. Her name was Antoinette Woordmaan but she went by the handle, 'Antwoord'. She was a thin woman with short spiky hair and a thing for bright red lipstick and large eyelashes. Her striking green eyes made her pale skin prominent.

"Antwoord," said Moodswing simply.

"*Your Majesty*," she replied. Their racing history – particularly their racing wars over the Crown were something of legend on the scene but it left them with a prickly relationship. "So, who's the new chick?"

"My protégé."

Antwoord laughed. "Your protégé? Oh please. Moodswing, everyone here knows you care about no one but yourself. Now we're supposed to believe that you have an apprentice."

But Moodswing merely lifted a hand. "Antwoord, I'm going to stop you right there. There's no point of doing our usual dance that leads to a race because I'm not racing tonight. But if you're so willing to tango..." Moodswing gestured to Stevie, still sitting dead still.

However, Antwoord just scoffed. "Na-ah. I don't break in the new guys. It's either feature race or nothing."

"You're not King anymore, Antwoord. Demands like that don't work unless you're me."

"Maybe, for now. But that's still how I roll. Either way, you're going to have to find another racer to pop your girl's cherry."

"How about Tyger?" It was Solo who spoke, having watched Moodswing and Antwoord banter, amused by it. "Isn't he always bragging that he's always up for a race?"

"That's because no one in their right mind wants to race him," added Antwoord. "Unless they're desperate that is." Antwoord then looked at Stevie. "And I'd say she fits."

Moodswing saw Stevie look at him and gestured for her to dismiss Antwoord's verbal jab. However, Antwoord had given Moodswing an idea. "I'll be right back," he said to Stevie before starting for Tyger. "So much for being *the answer*," said Moodswing, mocking Antwoord as he walked past her. The racer simply swore, earning a smug smile from Moodswing.

As Moodswing made his way over to talk to the bald racer with a huge tiger patch on the back of his race suit, he looked around at the lot. While the second floor was designed much in the same way as the first floor, downstairs, it was occupied in a very different way with three things setting it apart. For one, while there were roughly the same number of racers, there were almost double the amount of people as each racer had two people with them. While it was under the guise of being part of the team, the honest truth was that they were either girlfriends, friends, muscle or just very lucky fans.

The second thing that set the second floor apart was the wild things that some of the racers brought with them on race night. While most of the racers – especially the ones downstairs – set themselves apart by the colour of their vehicles, the vinyl stickers on them and their complimenting race suits and helmets; racers on the second floor went all out to make themselves special.

Moodswing believed the epitome of this was one racer, a gorgeous female racer who always arrived swimming in a glass pool that had been built on a trailer that was pulled in on a bakkie. And the kicker: she swam in it naked. But luckily for those that valued *not* being distracted before a race, she dyed the water so that no one would see her naughty bits. Of course, this did not at all stop her from inviting fellow racers to join her.

It was always a mission to resist, what with her breath-taking good looks and sheer grace in the way she moved in the water. But it was obvious that *that* was her mind game: distraction through seduction. She had her opponents thinking about her body instead of the road which would lead to her smoking them. Her name: Siren.

Moodswing moved past Siren, blowing her a kiss when she winked at him. He looked around the lot and saw the guys that brought to mind the third thing that set the second floor apart from the first: the DJs. There were three of them and all of them were mixing at the same time. The secret: they were using the silent disco format.

Scattered across the lot were people nodding their heads to beats and even dancing yet there was no music, at least none that Moodswing was hearing. Instead, all the people jamming to music were wearing Bluetooth headphones and were in fact jamming to what they were hearing through them. It was an innovation brought from overseas but one that became perfect for the scene. Now they could play music however they wanted to without ever worrying about a noise complaint alerting the authorities.

Moodswing hurried past the DJs and finally got to Tyger. The racer known only as Tyger was currently leaning against a bronze and black tiger-striped race car named the *Bronze Bruizer*. "Hey, Shere Khan, you got a minute?" Moodswing had never cared for tact. So, he didn't care if he was coming across disrespectful. He was the King.

"If it isn't His Majesty," said Tyger in a raspy voice. Tyger's voice had been raspy ever since an accident against a fellow racer a few years ago injured his larynx. Already feared for having a reputation that saw his opponent's end up in collisions – mostly minor – the voice had ironically only added to his mystique making him the last person you wanted to mess with. But Moodswing had never cared about how scary a racer was, just how they raced on the blacktop. "What can I do for you?"

"I want to know if you'd be interested in racing a guy? Well, a girl, actually," said Moodswing, correcting himself.

"You mean victim," said Tyger, darkly. Tyger thought for a minute before catching a glimpse of Stevie in her bright pink vehicle. He shrugged. "I could eat," he said menacingly.

Moodswing wanted to roll his eyes. "Great, then it's a," Moodswing smiled when he thought of the perfect metaphor, "a meal. Now get ready. Your guys' race is next."

As Moodswing made his way back to Stevie, a dark thought went through his mind. There was a part of him that wanted to let the chips fall where they may: just let Stevie race her race and if she got injured, then so be it. It would definitely send a message to Tar. But no, Moodswing had a plan and he was going to stick to it. And that plan required Stevie to succeed in her first race.

"Okay Stevie," said Moodswing when he got to her, "you versus Tyger is a go. And it's next so in a few minutes, you're gonna go down to the start line."

"Don't they have to check that the car is the same spec as his?" she said, her helmet muffling her voice.

Moodswing dismissed this. "Don't worry about that. I've got some pull around here." When she reopened her visor to give him a suspicious look, he raised his hands. "Hey, all I mean is that I got them to check it earlier." She still didn't believe him. "Hey. You win this race and the car is yours. Once it's yours, you can have them check that it's up to spec for every race if you want to." That seemed to calm her down.

"Uhm," she said, not done being suspicious, "Tyger: isn't he like the most dangerous racer on the scene?"

Moodswing had anticipated this conversation so he knew how to shape the narrative. "The truth: yes, he is. But I'm not worried. Do you want to know why? Because I know how he drives. Stevie, there are rules. Rules which dictate that you cannot under any circumstance use your vehicle to damage another racer's vehicle. So contrary to his reputation, he can't physically harm you."

"So, then what does he do?" Moodswing smiled. If she was already willingly listening to his advice, to his influence, then his plan was working perfectly.

*

A few minutes later, Stevie was at the start line standing opposite Tyger, ready to take him on. Meanwhile, Moodswing was upstairs, on the second floor watching from his tablet. The website was already streaming. Moodswing smiled as he saw the comments below the video with almost every commenter asking who this "pink racer" was while the other few were convinced that she was toast against Tyger. However, Moodswing's good mood was interrupted by a familiar voice.

"So, who's the new guy, Moodswing?" said Max as he approached Moodswing.

Moodswing didn't bother turning around. "All in due time, McKay. So, what, you think because you defeated Bomba tonight in, what, your *second* race that you're allowed up here?" Moodswing had watched McKay's race earlier in the night. While he hated the boy, he had to admit that he had some skill.

205

Max opened his hands as if it was obvious. "It's a free country, is it not?"

"Yeah. It's also a democracy where popular decision commands respect."

"Oh, so not you then?" said Max, ever quippy. He dramatically turned his head, looking either side of him. "Where are your goons? Or are they your mooks. It's confusing."

"I see you're confused, considering I just told you to get lost because you don't belong here and yet here you still stand."

"Relax, I'll go, when I've said what I need to say."

"And what's that?"

Max didn't speak immediately and instead opted to stare Moodswing down. "That's Stevie, in the car, isn't it?"

"Oh, is it? That's funny. I never heard anyone say that it was."

"Tar told me that she hasn't worked a single shift at The Dive this week—"

"Is that so—"

"And I think it's because she's been with you."

"You have quite the imagination, McKay."

"Is that her in that car or not?"

"It seems everyone wants to know who's in the car," he said pointing to the tablet. "I guess you'll have to wait to find out just like them."

Max scoffed. "So, what, you wanna hide behind the unwritten rules of the scene? Once she's raced one race, she's one of you and what, Tar can't touch her, is that it?"

Moodswing wanted to smile. He'd nailed it. He'd figured it out. But Moodswing felt compelled to correct one detail. "One of *us*, McKay. You're one of us now. You're a racer. Which means if you want to stay, you'll have to obey those *unwritten* rules. And one of them dictates: that you don't get to be on the second floor unless *you've earned it*!"

Moodswing had suddenly raised his voice which had gotten the attention of the others in the lot. This time Moodswing did smile when they began giving McKay the evil eye. He really *didn't* belong here. Not after only two victories. Moodswing watched as Solo walked up to him and put an arm around him, leading him away. It irked Moodswing that Solo was being nice about it. *You're a feature racer for Heaven's sake, Solo. Big leagues. Act like it.* But it didn't matter as McKay was gone... but not without his last words.

"Rules or no rules, Moodswing. Tar's going to put a stop to this, and you know that. And when he does, you're dead meat. You hear me, dead meat."

"Goodbye McKay," said Moodswing mostly to himself who then went back to what he was doing just in time to see Stevie take off speeding from the line.

The race itself was a stunning contest. Moodswing watched with pride as Stevie followed his instructions to the letter and anticipated Tyger trying to draw her in the overtake on the freeway before moving away to make her hit traffic. Instead Stevie remained resolute like Moodswing had told her and played her own game.

Moodswing was surprised by how much of the race he got to see live as he seldom streamed the races since he didn't care much about the other racers. But now, he was understanding the appeal of watching the races like this and also understood the massive underground fanbase they'd procured.

He looked at the comments section and smiled as he saw comments praising Stevie's moves and being good competition for Tyger. He also saw one comment about Jeremiah Smyth and what Tyger did to him, but Moodswing ignored this. He hated when someone brought up something negative about the scene. It had been a dark time and people needed to forget about it. Jeremiah was gone.

Moodswing was so busy minding the comments that he almost missed Stevie finally overtake Tyger on the M1 as the two gunned it down the straight with Stevie's vehicle showing more staying power than Tyger's *Bronze Bruizer*. From there on out, Stevie had it in the bag as she maintained her lead for the final major turn and sped down the main road to cross the line first.

Beaming from ear to ear, Moodswing made his way down to the finish line just in time to hear Admin say the line he'd specifically asked him to say *after* the race. "Ladies and gentlemen, introducing to the scene, the winner of the race and driver of the *Candyfloss*, I give to you: Darcy Stevens."

Admin had spoken the words to a man holding a smartphone, filming him, instantly beaming the video onto the website so that Stevie had now been introduced to the entire fanbase. Moodswing knew that the racers inside had been watching the stream too so now, they were aware. But this phase of the plan wasn't complete until Stevie climbed out of the *Candyfloss* and took off her helmet and revealed herself to the world. And the moment she did, Moodswing knew his plan was working.

What made it work though were the parts he couldn't have planned for like the way Stevie had stood on her seat to take off her helmet and the way she'd looked to the heavens when she did with that glorious smile of hers. It was like she was born to be an XF racer... which was *exactly* what Moodswing needed: not just for them to love her but for her to *love it*. And boy did she love it.

However, there were few who didn't. Three people, in fact, as Moodswing saw, even from this distance, standing on the first floor looking down on them. They were the only two people not cheering: Max McKay and Thompson Mashaba. There was also someone else who seemed upset at what he was seeing: way on the roof. Moodswing's next biggest challenger: Shade. *Why was he upset?* But that didn't matter. Not to Moodswing. In fact, the more upset they were the happier he was. In fact, he wondered if he wasn't happier than Stevie herself. And the best part was that he was about to be even happier with what followed. It was time for the next phase.

CHAPTER THIRTEEN
THE OLD WAY

Max was beginning to think that going to The Dive on Saturday morning was becoming a thing. While Max had asked Thompson if he wanted to come with, Thompson opted to sleep in, claiming that whenever they weren't in school or on the scene, he spent every waking minute trying to learn more about open wheel race cars. Max really had to buy that guy a beer one day, thank him for all his help in orientating him. He wondered where he would have been without Thompson.

When Max arrived at The Dive, he realized quickly that it was to a very different atmosphere. He walked in to find Tar *not* behind the bar, but rather pacing in front of

Solo, Touch and the third racer in their trio who he'd finally learnt the name of: Shannon Kelly – a tall, lanky man with a youthful face and strawberry blonde hair with bangs he didn't seem to know what to do with since he was forever hand-combing it out of his face. Due to what they perceived as a girlish name, they called him Canon.

"Tar, I swear if I'd known it was her then I would have done something," said Solo, clearly feeling guilty.

"Yeah man," added Canon, "we all would have done something."

"I don't blame you guys," said Tar, still fuming. "I blame *him*." Clearly Tar had no interest in making his friends feel guilty when the real culprit was a man, he already hated the guts of.

"Say what you will about Moodswing, but he's smart." said Touch. "The man didn't show her face until after the race and by then—"

"The damage was done," added Solo. "The fans love her, and the other racers love her. She's in."

That was the one thing that Tar didn't want to hear. "No, she's not."

"Tar, you know how it works," said Canon, adding petrol to the fire. "It only takes one win to become part of the scene..."

"And two to start contending for a title," added the still furious, Tar. "Yeah, *I know* how it works!" Tar had raised his voice but then calmed himself down again, remembering that he wasn't mad at his friends.

"Yeah, so there's nothing you can do," said Touch.

"The hell there isn't," said Tar.

"Tar," said Solo, trying to reason with him. "She's in. There's only two ways out: either she gets exiled or she chooses to leave."

As Max stood there listening, he remembered Thompson covering these rules: the unwritten ones that him and Moodswing had been arguing about. Max remembered the first thought that popped into his head when Thompson first said that "there were only two ways out". *Oh crap, is this the mafia!? You only leave by going to prison or in a coffin?* But then Thompson had continued, and Max realized just how level-headed the scene was. Of course, Tar had told him just a week ago what the scene was designed for: fun. So, if that was the case, then how had they gotten here?

"I don't care about that. Guys, she's *fifteen! Come on!*" This time, Tar *was* shouting at them.

But Solo, ever the level-headed and fierce friend, continued to try and reason with Tar. "Yes, she is. But she chose to do this. And there are rules."

"Who gives a damn about rules?" It was Max who asked the question, having been standing in the doorway the whole time. He took off the hoodie he'd been wearing up until now as if to announce himself like a gentleman taking off his hat when entering a house back in old fashioned days. Max walked into the conversation. "Seriously guys. Did Moodswing give a damn about rules when he went after Stevie? She's an innocent girl."

"Not anymore," said Touch, which got Tar to stop pacing. Touch saw the look in Tar's eye: like he was ready to kill someone, perhaps him. "All I'm saying is that, she knew what she was doing when she got inside that car."

Tar got in Touch's face. "And all *I'm* saying is that I. Don't. Care!" Tar began pacing again. "She's my little sister and I'm getting her *out!*"

"No, you're not!" It was Stevie who spoke these words as everyone turned to see her standing in the doorway just as Max had a minute ago. She had a defiant look in her eyes. "And I'm *not* your little anything."

"You're not what!?" said Tar, not bothering to hide his anger. "My little sister!? You damn sure are!"

Stevie didn't back down. "That changes nothing."

"It changes *everything!* Stevie, what the hell did you think you were doing?"

Stevie didn't answer immediately. "I think you mean, 'what the hell do I think *I am* doing'."

"Dammit Stevie, no."

"I'm not asking permission."

"No!"

"You can't stop me from doing this. None of you can," she said, finally acknowledging the rest of them.

Tar looked like he was beside himself, not sure what to do. "What about the fact that it's illegal."

"That didn't stop you."

"Except that I *did* stop."

While Stevie hesitated a moment, she didn't get stuck. "It didn't stop *them*," she said, pointing specifically to Solo, Touch and Canon. "Don't tell me about how illegal it is when your best friends are doing the same thing."

"Actually, my best friend is paralysed, because of the same thing that you're adamant on doing."

Instead of feeling guilty, Stevie looked ticked off like what Tar had said was below the belt. But she kept her composure. "Tell that to them. Maybe, just maybe, if they quit, I'll quit."

Tar saw that going this route wasn't going to work. "I'm not telling them anything. I'm telling *you*. *You're* fifteen and they're not." When Tar saw no expression change on her face, he pushed on. "You could get hurt, Stevie."

"You know, I faced the most dangerous XF racer last night and here I am, unscathed."

Tar swore. "You could go to jail. Do you want another member of our family in prison?"

Stevie sighed. "Then by all means, call the cops. Shut us down. Because it *will* work. That *will* get me out but then what?"

Max watched this argument not sure what to say; not sure what to do. He couldn't believe how hard these two were arguing with each other, made worse because he knew that they loved each other. Perhaps that was why the shots they were firing were so powerful: because there was so much emotion involved. Even looking at them, both having gone silent from sheer exhaustion. Max didn't know how Tar found the stomach to continue arguing but what choice did he have? He *had* to get her out.

"Stevie, just tell me why?"

"Why am I racing? Do you have to ask? You know I've always been interested in the scene."

"No. No, why did you go to Moodswing? Of all the people you could have gone to, to try and break into the scene, you go to *him*?"

"He came to me, Tar."

"And *that* didn't strike you as odd? Stevie, he's only using you to get to me."

Stevie completely evaded the notion that Tar had just expressed and continued. "Even if I did go to him, what other choice would I have? Huh? When my own big brother would rather help a stranger," she said pointing directly at Max, "than his own sister, then what choice did I have?"

This time, Tar ignored her statement. "Stevie, did you hear what I said? I said Moodswing is using you to get to me."

This time Stevie acknowledged what Tar had said. She sighed before answering. "I suggest you take *that* up with Moodswing. Bottom line is, you're not getting me out of

219

the racing scene." Stevie then added the ultimate insult by turning around and walking away.

"Stevie. Stevie! Stevie, get back here! Get back here!"

"She's gone, man." said Canon.

"But gone where?" asked Touch. "Did she quit? I know she's in, but did she just quit The Dive? She can't quit."

"Well can she do both?" asked Max, innocently.

Tar, who had calmed down out of sheer exhaustion, looked at them. "You guys are talking like it's over." Max and the others didn't know what Tar had meant by that but left it alone when Tar seemed to drop the issue, utterly defeated.

*

Max was still thinking about Tar's last words when Thompson called him. "Hey, wake up man, we've got work to do."

They were currently on the racing scene where Thompson was giving him his latest lesson in how things work. It was crazy to think just two weeks earlier, he was in Brisbane, Australia not knowing when he would next set foot in South Africa. Now he was here, with an open wheel race car he got to call his own *and* a gorgeous girl he still had to take out on a date.

After the beach party had ended in the disaster it was, Max and Lisa had decided to take it down a notch on the dating front. Instead, they opted to get to know each other with phone calls and during break times, even in detention when they happen to be there at the same time. It had gone surprisingly well, and Max had finally learnt her favourite colour. But he felt like it was time to take her out on an actual date.

"Max, Max man, you need to focus."

Max rolled his eyes. "Stop telling me to focus and say what you want to say already," said Max, pretending to have been with him this whole time.

"Look, I know it's Saturday night and you most likely would rather be elsewhere but—"

"No, I wouldn't rather be elsewhere. I'd rather be here," said Max a bit too quickly.

"Wow," said Thompson. "Says a guy with a girlfriend."

Max didn't want to explain what he and Lisa had agreed on. "It's complicated."

"Already!? Wow, that must be a record. Anyway, it's none of mine. What I was *saying* was that now that you've won two races, you get to decide which title you want to go after."

Max liked the sound of that. "Is that right? So, I just win two races and I get a title shot?" Max remembered what Tar had said earlier at The Dive.

However, Thompson made a face. "Nooo, no, no, no. You win two races and you go onto the list of contenders. From there you have to climb the ladder." Thompson saw Max's face drop. "It's not Christmas, man."

"Aha. Okay, so who am I racing next?"

"Well that depends which title you want to go after." Thompson continued speaking but Max barely heard what he said as he saw someone dressed in a hoodie move through the crowd. There was something about the way he was moving, like a man on a mission that didn't sit well with Max. And judging from the way he was looking at the vehicles, he was clearly looking for someone. Max had a suspicion he knew who this was. He then heard Thompson once again ask which title he wanted to go after.

Max answered on autopilot, still looking at the stranger. "The one Moodswing has. The King's title." Max saw the man head for the stairs, clearly not finding who he was looking for. For Max, this confirmed who this was. "Thompson, I'll be right back."

Max then broke into a sprint towards the stairs. He needed to catch him before he did something he couldn't take back. While he knew that the racers here now preferred exile to get rid of bad elements, he was sure they'd make an exception for someone who was only here to beat someone up and revert to the old-fashioned way of breaking knees.

When Max got to the second floor, he saw Tar, hoodie still on, and sprinted for him as he made a bee line for Moodswing. Solo had managed to see him from wherever he had been standing and started for him too. They had just managed to get to him as he lunged for Moodswing. He'd barely managed to grab his jacket when Max and Solo managed to restrain him.

"Tar, Tar, don't," said Solo, trying hard to keep his voice down. But Moodswing had no such intention.

"Well, well, well," he said in his usual booming voice, "what have we here? Is that you, Tar?"

"Moodswing," said Tar, clearly not eager to hide his presence either, "you crossed the line, man."

"Did I? How do you think?"

"You went after Stevie because you were too much of a coward to face me yourself!?"

"Oh, is that what I did?" continued Moodswing, sarcastically. He then pretended to think. "Do you want to know what I think? I think you give me too much credit." Moodswing didn't flinch when Tar tried to lunge but was held back. "Honestly, I do. I'm not the one who told her to get secret racing lessons. I mean, did you know she was doing that? I'm not the one who told her that she *had to* race down here. I only gave her the keys to a car and said: if you want to, have at it."

"She's a fifteen-year-old girl."

"You say that like she's some ordinary teenage girl. By my count, she's already had to grow up fast. She even has a job if I'm not mistaken. She doesn't sound like a little girl to me."

However, Tar wasn't letting any of this in. "If you want me, Moodswing, I'm right here," said Tar, ready for a fight. But Moodswing shook his head.

"But that's not the way. Remember what you said to me before: that everything needs to be handled on the asphalt. What did you call it, the old way? That's right: the old way. So, what do you say, Tar? You versus me? The *Dracula* versus the *Queen Nandi's Revenge*?" Moodswing saw the hesitation in Tar. "I'll even sweeten the deal: you win, I'll get Stevie out. She resists, get her exiled," he said with a shrug of a shoulder. "Nothing a short race can't do. Point is this: her career here will be over before it even begins. That's if you can win. So, what do you say?"

As Max continued to struggle against Tar who was still eager to hit Moodswing even with such a sweet offer at his fingertips, he couldn't help but be impressed with Moodswing's plan. There was a brilliance to it. Get Tar angry by going after his sister and then challenge him to a race to end things once and for all, perhaps even embarrass Tar for everything that Tar had 'done to him'. Unfortunately, the epic showdown of a race that Max had built up in his head was all for nought when Tar finally gave his answer.

"That's not going to happen."

Moodswing raised his eyebrows. "Even for the sake of your sister."

"I'm *never* getting back in the seat of that vehicle, Moodswing." said Tar through gritted teeth. "Never!"

"Then we have nothing to discuss." Moodswing then spoke to the crowd that had slowly gathered around to

226

watch the faceoff between the once-dominant Tar and the current reigning King. "Ladies and gentlemen, this man came here, into this place that's like a second home to us not to enjoy the show, not to participate but to incite violence. He would rather use his fists than get behind the wheel of a car to prove himself better than me. Now I ask you, what do we say to that?"

There was a beat before the answer came. And what an answer it was. Instead of heated shouting or a charging of some sort, the gathered crowd began to hiss. The hissing was loud from the moment it started. It was like falling into a pit of snakes and with Max standing right next to the person they were all hissing at, he began to get frightened.

"What the hell is going on?" he asked Solo, standing right next to him.

"That means it's time to go." Solo had spoken the words to Tar who, this time, did not argue at all as they turned around and started for the exit. As Max and Solo escorted Tar out, the hissing did not stop. The crowd had followed until Tar was off the property at which point it went dead quiet and they went back inside.

Max understood why that had worked, perhaps even better than if they had attacked him. It was their uniformity. The crowd had all acted as one and there was nothing scarier than that. At that point, they didn't need to throw a single strike because the fear that they *might,* alone, was enough to frighten a man to run. Max still wore an expression of fear on his face as Solo quickly took note.

"Don't worry. They're not going to come back."

"What the hell was that?"

"The alternative to kneecapping," said Solo before turning to Tar, "which is exactly what would have happened if you landed even one punch on Moodswing."

Tar rolled his eyes, shrugging his whole body as if over everything. "Oh, c'mon, Solo. Do you really think I care about my kneecaps right now?"

"You should if you still care about getting into the Navy." Solo had him there and they all three knew it. "Tar, you need to think. About his offer, preferably."

"What, no." said Tar loudly and adamantly. "I am not—" he said before lowering his voice. "I am not getting back in *Queen Nandi's Revenge* or any other race car, do you understand me?"

Solo struggled to accept this. "Well Moodswing needs to be taken down for all of this. That race would have done the trick."

Tar was already shaking his head. He then looked at his friend. "And you? Why don't you take him down? You've faced each other before."

Solo shook his head too. "Yeah, too many times. You know the thing about popularity. For the race to happen, people need to *want* to see it, *especially* if it involves the King and big-time stakes which is what you need to take him down. *No one*, wants to see Moodswing versus Solo, one hundred and fifty-five."

Max knew that Solo was exaggerating about that number. But he was still thinking about the dilemma ahead of them. It had been one thing to help Tar try and get Stevie out. Max didn't know how he could help there. But if they were talking about simply taking Moodswing down, surely, he could help *there*?

"What about me?" said Max.

"What about you?" said Solo, as both him and Tar looked at him.

"What if I faced him? What if *I* took him down?" Max watched as Tar and Solo shared a look. When they both shrugged as if to say, "worth a shot", Max knew that his idea was sound. So, that's what was next for him: taking down the King of the XF racing scene. *Nothing like the easy ones*.

CHAPTER FOURTEEN
GAME PLAN

When Max had suggested that *he* be the one to take down Moodswing, he hadn't expected that to mean that he'd lose his Sunday morning to sitting at The Dive and planning his next move. Yet here he was, sitting across from Tar and Thompson who he'd invited as they laid out exactly what he needed to do to get back at Moodswing.

"Okay," said Thompson, ever the planner, "so what do we need to take down a King? Well first thing's first," he showed them his tablet. "You're now officially on the list of contenders for Moodswing's title."

"Well that's definitely the first step," said Tar, "but now you need to think of your opponents. You need opponents that are going to get you close to Moodswing."

"What do you mean?" asked Max.

"He means that every racer you face must get you up this list until you're number one."

"Right," said Max. "As in number one contender."

"That's right," affirmed Tar. "But this ain't combat sports. Here, you can take short cuts."

"Short cuts?" said Max.

"Yeah," added Thompson. "What he means is, there is no points system. There's no complicated league with scoreboards and logs. Moving up and down is almost exclusively dependent on whether the fanbase wants you to or not."

Max thought about that for a second. "That sounds like wrestling."

Tar nodded. "Remember what I told you, about how the first generation came up with all this?"

"Right," said Max. "But wrestling is scripted. The guys that run the show can shape the narrative and dictate who's rising to the top. How do I do that here?"

"By choosing the right opponents," said Tar and Thompson in unison. Tar continued. "When it comes to your opponents, it does you absolutely no good choosing easy opponents. Only someone not interested in getting to the top does that. What you need to do is choose opponents who either have a prestigious history or a popular one."

Thompson added on before Max could ask what he was talking about. "Because the two things you need to make it in the XF racing scene," he said putting up two fingers, "are skill and popularity. One is useless without the other. For example, Touch is very popular but his racing skills, well, they haven't won him the Crown yet."

"Hey," said Tar, defending his friend.

"Well it's true," said Thompson upon seeing Tar's look. "On the other side of that, Canon Kelly is very good behind the wheel but is as bland as can be."

233

"Okay, are you done insulting my friends?"

Thompson continued, ignoring Tar. "My point is, while they might have earned a spot on the second floor, it does them no good in getting to the Crown. Solo on the other hand managed it by balancing his skill behind the wheel with this cool thing he does." When they both looked at him, Thompson explained. "Haven't you guys noticed that Solo has this ultra-cool presence about him? It's like nothing fazes him."

Max raised an eyebrow. "Wow, he really is his biggest fan, huh?" he said to Tar.

"I'm just glad he's praising one of my friends for a change."

"Whatever," said Thompson, dismissing their teasing. "But people like me who watched his races online and liked what they saw in the man put him on the Throne. Which happens to be my point by the way."

Tar shrugged, affirming what Thompson was saying. "That's why you'll find some racers who are good behind the wheel develop gimmicks that can feel straight out of

234

wrestling. Because they need people to *want* to see them race. They need a thing."

Max thought for a moment. "Okay, then what's Moodswing's thing?"

Thompson and Tar shared a look before answering. "That he's a jackass." They all laughed, in complete agreement on that one.

"Okay," said Max, trying to get to the meat of the matter, "so if I've got this right: I need to be as popular as I am fast and in order to take down Moodswing, I need to climb this list by beating people who are also popular and fast." They both nodded. "You said prestigious history and popular history."

"Yes," said Tar. "So, you need to face former Kings and racers who had iconic rivalries or legendary races."

Thompson looked at Tar and engaged him in a short conversation. "Former kings? Shouldn't he also face former Dukes and Barons too?"

Tar shook his head. "Only if he's going to face them in the races of their division."

"Okay, so if he faces a former Duke of Drag, it would need to be in a drag race?"

"Exactly. But since we're focusing on getting him up the King's list of contenders, I would suggest refraining from facing former dukes in drag races. Unless—"

"Unless they're also on the King's list because then he would climb up the ladder."

While Tar and Thompson had gone on, Max had picked up Thompson's tablet and looked at the list. "You guys."

They didn't hear him. "Well I was thinking he should face Siren," said Thompson.

"The woman who's always swimming naked in her trailer pool? Why her?"

"She recently had a rivalry with what's-his-name, sent him packing."

"Oh please," rebutted Tar. "I think you only want him to face her because you think she's hot."

"You guys," repeated Max.

"What?" said Thompson to Tar. "She's also on the list of contenders. That's why I want him to face her."

"You guys!" Max finally got their attention. "I think I know who my next opponent is going to be. Max showed them the name he'd pointed out.

"Dumo?" said Thompson.

Tar had tapped his name and read his credentials. "Damn, he's perfect. Former Duke of Drag with over a hundred-day reign; won a revenge race against Tyger upon returning from a six-month hiatus due to damage he'd received in a previous race with him. And, he's fourth on the list."

"Huh," said Thompson, thinking on the idea. "Both skilled *and* popular. Nice one spotting that, Max."

"Yep," said Tar. "But do you know what race you need to challenge him to?" This time all three of them answered in unison. "A drag race."

After they'd finished up and Thompson had left to salvage whatever he could of his Sunday, Max stayed behind to ask Tar if he would come to his practise session just to give him some pointers on his technique. When Tar asked why he didn't ask while Thompson was still around, Max mentioned that he wanted to do it tomorrow morning, during school hours.

*

Lisa didn't really know what the hell she was doing at the mall on a Sunday. She'd never been the type to hang out at malls. She never understood the point. Well that wasn't true: the point was to buy things. But that was her issue. If she didn't have anything that she wanted to buy, then why would she go to the mall? Yet here she was.

She wanted to blame Angela who had dragged her to come but she really couldn't. Even if Angela had guilt-tripped her into coming, by once again suggesting that she had abandoned her during the beach party, Lisa could have said no. She'd blown off Angela so many times, she'd probably perfected the art by now. Yet, she'd agreed to it. And looking at Angela now, she knew why.

Angela was currently standing in Mr. Price Sports talking with a handsome young man that worked there. Judging from how Angela was holding a black one-piece swimming suit to her body as if modelling it, she was probably talking about the fit. Lisa rolled her eyes knowing very well that Angela didn't care at all about one-pieces, let alone how they fit. In fact, she was sure that the only reason she had it up to her body was to put the visual image in the man's head.

While Lisa wasn't sure whether Angela's plan was working, she was sure of something else. Watching Angela get her flirt on reminded Lisa of him. It reminded her of Max. Since they'd agreed to slow things down and go to the basics of courting by getting to know each other before going on a proper date, Lisa had yearned for one. She wanted to spend time with him *outside* of school. But there was a reason they'd decided to go to basics. The events of the beach party had scared them. They wanted to make sure there was something worth exploring before they tried to eliminate the memory of that night by replacing it with another. But Lisa was over it.

It sounded strange to think it, but Lisa wanted to date this boy. She wasn't desperate for it or anything, she just loved his company so much that the idea that they were holding off for whatever reason was bothering her. She adored the way he made her smile; the way he made her feel and how he challenged her just by being so different from her. *Argh man, why am I being such a girl about this boy?*

In an effort to get her mind off of how she wasn't dating her boyfriend, Lisa walked through the opening between Mr. Price Sports and Mr. Price Home, wandering two of the isles before passing through the next passage into Mr. Price itself. Standing in front of the women's section, Lisa was suddenly grateful that Angela wasn't here. Otherwise, not only would Angela tell her to purchase, basically, everything. She'd also tell her to burn what she was wearing: a red and black flannel shirt with jeans. However, not a moment later, she almost wished she had burnt her clothes.

What is it with this boy and always finding me when I'm not dressed better? Standing there, right in front of her, across from the main isle that ran between the Men's and Women's section, was Max, dressed in a dark hoodie over a white t-shirt and old blue jeans. He smiled upon seeing her. *Oh, here we go with the crooked lip thing.* This time, there was no resisting the urge to blush.

"Why hello there," he said, oozing confidence as always.

"If it isn't the driver of the *Baby Cradle*," she said, smug that she managed to say something smart. "Are you stalking me?"

"You wish," he said as he approached her. "You're going to have to blame destiny for this one."

"Destiny?" she said, sceptically. "You believe in destiny?"

"Well it brought me to you, didn't it?" Before she could say anything else clever, Max planted a kiss on her cheek

Lisa took a moment to ponder whether she actually squeaked. *That was so perfect*, thought Lisa. The perfect balance of intimacy and politeness. How could a badass underground racer be such a gentleman too? Lisa found herself lost for words and all she could do was smile. Max inadvertently bought her time to recover.

"So, what brings you here? I thought someone like you would at least shop at a place like Edgars, if not Woolworths or Truworths."

"Funny," said Lisa, "I would have thought the same of you."

"I actually am a Truworths guy. My favourite leather jacket and denim jacket came from there."

"Then what are you doing here?"

"I believe I asked you that first." When Lisa simply gave him a slight lift of an eyebrow, Max continued after being a bit flustered. "My mom's idea. I only brought one bag from Australia, so this is me, finally buying myself a wardrobe. You?"

"Apparently, Angela's wing woman. Although judging from her having the longest conversation I've ever seen in my life about a school swimming costume, I'd say she doesn't need me."

"Hmm. Then perhaps I could procure your services."

Judging from how much traction she'd managed from the single raise of an eyebrow, Lisa followed on by simply

242

smiling which earned a huge grin from him. *Hmm, I think I'm getting the hang of this flirting thing.*

Max had asked Lisa to help him pick out some clothes which had basically turned into a one-man fashion show with Max modelling each set of clothes that Lisa had picked out. Even though Lisa had made up her mind basically the minute she picked them off the shelf, she still made Max wear each piece of clothing, taking a particular liking to the ones that were one size too small and hugged him tightly in all the right places.

After finally getting everything he wanted, or more like *she* wanted *and then some*, they headed out of the shop and found a bench outside Mr. Price Sports to wait for Angela. While a part of Lisa wanted to wait for Max to be the one to ask, the part that had been raised to be an independent woman won out.

"So, when are we going to go on a proper date?"

Max didn't miss a beat in responding. "And what do you call this, pray tell?"

"I call it: you running into me at the mall. I'm talking about the whole sitting at a table eating a meal and sharing some laughs."

"Oh that? Hmm, well," he said pretending to think. "Well I take it we're not counting the beach party where; you know, we did exactly that?"

"Nope," said Lisa, matching Max's sense of humour beat-for-beat.

"Okay then. How about, we have one sometime next... when do you want to go on a date?" Max's facial expression had changed at the exact time his sentence changed to a question.

Lisa burst out laughing. He still had that effect on her. "Okay then. What about tomorrow after school?" Lisa found that it didn't even bother her that she wouldn't be going to the Shop in order to go out with him. She clearly cared for him more than she'd thought.

However, Max's expression changed again, this time to a slightly more serious one. "I can't do tomorrow, Lisa. I'll be busy then."

Lisa understood what that meant: the racing scene. And she wasn't mad about that. Just confused about how the two would conflict. "I thought the scene only starts after the sun goes down?"

"Yeah, but I'll still be busy until then."

A detail caught Lisa's attention. "*Until* then? Are you going to miss school again?"

Max barely hesitated to answer. "I need to prepare for tomorrow night."

"So, you're going to miss another *whole day* of school?"

"I have to. I've never competed in a drag race in an XF vehicle before and I have to win." When Lisa gave him an exasperated look, Max tried to explain as briefly as he could what was at stake and why it was important. It hadn't helped matters as Lisa's disappointment had increased rather than decreased. "Lisa, I'm sorry."

Lisa shook her head. "I'm not mad. I'm just..." Lisa didn't know what she was. "I guess I just can't believe that you're this deep already. You haven't been here two weeks and what, you want to be King already?"

"It's not like that. I'm not taking him down because I want the Crown. I'm taking him down because he has to go down, after what he did to Stevie. To Tar."

"Oh, that I have no doubt. No one likes a jackass. But Max," said Lisa, yearningly, "you're going to go to bat for people you've known less than two weeks?" That wasn't at all the question that Lisa wanted to ask. What she truly wanted to ask was why she couldn't be considered just as important since he'd known her for just as long. But, unfortunately, she knew what she'd sound like: a girl who wanted to be prioritized above all else.

Not wanting to make things more complicated, Lisa stood and luckily, Angela walked out of the shop just then. "Hey Angie, ready to go?" She nodded. Lisa turned to Max. "See you around Max."

*

Admittedly, Max was still distressed the following night when he drove up to the start line for the drag race.

'See you around, Max?' What the hell did that mean? Were they broken up now? Did this mean the next time he saw her, he had to act all awkward or could he still flirt with her? *But were we even dating?* How did one qualify the point at which someone is dating? Surely you needed to go on one date to count as dating?

Max had been so busy thinking about his argument with Lisa at the mall that he almost missed the young woman signalling the start of the race. Lucky for Max, he was used to having his mind elsewhere just moments before a drag race.

While he had never been in a drag race in an open wheel car before, he had been in motorcycle drag races before. And armed with the tips that Tar had given him during his practise session, Max was confident that he had this in the bag.

One of the things that Thompson and Tar hadn't explained until earlier this morning was that Max was going to have to instigate something with Dumo in order to get the race he wanted. Lucky enough, Max had just the thing when he heard the name of Dumo's vehicle: The

Lightning Rod. After insinuating that Dumo was cannon fodder and that he could beat him any day, Max proceeded to make fun of his name being one letter short of Dumbo before moving on to his vehicle saying that it should have been named the frightening rod because that's all it was good for: frightening people. That was of course, besides also being the thing that was shoved up his backside to get that look on his face. That had been enough to get the former Duke of Drag and current number four contender to accept Max's invitation to the start line drawn on the M1.

During the race, Max made sure to cycle through his gears the way that Tar had told him to, taking advantage of the fact that his vehicle was analogue to his opponents' digital. The ploy worked as Max ended up crossing the finish line first. The one thing that Max noted was that the race had ended so quickly. When he saw Thompson come over to him, he expected a big smile to be on his face but instead, he looked at his tablet and his face fell.

"What's wrong?"

Thompson showed him the screen, which showed a visual of the next race: another drag race. This one was for the Duke of Drag title. And the person who the Duke of Drag – a large man named Tiny – was defending against, was none other than Stevie.

"What the hell is this? Is this next?" Max's question was answered by someone asking him to move his car from the finish line. "Is this *now*?" Max judged Thompson's silence to be a confirmation. "What the hell? How did this happen? I thought you needed *two* victories to become a contender for any title?"

"Moodswing must have tricked Tiny into challenging *her*. Bets are off when the champion makes the challenge."

Max just looked at Thompson. "But there's no way she's going to win, right? I mean this is her *second* race." But Max wanted to swallow his words as soon as he said them. After all, didn't he beat the King in his *first* race? It was a good thing Max wanted to swallow his words himself because a minute later they were joined by Stevie who did the unthinkable and pulled off the victory and thus became the *Duchess* of Drag.

Max and Thompson watched in disgust as the King himself, seemingly coming out of the night itself, walked up to Stevie and gave the girl her shiny new helmet. He posed with her for a selfie with both their golden helmets before leaving but not before telling her that he'd see her back in the parking lot.

Just before climbing back into the *Candyfloss*, Stevie finally took notice of Max and Thompson who had not lost their disgusted looks. "Something wrong boys? What's with the long faces? This is a time to celebrate. We're all winners here, aren't we?"

"What you're doing is wrong, Stevie." As Max started, Thompson's tablet vibrated.

Stevie rolled her eyes at Max's incoming speech. "Oh c'mon, not this."

"No, listen to me, Stevie. You're—" But Max was cut off by Thompson who directed him to the screen. On the screen was a video of three racers standing on the start line. They were quickly joined by Shade. Not a minute later, the race began. To let them know that this was real and happening now, they were directed off the M1 and told to either wait until the race finished before heading back or take an alternative route.

While Stevie opted for the alternative route, eager to get away from Max and Thompson, Max and Thompson moved to the side and stayed put. Max had to admit that he was very happy to have made that decision as they got to witness the vehicles zipping past them, closer up than they'd ever seen them. But Thompson had pointed out that they had another problem.

Thompson suggested that they had missed a critical element in their plan: the *current* number two contender: Shade who was just as hungry as Max was. Thompson suggested that Shade taking on three opponents was just as much a strategy as theirs was. When Max asked how that was, Thompson pointed out Shade's opponents as being the number five, three and one contenders. Max swore, realizing that their plan was going up in flames.

CHAPTER FIFTEEN
THE TUTOR

Max had never been one to follow school rules, so he was not shocked to be in the Grade 11 H.O.D.'s office right now. The name on the door had read Mr. Pillay but Max was currently sitting in front of a Caucasian lady who'd introduced herself as Mrs. Turner. He assumed it was an old sign or that Mrs. Turner had been newly appointed in Mr. Pillay's stead.

"So," said Mrs. Turner, "I assume you know why you're here?"

Max shrugged. "You want me to be the Captain of the inter-grade rugby game?" he said, playfully.

Mrs. Turner shook her head. "This is not the time to make jokes, Mister McKay," she said pronouncing his surname wrong. "You're travelling down a very dark path."

"A dark path?" said Max, surprised by her words.

"Yes. You are well on your way to being Grade eleven's biggest discipline case which is a feat considering that you've been here just under twenty days."

Max wanted to laugh but refrained. "Oh, that. I wouldn't say that's *dark*. Just a little bit grey, maybe."

"Mister McKay."

"I think this is the part that I tell you that Mister *McKay* is my father," he said, emphasizing the proper pronunciation of his surname.

"Not on this island," said the teacher, coldly.

"Ouch," said Max, not flinching at all from the quip.

"Perhaps that's the reason that you are such a difficult student to discipline: no father figure in your life."

"He's not dead, ma'am. Just on another island."

"Yet when you were on that island, it seems you attended school just as sporadically as you do here." Max didn't answer. This was the point in the scolding where, as the student, he should just sit there and listen, sulking, to all the reasons he was the worst student in the world. "Max, you have missed nearly a week's worth of school days and have no doctor's letter or note from your mother as to why."

Sometimes Max actually forgot that he had a mother, what with days going past before they ran into each other in the morning. It was some kind of miracle that she had yet to notice that he came home late some nights. He was even more surprised that she didn't know that he had been missing school. Didn't the school try to get a hold of her?

"Do you have anything to say for yourself?" asked Mrs. Turner.

Max shook his head, still sulking. "I think you've said everything there is to be said, ma'am."

Mrs. Turner clenched her jaw, notably. "You also need to watch that mouth of yours. You're too clever for your own good."

Max almost laughed. "I've never been accused of that."

"And there's no surprise there, considering that at this rate, there will be no way of telling how smart you are anyway." Mrs. Turner saw that he was lost. "You missed a see-tee-ay test."

Oh crap! That's bad. C.T.A. tests, those are important. Control Test Assessments were rumoured to be the entry tests to the end of year Grade 11 exams. Even *he* wasn't stupid enough to miss those. Except, somehow, he had. Lisa. *Dammit, Lisa. Why didn't you tell me about this!?* Was she that angry with him? But he couldn't blame her for *his* mistake.

"That was a mistake," said Max.

This time, Mrs. Turner had to stop herself from laughing. "I hope all your absences were a mistake. Because while you were off doing God-knows-what, we were marking down an A-for-absent on your paper."

Max swallowed, not sure how to respond to that. He was finally paying attention to how serious this was. "Surely there must be a way to make it up."

Mrs. Turner didn't respond for a long time, clearly trying to make him sweat. It was working. "I'll let you retake the test but you better study and pass it. Because after that there's no coming back for it."

"Thanks, Missus Turner," said Max standing up. "In fact, I'm going to get right on that right now."

"I hope that's not true. You've got English to go to. You study in your own time."

"Right, right," said Max, beginning to leave. "English, class then study. Got it."

"I guess you're dismissed then," said Mrs. Turner, rather glad to be rid of him having achieved something. This was made obvious when she sighed as he paused, turning around. "Is there something else, Mister McKay?"

"Yes. I don't suppose you know where I can find a tutor.

This truly did surprise her, although Mrs. Turner didn't dare show him that. "For a Grade eleven tutor, you're going to want to speak to Christina Langa."

"Great. Thanks ma'am," he said before finally leaving the H.O.D. in peace.

*

The quest for Christina's help had to be delayed as Max had to attend to English class where he didn't get the chance to speak to her. The next class Max had was one that he didn't share with Christina, so he lost track of her. In fact, Max wouldn't get a chance to speak to her until lunch break and even then, it was a mission figuring out where she was. Eventually, Max had to do some old-fashioned deduction and figured that the smartest person in class would probably be in the library, studying.

When Max walked into the library, he was relieved to see her sitting right there at a table in the middle of the studying area. However, before Max could smile, he saw another familiar face sitting with her: Lisa. After their last conversation, Max hadn't been sure what to say so he'd said nothing to her. Now somehow, the situation was worse as Max also felt guilty because she had been right about missing school. Look where that had gotten him.

Unfortunately, Max had to swallow his pride and approach the table. He needed Christina's help whether Lisa was there or not. What happened next, Max didn't know whether was unfortunate or fortunate as when Lisa saw him approach their table, she quickly gathered her stuff and left. When Christina protested her exit for the sake of their assignment, Lisa simply apologized and turned for the door. On her way out, Max caught a glimpse of her expression before she turned her face to the floor, avoiding eye contact. She looked like she felt guilty. *What the hell is she feeling guilty for? I'm the jerk that messed up.*

When Max got to the table, Christina looked up at him as if offended by his presence. "Can I help you with something?"

"Yes, actually." Max sat down, uninvited. "I need your help with something. I missed my C.T.A. test and now I need a tutor to help me prepare for my make-up test." But Christina gave him a blank look as if saying "so?".

"Missus Turner said that you're the best person to ask for that."

Christina thought for a moment before answering. "Pass."

This surprised Max even though it was a long shot in the first place. "What, why?"

Anticipating the question, Christina answered immediately. "Why did you miss the test in the first place?"

"I wasn't at school."

"Why?" she said, barely giving him time to answer.

"I was busy."

Christina pointed her pencil at him like a teacher disciplining a learner. "That's why. I can only tutor people who want to be tutored. And the first sign that they're at all interested in this learning thing, is showing up to school." Christina then added insult to injury by simply turning back to the textbook in front of her and reading as if he wasn't even there.

Dammit Christina, "Look," he said, trying his luck, "the reason I didn't come to school that day is because I was helping a friend, okay. He thinks," said Max, softening his voice, "he thinks that his sister is being used in some kind of revenge plot against him."

Max wanted to smack his palm to his forehead. He realized just how preposterous that sounded having said it out loud. What only made it worse was that he'd only been here just over two weeks, and now he had friends who had sisters who were being used in revenge plots? At this point, Max wanted to ask *himself* to give him a break.

However, Christina surprised him by believing him. "The sister: that's that girl that got on the bike with that," she struggled to describe him, "notorious underground racing guy. What's his name?"

"Moodswing." Max saw that Christina genuinely *did* believe him. It was now that Max remembered that Christina had been standing right next to them that day Moodswing had come to the school and picked up Stevie. How could he have forgotten? Was it possible that that day of misfortune would work in his favour here?

Christina made a face suggesting that despite understanding, it wasn't going to change her mind. "Still. Someone else's problems shouldn't affect your school life. This stuff is important."

Max let out a deep breath. "I know." Or at least, he knew now. "That's why I'm here. The words 'make up test' have never been more important, as I'm really trying to make up for the mess I've put myself in."

Christina gave him another thoughtful look, contemplating him, before answering. "Okay, I'll tutor you, but we can only work during break times." Christina didn't react to the smile on his face, but she did react when his cell phone rang. "And for Heaven's sake, turn off your cell phone when we're busy."

"I know. I know," said Max standing to answer it and take it outside only to find that it wasn't a phone call at all.

"You're not even supposed to have your cell phone on in the library let alone take calls."

"It's just a notification," said Max starting for the door.

Christina rolled her eyes. "Just turn it off next time."

Max got outside and looked at the screen of his smartphone. On it, was a notification from the app that Thompson had downloaded for him. It was for the deep web website that streamed the races. The notification was an alert that was telling him about an upcoming race tonight:

NUMBER ONE CONTENDER'S RACE
SHADE VS. MAX MCKAY

Max's jaw dropped. *Whoa!* Max remembered being bummed out when Shade did the unthinkable last night and defeated all three of his opponents thus proving his dominance and why he should be Moodswing's next opponent. He remembered being beside himself that the plan was going down the toilet right in front of his eyes.

While conventional wisdom would tell anyone else that Shade becoming Moodswing's next challenger for the title and taking it from him achieved the same goal, the fact and the matter was that it didn't. Thompson had even explained to Max that all it did was tie up the title picture for a series of racing battles between Moodswing and Shade that could easily see Moodswing regain the title in a return race. The reason the plan required Max to take the Crown was because their plan had Max leverage the Crown to get Stevie out as that was the true endgame for Max, Thompson and most importantly, Tar.

So, when Shade put their plan on fire by burning through the rest of the top five contenders – sans Dumo – it had really given Max, Thompson (and Tar when they told him) a headache. All each of them could think was: "now what are we going to do?" Following last night, they had been sure Shade would be named number one contender. But seeing this message now, changed things.

Max wondered how this happened. How did the question of the next challenger to Moodswing's title become a coin toss between him and Shade? Max thought about it and wondered if it was less to do with his and Shade's victories and more to do with all the other top five contenders' *losses*. That had to be it. Between him and Shade, they had basically made all the other top contenders, losers. And in a big way particularly for Shade's opponents.

This was great. This was truly great news. It meant that their plan was back on track. If anything, it had been fast-tracked. Now all they had to do was contend with one of the best racers on the scene: the enigma and all-round badass driver, Shade. *Yep, there really is nothing like the easy ones*.

Max walked back into the library thinking about Shade when he saw Christina who was looking at him. Just as he thought she was going to give him lip about his "phone call", he saw *her* slip her phone into her bag. When he got back to the table, he gave her a playful look.

"I thought you said no cell phones in the library."

"It was a text and it was important." Feeling the need to explain herself, Christina went on. "It was from Lisa. She was just asking to reschedule a time to continue with the assignment."

Max refrained from quipping, realizing why Christina might not have wanted to tell him about the text. Things really were strained between him and Lisa if Lisa had to exit stage left upon seeing him and then text Christina about rearranging a homework session all in the vain of avoiding him. *Man, I really messed up big time with her.* Max knew that he was going to have to find a way to make it up to her. But that would have to come later. Tonight, he was going to have to defeat the undefeatable.

CHAPTER SIXTEEN
UMTHUNZI

When it came to coming up with a game plan for taking on Shade, Tar and Thompson had been at a loss. They'd told Max as much, saying that what made Shade so formidable was that he was adaptable: a true chameleon. Thompson was notably worried about the race while Tar said that he maybe, *maybe*, could figure out a strategy to defeat him if he were there, watching the race and feeding Max info in real time as part of his tech support. But when Max invited him to join his team, Tar declined, claiming it was because he wasn't welcome there but in reality, it was due to his principles.

This left Max and Thompson to figure out just how in the hell he was going to defeat Shade. Thompson had told Max all about Shade's history as they prepared after school including how Shade won the Crown a few months ago. Apparently, he had beaten Solo for it which was a big deal since he had just come out of a big-time rivalry with Antwoord which had involved Moodswing at some point. This had made Shade's victory an accomplishment and had cemented him as a feature racer. As an aside, Thompson also mentioned that it was Moodswing who had ended said reign so there was a dog in this race for him as well.

"Is that how Moodswing got the Crown?" Max had asked.

"No," Thompson had answered, "his current reign is actually three reigns removed from the one where he beat Shade." On Max's confused look, he had added, "so after he won it from Shade, he lost it to Antwoord who lost it to Solo who then lost it to Moodswing."

At this point, the confused Max asked how many Kings there had been, and Thompson had said no more than twelve. When Max had given him a sceptical look, Thompson had qualified his answer by saying many of those twelve had multiple title reigns. "Sounds like they've been playing hot potato with that thing."

Currently, Max was standing next to *Baby Cradle* as Thompson checked the new tires. Max glanced over to Stevie who now occupied the parking space across from him. She'd tried to get herself moved to the other side of the first floor but to no avail as most of the racers had become comfortable with their spaces. Max had wondered why she hadn't used her relationship with Moodswing to get a spot on the second floor but didn't care to ask her. If everything went according to plan, she wouldn't be on any floor for that long anyway.

Stevie looked up and caught his glance. The look in her eye was an anguished one. It was as if she wanted to be her old fangirling self and gush over how cool it was that he was going to go up against Shade but instead refrained from it. Clearly, she wanted more than anything to get along with Max. But with Max wanting nothing more than for her to go home, she remained distant, intent on avoiding any more speeches.

As much as Max hated to admit it, Stevie had some real raw talent as she'd just come back from her own race against the *former* Duke of Drag, Tiny where she managed to defeat the man in a drag race for the second time in two days. Despite being Moodswing's apprentice, she had done the honourable thing and given the former titleholder a return race for the title just twenty-four hours after he'd lost it. Many, including Max, had been surprised by this. But maybe there was more honour in Stevie as a racer than any of them had given her credit for. After all, she wasn't complaining about being on the first floor. In fact, she seemed to like being down here.

Thompson came around the vehicle and gave Max the all-clear just as Admin called out his name for him to go down to the start line. After taking a deep breath, Max put on his helmet and climbed inside *Baby Cradle* and fired it up. The engine came to life at his touch and he started for the rampway. But before he was out of the building, he heard it.

269

"Mthunzi!" The Admin's call was followed by a soft cheering from the others. "Mthunzi! Mthunzi! Mthunzi! Mthunzi!" There was something about them cheering in these lowered voices that made it even more thrilling than if they had been cheering at the top of their voices. It was like it added something to Shade's aura.

Max heard the faint sound of an engine being revved loudly coming from up above. It was Shade who had gotten into his vehicle. Max took off down the rampway before Shade came charging down and was nearing the start line when the enigmatic racer came speeding out of the parking lot, skidding to stop next to Max just as he'd stopped.

Still with his visor up, Max gave Shade a stare which he must have felt because his dark helmet slowly turned to him so that he was clearly looking at him. Max then shut the visor, hoping it came off more badass than it used to during his street biking days. But Shade simply and slowly looked away, back dead ahead of him and Max knew then, that it hadn't been the least bit intimidating.

There was this moment of utter silence before the red cloth was dropped at which point, both vehicles screeched off the line and sped away! Max knew right away that he was in one hell of the race as Shade seemingly adapted to Max's intentionally more aggressive style of driving almost instantaneously.

Max was intentionally trying to box Shade in on his side of the road so that he would be forced to pull behind Max and operate from a losing position. But instead, Shade intimidated Max right back by twitching his wheel towards Max and threatening to bump tires. While *actually* bumping Max's tires would be considered against the rules and possibly lead to Shade getting exiled, Shade knew that there was no way Max would let that happen and thus, every time Shade made the threat, Max had also twitched, backing off from him.

This game continued until they hit the freeway which was where things got interesting. With almost no traffic, both of them gunned their engines to 250 kilometres per hour. However, where Moodswing had opted to hang out in the emergency lane, Shade remained right next to Max

271

on the far left of the freeway, next to the concrete divider keeping the opposing sides of the freeway separate, making him very uncomfortable.

"Jeez," said Max, "hasn't this guy ever heard of personal space?"

"He's trying to intimidate you," explained Thompson, "get you to slow down."

"Well it's damn well working." Max tried hard not to panic as he saw Shade's tires inching as close as possible to his. "Damn, is he crazy!?"

"Don't panic. He won't touch you. The moment he does, he's disqualified, eighty-sixed and it's all over for him but the crying."

A scary thought passed through Max's mind. "What if my wheels touch his?"

Thompson thought about that. "That's what he's trying to do. Dammit, he wants *you* to touch his wheels." Thompson quickly thought of a strategy. "Max, you have to keep away from him."

"That's your strategy? I was hoping for something less pedestrian."

"Well what do you want me to say? There's no nitrous button."

"You are so not helping." Max didn't say anything else as he concentrated hard on keeping their wheels apart. A part of him did think of trying Shade's trick of twitching the wheel towards him but deep down, Max knew that it wouldn't work. In a situation like this, there could only be one attacker and one defender. Once the defender tried to attack, disaster would strike. And that was the genius in this move.

In order for the move to work, the attacker had to have nerves of steel as they were basically risking life and limb on a gambit: that the defender valued their life more than the attacker valued their own. It was a dark gambit but a very good one. But only if the attacker had balls for days. And clearly, Shade had a pair on him.

Max was about to do the only other thing he could do which was pull back and try to regroup from second position – which was really last position in a race like this

273

– when he was spared the embarrassment by Shade suddenly pulling away and swerving across the entire freeway. Max knew exactly why he did it and immediately followed and just made it onto the offramp without losing speed.

Now behind Shade, Max had some catching up to do. Lucky for him, the M1 offered that long stretch of straight road with almost no traffic to speak off. All Max had to do was gun his engine and keep away from Shade when he passed him. Unfortunately, Max quickly found out that tonight, the M1 was *not* without traffic. Not by any stretch of the imagination.

"Holy crap!" Up ahead was a line of cars with bright red and yellow lights lighting up the night sky as the Metro Police had set up a roadblock. It was only when the cops saw Shade and Max coming, that they switched on their sirens which let out that deafening sound. Max watched Shade screech his vehicle to a stop and Max did the same.

"What's wro—" But clearly, Thompson must have seen what he was seeing from the streaming video. "Oh no, cops."

"Not just cops, Thompson. Metro cops." While it had been years since the last time that Max had been on the island, he knew about the reputation of Azania's Metropolitan police departments – particularly the Ngelosi Metro P.D. They were legendary. Max didn't know if the media was just putting a spin on it, but they sure as hell made it seem like they were the only cops in South Africa who knew how to get anything done. These guys didn't know the meaning of red tape, compared to the S.A.P.S. It was a common conception that when the Ngelosi Metro P.D. were on the case, things got done; cases got closed and bad guys went to jail. Unfortunately for Max, tonight, he was that bad guy.

Max looked on in agony at the Metro cops and their expertly laid roadblock. They had them pinned on this side of the freeway as there was a metal barrier preventing them from crossing onto the other side of the freeway. While the metal barrier was something of a joke in protecting anything in a high-speed collision, here it did the job as it prevented them from going anywhere. To their left was just wilderness so there was no going that way. Max swore.

Luckily for Max, he wasn't the only bad guy out here tonight. He watched as Shade revved his car back to life and then spun it around and started back where they came from. Clearly, he must've known something Max didn't so Max repeated what he had done and followed. Max had expected Shade to try and double back up the offramp but instead, went right past it. As Max thought, maybe he was being safe and going for the onramp on the other side, under the bridge, Shade showed this to not be the case as he drove past that as well.

"Where the hell are you going?"

"What happened? Did you lose them?"

The question was answered by a wailing of sirens trailing behind him. "No. They're still on me. I'm following Shade. He seems to know something I don't. We're going the opposite direction, up the Mike One. Any idea where he's going?"

Thompson thought for a moment. "Do I know? No. Do I have an idea? Maybe."

"Care to share?"

"Hold on a minute."

"I don't have a minute!" But with bigger problems than Thompson needing a minute he didn't have, Max continued to follow Shade. As they blazed further down the M1 with the city of Ngelosi whipping past them in the distance to their left, Max wondered if they were going to follow the M1 right out of town. But unfortunately, this looked to be an impossibility as, to his horror, Max saw sirens up ahead as well with *another* roadblock of Metro cop cars.

"You've got to be kidding me," said Max mostly to himself.

"Hey, so I spoke to Stevie. I know where Shade's going."

"I think it doesn't matter, man. There's another roadblock up a—" Max cut himself off at the sight ahead of him. Max had fully expected Shade to slow down again

277

as they approached the roadblock. Instead, he seemed to speed up. Max wasn't sure if it was a good idea but since he'd followed him this far, he decided to speed up as well. When they got closer, Max realized why Shade had sped up.

Up ahead, at the roadblock, Max noticed that the cops had made a mistake. *This* roadblock wasn't a line of cars but rather two police cars on either side of a plastic barricade that was basically two pillars holding up this bar that ran across them. And if Max's calculations were right, their XF race cars were *just* low enough to fit right under it.

Max fell in behind Shade and began drafting her, entering into a slip stream. The two of them increased the speed so that when they zoomed right past the barricade, the sheer speed of their vehicles had toppled over the barricade and had the cops standing there ducking away at the sound of the cracking their vehicles made as if breaking the sound barrier.

"What happened?" asked Thompson.

"We got past the roadblock," said Max, now smiling.

"That's good. Like I was saying: I know where Shade is going. Apparently, there is this route that they have here called the contingency in case of cops."

"Okay?" said Max, trying to hide the shock of why he was only learning about this now.

"It goes through the old power plant by the dam."

On cue, Max saw the dam come up on his right as the M1 began running alongside a river. "Okay I see the dam." Max followed as Shade took the next off ramp. "And Shade just took the offramp. Okay, I think he's going where you think he's going."

As they continued to drive, Thompson explained that the power plant was actually converted to a hydro-electric power plant some decades ago and specifically built at the riverside with anticipation of the later conversion. Max commended the foresight of the developers but asked what this had to do with this being a getaway route. But the question was answered immediately when Shade and Max entered the plant.

Unlike Thompson's hiding spot, this plant was very much still functional. However, the route that Shade was taking them along seemed to belong to the old thermal power station as it had many pipes, some of which were low-hanging and whizzed terrifyingly close to the top of their vehicles. But Max understood this to be precisely the point. The pipes hung so low that only an XF race car *could* navigate this route.

The route took them all the way to the other side of the dam where Max noticed Shade notably go slower as they travelled down the quieter backroads on the opposite side of the river. As they continued, Max smiled as he heard the sirens but far in the distance, trapped on the other side of the river. He wanted to start celebrating when Shade suddenly swerved and slid off the road into the bush.

Max saw that it had been a cow he'd been avoiding and managed to slow down and avoid a collision himself. But upon coasting past Shade, he saw that while his car looked like it was in one piece, Shade was failing to turn it over. As Max stopped the *Cradle*, took off his helmet and jumped out, intent on checking on Shade, he noticed the fearsome driver lose his head with rage. Shade got out of the vehicle and kicked it in frustration.

Max had never seen the usually cool-headed Shade look like this. Max was about to walk over to him when he stopped dead in his tracks at the sight in front of him. Shade was fiddling with his helmet and lifted it off. Max expected, perhaps, that he would be wearing a protective mask, but he wasn't. Max realized that Shade had, perhaps, made a mistake. But Max realized immediately that it was *him* who had made a mistake, as Shade wasn't a *he* at all.

"Christina?" Max had recognised the blonde-streaked plaits first before noticing the light brown skin tone. But when she turned and gave him a scowl that Max would recognise anywhere as belonging to the smartest girl in his class, Max knew that it was her. "You're Shade?"

However, Christina clearly didn't give a damn that she had just revealed her secret identity to him. She simply looked at the damaged *Tumbler* and swore. "It won't start. Dammit!"

Still in shock over the reveal of what he believed up until now to be a badass *male* driver, Max barely registered that Shade was facing a major dilemma. *Why the hell am I still calling her Shade*? But before Max could correct himself, he heard the sirens again. While they were still across the river, they were definitely closer.

"They might be far off, but they'll still get here," she said, finally registering that Max was there. "They'll be taking the bridge which is about a kilometre down the river. The one behind us is even further away."

Max nodded in approval. "Ha, the perfect getaway route."

Christina nodded. "Yeah. Hasn't been used though since the rich kid generation. But in order to actually get away," she said, kicking her vehicle again, "you need to be able to drive."

Max looked at Christina as if seeing her for the first time. It might as well have been the first time since he was definitely seeing her in a new light. Max looked back to his vehicle then back to Christina, calculating. "C'mon."

282

"What's your plan?" she said, not following him to the *Cradle*.

"You'll see," he said, with authority in his voice. "Now c'mon." Christina did as he said. And while Max came up with a plan to evacuate himself and Christina out of the area, all he could think of was how he could be so blind as to not notice that someone in his own class was a fellow racer; one of the best racers. Clearly, come tomorrow, Christina would have some explaining to do.

CHAPTER SEVENTEEN
THE DRIVER OF THE TUMBLER

It had definitely been a weird experience transporting Christina to safety the night before. She had been forced to jump on the top of *Baby Cradle* and hang on for dear life as Max got them out of there and off the road. Once he'd done that, it was just a matter of calling Thompson for a ride and getting them back to North Ngelosi.

While Max had learnt Christina's secret identity as Shade, it was clear that she had no interest in anyone else learning it, as she kept her helmet on and her mouth shut as Thompson gave them a ride back. Now that Max knew that Shade was a girl, it was almost as if his eyes had been opened.

Christina had always been a girl with notable feminine curves but as Max had looked at her now, he noticed that she had taken strides to hide them as Shade by walking with a different gait and almost always folding her arms to hide her well-endowed chest. Max had decided not to interrogate her about it then. But today, as he got to class and saw her at the back acting like everything was normal, Max was going to get some answers.

Max had tried to get those answers the first time he saw her, but Christina had shooed him away with just a stare. *Man, she has a cold stare*. Her stare was truly icy. It was at this point, they went about their lessons like nothing had changed, and Max realized that there had been so many clues that Christina was Shade.

Thinking back, Max began putting things together starting with the last conversation – well second to last now that he knew she was Shade – that he had with her where she had understood immediately why Max had skipped school. It hadn't been because she'd been there when Moodswing had picked Stevie up that day. It had been because she was Shade and knew exactly what Moodswing was doing, using Stevie to get to Tar.

Thinking more specifically about yesterday when Max had seen Christina at the library, Max suddenly remembered that she had fiddled with her phone just around the time that Max had gotten off his. She hadn't been getting a text from Lisa! No, she had been getting a notification about their race last night! It all seemed to make sense now.

Except that none of it makes sense, thought Max. Why the hell would the smartest girl in class – a shoo-in for Head Girl – be moonlighting as an XF racer? When First Break came along, Max caught up to her in the hallway and was about to ask her again about last night when she shut him up and said that if he *must* know, she'd tell him all about it but only during Second Break as she had to get some headway with the assignment and was meeting up with Lisa now.

Second Break couldn't have come sooner as Max hurried off to the library and found Christina sitting exactly where she had been sitting just twenty-four hours earlier: at the large table all by her lonesome. Max sat down across from her, this time very much invited, and waited patiently for Christina to say something.

"Okay, Max, what do you want to know?"

Is she serious right now? "Why?"

Christina rolled her eyes. "Why what? C'mon, you've been bothering me all day and now you're asking incomplete questions?"

"Why, as in why Shade? Why do you race as Shade?"

Christina thought about her answer. "Why do you race?"

"Because I enjoy it. The thrill, the speed."

"There you go."

"Yeah, but I don't do it in secret."

"Well, I don't want people knowing that I'm an XF racer, so I race as Shade."

"But that's what I want to know. Why would a girl, as smart as you, with everything going for her, go and involve herself in an illegal, underground racing scene?"

"Well I guess because of what you just said. And I'm tired of hearing it. I'm tired of being seen as the good little girl who does as she's told and gets full marks. I wanted to do something dangerous. And as it turns out, I'm very, *very* good at it."

"Yeah, I've heard that you won the Crown a couple of times."

"Aha" she affirmed. "And I'm going to win it back." For a second, Christina's tone of voice suggested she was channelling her 'Shade' side.

Max didn't respond to that. "Just tell me one thing. Fine, you want to race but you're the smartest girl in school. But, so what? Why hide who you are? Like you said, you're good at it. That should be enough for people not to judge you."

"Oh yeah, how's that going for Tar's sister? You're telling me Tar's not giving her a piece of his mind every day?" Christina had a point. "Look, I know that we live in Azania: the paradise that knows no colour, but all that means is that *racism* is dead. All the other ways in which people judge people, those are still alive. In one way or another people are judgy. Always have been. So, to answer your question about why the big secret: because I wanna have my cake and eat it."

Max just looked at her. "I didn't know you were so cynical."

Christina shrugged playfully. "I guess that's my Shade side," she said smiling. She sighed. "But I guess eating my cake is not an option anymore."

"Why?"

"The *Tumbler*. It's totalled, remember?"

"So, have it repaired."

Christina gave him a curious look. "You do know that we're rivals out there, right? Only one of us can be King?" She then mumbled something about that definitely being him.

"Hmm, definitely your Christina side." When she looked up, Max leaned forward. "Shade wouldn't give up this easily."

Christina played with her jaw, amused by Max's words. "Well, baby cradler," she said teasing him, "even if I could take the *Tumbler* all the way to my guy at Noresto—"

"What the hell is your mechanic doing all the way out there?"

"—it doesn't solve the problem of where the car is right now."

"Yeah it doesn't. Getting your car to Noresto to get fixed and then having it back by tomorrow would be next to impossible."

"You don't listen well, which won't serve you any good for our study session. By the way," she said as an aside, "where are your textbooks?" When Max took them out, Christina smiled, impressed. "Like I was saying, the immediate problem with my vehicle is where it's currently located."

Max heard her this time. "Why, where is your vehicle?"

"If it's not still by the side of that road, which I doubt, then it's in SAPS impound."

"SAPS? But it was Metro Pee-Dee that was chasing us."

Christina nodded, knowing this. "But all impounded cars are kept at the SAPS police station. It's some kind of jurisdictional turf war or something."

Max understood. It was the red tape stuff that gave the S.A.P.S. the bad reputation that they had – at least in comparison to the Metro Police Departmen. But Max understood better than that because if the S.A.P.S. had the car, then he could do something about that. "Hey, we kinda broke the law last night, right?"

Christina just looked at him. "We break the law like every night, Max."

"So, you wouldn't mind us doing it again, then?" Max smiled when Christina gave him a confused look. "Meet me after school."

*

Max lay in the pitch-dark space trying as hard as he might not to move, not to make a sound. Unfortunately, his companion didn't seem capable of keeping still, let alone keeping quiet.

"I can't believe I let you talk me into this," said Christina.

"If you want your vehicle back, then this is the way to do it."

"But we're in a boot." She was right. Max had a plan to get Christina's vehicle back, but it required them to be stuck in a boot for a little while. The plan involved Thompson as well as his car and the delivery truck. It was a simple enough plan, but Christina wasn't sold on it.

"It's going to work."

Christina gulped notably. "I'm sure it will."

"Then what's the problem."

"Never been a fan of small spaces."

"Claustrophobic?" This was surprising considering how much time she spent sitting in that small confined space they called the seat of a race car.

Christina scoffed. "Not likely. I'm not claustrophobic. I'm just not a fan of small spaces where I can't see, talk or freaking breathe for that matter. It would be much easier if we could talk."

Max contemplated this. *Oh, what the hell?* The quiet part of the plan was behind them now, anyway. "What do you want to talk about?"

Christina didn't take long to answer. "Why are you helping me?"

Nothing like the deep questions, thought Max. "I'm helping you because you helped me, last night. You led me out of a jam back there, you know, with the cops."

Max heard Christina laugh. "You know that was inadvertent, right? I was just trying to get out of dodge. I wasn't trying to *lead* you anywhere."

"Well you helped me out all the same. So now, I'm helping you out."

Before Christina could ask Max any more questions, they felt the car stop. They kept dead quiet and Max heard a short conversation and realized they were at the gate of the impound lot. The car was then driven inside and lowered off the flatbed that it had been sitting on. When they heard the flatbed truck drive out of earshot, Max used the emergency boot release to open the boot to reveal a yard of cars in a piece of land that looked like a regular rugby field. He could see the police station in distance on the other side of the field, but it was facing away from the lot.

"C'mon," said Max to Christina and led her down the aisle of cars before they came to the beautiful black XF race car. As Christina smiled at seeing the *Tumbler,* Max looked around and quickly caught sight of their truck. "C'mon," he said again as he led Christina to the truck.

Max then took out the spare keys and reversed in front of the *Tumbler* before going around and opening the back. It was empty as Thompson and Max had vacated it of *Baby Cradle* so that they had space for the *Tumbler.* While they struggled to push the vehicle up the ramp, they

294

eventually managed. They then moved on to the second part of the plan which involved moving the truck back to where they'd found it and locking themselves in the back with the *Tumbler*.

"You okay?" asked Max, remembering Christina's discomfort with small spaces.

"I'm good. I'm just wondering when the next part of your plan—" Christina's question was answered immediately when they heard Thompson's voice. He was with someone else and he was apologizing for having left his car in a tow zone before thanking him for being so kind to let him have his truck back. Max and Christina then felt a shift in weight as Thompson got in the truck and drove it straight out of the impound lot, free as a bird.

A few minutes later, the truck came to a stop. When Christina went for the door, Max stopped her. "If you still value your anonymity, I'd suggest you hold off on opening that door." Christina paused upon hearing these words. "I told Thompson that I was with you, well, Shade and that you would appreciate it if he didn't sneak a peek at your ride."

After five minutes, the two exited the truck and Christina saw that they were in the abandoned plant in Empiko. "Wow. I don't believe it. We did it." Christina jumped down from the truck.

"Mission accomplished," said Max, smugly as he stood still on the truck bed, folding his arms, looking like the hero he was.

"Now I just need to get it to Noresto and get it fixed as soon as I can."

"How long do you think that will take?"

"It should be ready by early next week."

Max wasn't satisfied with that answer and jumped down from the truck bed. "I've got a better idea. What if I told you that I knew someone who knows how to fix your engine?"

"I'd say I hope you do because if you don't, you'd have a problem one—"

"Yeah, yeah, Christina. I know you're smarter than me but just stick with me for a second. I'm talking about a mechanic in the neighbourhood who can fix your engine and have it ready in the next twenty-four hours."

"I'd say: what's the catch?"

"No catch. The fact and the matter is, if I can't beat Moodswing, maybe you can. It's not at all what I want to happen, but the fact and the matter is, if I have to choose between having that guy as King and you, then I'd choose you."

Christina smiled. "That's sweet. I hope you're not that sweet when I face you again to become number one contender."

Max returned Christina's smile. "Is that a yes?"

It was a yes. But getting Christina to agree to his help was the easy part. The hard part was the next part. Because he knew a mechanic that could fix the *Tumbler* alright, but he had no way of knowing whether she would agree to do it. With Lisa not even talking to him, he had no idea in hell of how he was going to convince her to fix Christina's vehicle.

CHAPTER EIGHTEEN
STAND/OFF

It had been a slow day at the Shop with not much for Lisa to do. Of course, that meant that Lisa got to do what she loved doing. After trolleying the *Yellow Prancer* out from the corner and into the working area where she could have some room to work, Lisa began.

She was currently working on the chassis, specifically how the engine would fit onto it. She pulled out the sheets of papers she had folded and placed into her pocket and unfolded them. On the papers, were the designs of what would eventually be the race car known as the *Yellow Prancer*. The finished product was still years away with Lisa having absolutely no idea how she was going to get some of the items she needed, but Lisa still persisted.

Currently, Lisa was pacing around the bare engine, trying to match it up with her drawings. She couldn't help but feel like she was trying to put together one of those model planes or war ships with a thousand pieces and model cement. It was going to take forever to complete but part of the fun was the construction.

Lisa had anticipated that she would be here all night working on the engine because that's what always happened. In fact, her father usually had to drag her out of the Shop because of how she would become completely lost in the construction of her precious engine. However, contrary to what Lisa had thought would happen, the last person she ever expected to show up, stood in the Shop doorway.

"Why hello there."

On instinct, Lisa wanted to smile, but she resisted. She didn't even turn around. "What are you doing here, Max?"

"Wow. Did I do something wrong?"

Lisa realized that he had a point. Max hadn't actually done anything wrong. Well, at least not to her. "I see you've been going to school religiously these days. How are the tutoring sessions going?"

"Not bad."

"Not bad? You missed a See-Tee-Ay test, Max. If you don't nail the make-up test, you're screwed. So, you better say it's going better than just 'not bad'."

Max scoffed playfully. "You sound just like Christina." Lisa was sure he could sense her smile. "By the way, why didn't you tell me about the See-Tee-Ay test?"

"Oh, that's my job now?"

"No," said Max, sounding a bit guilty. "But *this* is."

Lisa's brow furrowed and she turned around to see Max standing there, smirk on his face, arm extended behind him as if to say "voila". Lisa looked at what he was gesturing to and saw that there was an unmarked delivery truck across the street.

"You brought me a delivery truck?"

In one of the smoothest moves she had ever seen from a boy, Max simply stepped forward and arced his arm about his shoulder so that his extended hand was now facing her. Lisa was moved, her cheeks doing that involuntary twitchy thing they'd done just once before. She'd seen Max extend his arm like this before: on the beach. Lisa did as she'd done that day: stood up and took his hand.

What was it about this boy that she found it so easy to connect with him? Max led her to the back of the truck and opened it. Inside, Lisa saw what was unmistakably an XF race car.

"It won't start. I was hoping that you could fix it."

Lisa wasn't ready to answer that question, so she simply looked at it. "This isn't *Baby Cradle*."

"No," said Max simply.

Lisa raised her eyebrows. "So, what, you think because I'm building my own engine and I'm a mechanic that I'm now your guys' go-to repairs person?"

"Not even close."

"So, then what's the deal here, Max?" said Lisa climbing up onto the truck bed.

301

"It's a favour for a friend."

Lisa thought about that for a moment, thinking of Max's friends. None of them had engines that looked like this. Now that she was closer, Lisa gave the vehicle a closer look. While she wasn't at all a fan of the racing subculture; having grown up in Ngelosi, it was impossible to know nothing about the racing scene. And with her having a high interest in engines, Lisa had found that she was capable of recognising the race car engines by sight and sound. And right now, she recognised *this* engine.

"You're friends with Shade?"

Max tightened his jaw in an effort to keep from dropping it. He hesitated before speaking his next words, not knowing if he should deny it or not. "How did you know it was hhhhis vehicle? I thought you weren't familiar with the scene."

"You're right, I'm not. But I can still recognise an engine when I see one."

"Really? Is that your superpower?" But Max wasn't really interested in super-powers. "So, will you see what's wrong with it? She needs—" Max bit his tongue and seemed to change his words mid-sentence. "She needs to be done by tomorrow night."

Lisa looked at him curiously. "Since when did you start referring to race cars as 'she' instead of 'it'?"

"You're not answering my question."

Lisa sighed, thinking. "Tomorrow, huh?" While Lisa was more than willing to figure out what was wrong with the car, she didn't tell him that. No. She was going to figure out a way to turn this to her advantage. "If I do this for you then I'm going to need something in return," she said smiling.

"Well what did you have in mind?"

"There's this movie called Stand/Off that's coming out tonight. Take me to it?" Lisa had delivered her question with her raised eyebrow and a flirty smile that got Max flustered. She loved that.

"You want me to take you out? I thought I'd blown it."

"Have you now?" said Lisa, still flirting. Lisa wasn't lying though with the words she'd spoken. How could she hate a guy who'd paid attention to what she'd said? Wasn't he back in school? Wasn't he here, right now? Granted it was as a favour to another racer but surely that didn't make him a bad guy?

"So, what time is this movie?"

*

While Lisa had expected Max to say yes to the date, she had not at all expected him to take her *tonight*. When she'd asked him if he didn't have to be on the scene tonight, he claimed that he didn't have any place better to be than with her. So, for the first time since she could remember, Lisa left the Shop before six o'clock as they'd wanted to catch the 7:15 movie at the mall.

Since neither of them had a car – at least a private one – they took the train to the mall. The trains of Azania island were just as interesting as the ones on the mainland as every train car was made up of a collection of various subcultures, from church singers to street vendors to regular passengers. However, what set them apart was, like Johannesburg's Gautrain, they were subway trains –

at least in Ngelosi. The rest of the province used ordinary railway trains though.

As they made their way through the mall and upstairs to the cinema, they discussed the movie. "So, what's this 'Stand/Off' movie about anyway?"

"It's an anti-revenge thriller."

"An anti-revenge thriller?" asked Max. "What exactly is an anti-revenge thriller?"

"Well it's about these two former best friends turned bitter enemies who are terrorized into fixing their problems."

Max rolled his eyes. "And how exactly are they terrorized; may I ask?"

"Bad guy puts them in a room and stands them each on a landmine and says they're going to stay there until they sort out their problems."

"Hmm, well I'm glad it's not far-fetched."

"Well, I'll have you know, the trailer was awesome. All the tension lies in the fact that they can't stand on the

305

bombs forever." Max smiled, listening to Lisa talk. It was clear that he was loving seeing this side to her. When they got to the cinema, they found it packed and Lisa was glad that they'd arrived early.

As they stood in one of the shortest queues, Lisa wondered what she was going to get when she suddenly felt Max's hand tighten around hers. Lisa looked to see what had gotten Max's attention when it got hers too. Coming out of the cinema from the previous showing was Moodswing. But what had gotten their immediate attention was who Moodswing was with.

"What the hell is she...?" Lisa was so shocked; she couldn't finish her own sentence. "Are they on a date?"

"I sure as hell hope not," said Max who moved out of the queue and stood right in Moodswing's path.

Moodswing smiled when he saw Max. "Well, well, well. If it isn't my favourite person in the world. How you doing, McKay?"

Max's eyes moved from him to his companion then back to him. "Haven't you done enough, Moodswing?"

"Well hello to you too, Max." The person who spoke was none other than Stevie. It was her who had gotten their attention

Max blatantly ignored her. "Seriously Moodswing? She's fifteen."

"Hey," said Stevie, "hello. I'm right here. I can hang out with anyone I want to."

Lisa scoffed. "Hang out? Is that what you're calling it?"

Moodswing smiled. "Oh, did you think this was something else? Did you think this was like, a date?" However instead of denying it, Moodswing's smile widened. "And what if it is? What are you going to do about it?"

"Moodswing!"

"Max!"

Just before Max could pounce, Lisa and Stevie stood in front of their respective companions, keeping them from ripping each other a part.

"What, you're going to hit me now, McKay? Is that it? Is that what Tar is teaching you?"

"Moodswing!" said Stevie, clearly not happy with him goading Max. "Moodswing, stop."

"Stop?" said Moodswing. "What, he's the one about to break the rules."

"You can't keep hiding behind the rules, Moodswing." said Max, angrily.

"They're there for a reason!"

"Yeah," said Max, "so cowards like you can hide behind them."

Moodswing went silent, momentarily. Now he was clearly ticked off. "You're lucky that we're all laying low tonight otherwise I'd make mincemeat out of you."

Lisa realized in that instant that *this* was the reason that Max had gone out with her. It was because they were not racing tonight. However, considering the situation in front of them now, Lisa couldn't care less. Lisa began pushing Max back towards the entrance as two male cinema attendants headed their way.

308

She looked at Stevie as they made their way out. "Stevie, you should really reconsider the company you keep."

Stevie didn't respond and instead looked at Moodswing who was too busy staring a hole through Max. "I'm going to defend my title tomorrow, McKay. And I want you to witness it. I want you to see what it looks like when I'm on my A-game."

As Lisa left with Max in tow, she couldn't help but be impressed with how Moodswing had managed to *not* let slip anything about the racing scene. As far as anyone who wasn't in on the scene was concerned, they could have been talking about some local boxing or pro wrestling circuit that took place in high school gyms.

As they continued to walk out of the mall, the ever-perceptive Max picked up on her expression. "So, are you mad? About the fact that the only reason I went out with you tonight was because the scene was closed down for the night?"

Lisa thought about how to answer the question. "To tell you the truth, I want to be mad at you. I want to do the

309

disapproving girlfriend thing; to tell you to get out of the scene. But after the," she swallowed, "the disgusting scene we saw in there, I understand why you need to take Moodswing down."

"Lisa," he started. But Lisa silenced him by pulling him in and meeting her lips with his. The kiss was sweet, his lips perfectly soft. *Wow, this boy knows how to kiss.* It seemed to last forever yet when their lips finally parted, it felt like it had ended too soon. *Don't say wow. Don't say wow! You'll ruin the moment.* "Wow."

It was *him* who had said the word, to which Lisa smiled. But it was time to tell him the truth of the matter. "I know what you have to do, Max, but I can't be standing next you when you do it." She saw the solemn look on his face. "I'm sorry Max, but that scene is not *my* scene. Now go kick that man's ass and know that I don't hate you."

Lisa realized in hindsight that it was weird to say all that when they still had a train trip home. But it needed to be said so she was glad that she got it out of the way. Luckily enough, they did have *one* thing they could talk about. Max asked Lisa about the *Tumbler*.

"Oh, I already figured out what's wrong with it," she said smugly.

"You have?"

"Yeah. The fuel line is severed. I can have it replaced and all fixed up by sundown, tomorrow. Free of charge." Max gave her a look. "Getting to work on Shade's engine is payment enough. By the way, do you know who he is?"

Lisa had expected him to simply deny it but instead he kept quiet. Did he know? Because if he did then that made him the worst liar in the world. And once again, another reason she was so attracted to him. *Why oh why did he have to be both a catch and a racer?* Like life wasn't hard enough already.

CHAPTER NINETEEN
NORESTO

It was weird for Max walking into the class and being the only learner in the room. But since he was the only learner in his class who hadn't written the C.T.A. the first time around, this was bound to happen. As Max worked his way through the paper, he became more and more relaxed as he realized that the few tutoring lessons that Christina had given him had actually paid off.

Max found himself thinking about Lisa as he wrote the paper and what she'd said last night about not being by his side as he went to war with Moodswing. He had expected to feel upset or sad about it but instead he found himself glad. Despite her words basically amounting to a breakup, he now knew that she really, really liked him. Although the smooch was a dead giveaway. *Wow, that girl was a good kisser*, he thought.

Max now found that he had to concentrate harder on the paper as images of kissing the girl were swimming around in his head instead of the answers he needed to pass. But eventually, Max did finish and with fifteen minutes to spare. And with his make-up test taking place just before First Break, it gave him an extra-long break.

When Christina found him in the senior quad outside the library at the beginning of break time, he was already halfway through his lunch. "So, how did it go?"

Max smiled. "I think it went rather well. In fact, it went great. I felt like I knew all the answers."

"Well that's because we only studied what was going to come out." Christina explained that she'd used her knowledge of the paper she wrote to anticipate what they'd ask him. When Max pointed out that the papers asked different questions, Christina smugly said "yeah well I'm smart like that."

"So, I took the *Tumbler* to the mechanic I talked about and you'll be happy to know that she figured out what the problem is: the fuel line was severed."

Christina clung on to one fact. "*She*? Did you take my car to *Lisa*?"

"Yeah." Max gave her a confused look. "Is that a problem?"

However, before Christina could say another word, they were joined by the subject of their conversation. "Hey guys," said Lisa. "Am I interrupting something?"

For a second, Max wasn't sure if she was talking about interrupting their conversation or suggesting that Max was into Christina. Max answered both questions. "No. What's up Lisa?"

"Well I was actually looking for both of you." She looked at Christina. "I wanted to know from you if you're ready to continue with the assignment." She then looked at Max. "And I wanted to let you know that," her eyes darted to Christina before darting back to Max, "the repairs are done. You can pick *her* up after school."

Max smiled, amused at the situation in front of him. Here was Lisa making a point to keep the fact that she was talking about Shade's vehicle a secret while at the same time here was Shade, unable to say a damn word about the fact that the vehicle Lisa was talking about *was* hers. Another thing that got Max's attention was how Lisa had referred to the *Tumbler* as a "she", which was in turn a reference to how Max had almost messed up yesterday and referred to Shade as "she".

"Great," said Max. "I'll let..." Max realized now that he also had to pretend to keep the secret that it was Shade's car from Christina. "... the owner know that it's ready." Max responded to Lisa's nod with a nod of his own before screwing his brow in curiosity. "Wait, when did you get the time to finish between now and last night?"

"You remember that we didn't actually get to watch the movie, right? I went back to the Shop to work on her then."

Christina, having had enough of trying to keep track of who was supposed to know what, picked up a bag to

315

leave. "I don't know which I'm more curious in knowing: when you got a car," she said referring to Max, "or why you guys cancelled your date," she said looking at Lisa.

Both Lisa and Max shared a look before saying, "it's a long story," in unison.

"Whatever," said Christina. "Look, congratulations on your C.T.A. I hope it did go as well as you say it did. And Lisa, I'm ready to go do this thing when you are." Christina started away, taking out her phone to check something as she walked.

Meanwhile Lisa gave Max a beaming smile. "Your test, it went well?" He nodded. "That's excellent. Kind of just the right momentum you need going into your big race with Moodswing, huh."

"Well first I have to beat Shade before I get to Moodswing." On cue, Max's phone vibrated, and he checked it to see a text message from Christina.

I just got word that our race has been pushed to tomorrow night. Tonight, Moodswing wants to defend his title against some nobody. Trying to

send a message to us, I guess. Anyway, drop my
car off at my grandmother's place? It's in Noresto.

Max smiled at the message as he realized that Christina
hadn't actually asked him to drop the car off, but rather
had commanded him to do it. He guessed she was
channelling her 'Shade' side.

"About the race?" said Lisa, referring to the text.

Max shook his head. "No race for me tonight. That was
Shade telling me where to drop off the car."

"How did he know it was done?"

Max fought the urge to grit his teeth at the mistake he
made and thought of how to recover. "Well how does
Shade know anything, really? He's a mystery from top to
bottom, that guy." They both shared a laugh. It was great
that they could get along even after their understanding
last night. But even with that, Max couldn't help but want
more with her. He was haunted by that kiss from last
night. He wanted this girl.

*

Max remembered where Noresto was from when Joseph Sibusiso had pointed it out to him on the way from the airport. Unfortunately, he didn't know his way around the area itself, so he'd asked Thompson for directions. Armed with the address that Christina had given him later, and the delivery truck that he'd left at the Shop last night, Max was on his way.

As Max drove from the freeway onto the main road that ran through Noresto, he remembered what Joseph Sibusiso had said about the place: that it had evolved so much that it shouldn't be called a township. But Max wasn't sure about that. Yes, the place definitely didn't look like what one might imagine a township to look like. It had nice family houses complete with gardens; parks, soccer fields, playgrounds, public libraries, good-looking schools, community halls and more than one mall. But the place also had informal settlements, litter about the side of the road and an overpopulation of street vendors that made the place look far busier than it should be.

Max followed the directions that Thompson had given him until he went down a dead-end road. It was a lovely road with the large trees lined along the side of the road billowing over the road providing great shade. When he got to Christina's grandmother's place, he found a small but charming two-bedroom house that had another dwelling behind it. Max was about to honk the hooter when a boy not older than 14 years of age came outside.

"Hola," said the boy after opening the gate and coming to the driver's side. "Max, neh?"

"Christina told you I was coming?"

"Yah." The boy then told him to just bring the truck into the yard in reverse. He'd spoken Zulu but luckily for Max – the one thing that his mother had insisted on him learning which he was thankful for – Max understood and obliged.

While Max understood Zulu perfectly – which was a must in a province where even Caucasians were fluent in South Africa's mother tongues – and even spoke it well, he had admittedly lost some fluency after spending so much time in Australia. However, that didn't keep him from being able to communicate with this boy just fine.

His name was Sipho Langa and he was Christina's cousin. Max couldn't help but smile at the similarities between his name and his mother's. Sipho was currently living with his grandmother as his parents were overseas. And as it turned out, he was a big fan of the XF racing scene. It was at this moment that Max realized just how big the fanbase was of the racing scene. Sipho admitted that he had really enjoyed Max's races, believing that he was a natural. However, he also believed that no one was better than his cousin.

"So, I hear that you and umzala are going to face off tomorrow. Are you ready?"

"Ready as I'll ever be."

Sipho gave him a credulous look. "Hey wena, don't think just because you now know that Shade is a girl that she won't bliksom you. She's gonna moor you."

Max smiled, amused by the boy's slang. It wasn't surprising as the cultures of South Africa had found a weird and wonderful way of mixing here on the Island Province of Azania. Where the mainlanders were proud of their individual cultures originating in their distinctive provinces – and they should lest they be forgotten forever – Azania had always been the home to where all those cultures mixed and blended together to form their own sort of subculture that was truly South African.

After Sipho and him successfully unloaded the *Tumbler*, Christina's grandmother came out to greet Max and then told Sipho to go and buy a cool drink for him. Max knew better than to say 'no thanks' and gratefully accepted. But he decided to accompany the boy, not wanting him to do all that leg work by himself.

As they walked, Max asked why they hadn't hidden the *Tumbler* behind the house or put a tarp on it as anyone who walked past the house could see it. Sipho had dismissed this and claimed that no one stole anything in this part of Noresto. But that was not what had concerned Max. Surely Christina didn't want her grandmother's neighbours knowing her secret?

When they had gotten to the tuckshop, Sipho bought the cooldrink, which was a Lemon Twist in a 1.5 litre glass bottle. Having taken a liking to the kid, Max gave him a ten Rand bill for him to buy anything else he wanted. Sipho added a two Rand coin to the green bill and then proceeded to buy a portion of slop chips – which they called amafried – which he then drowned in tomato sauce, mustard and hot sauce, smiling widely as he did.

Sipho graciously shared the chips with Max as they walked back. But just as they got to the house, three dodgy looking young men approached them.

"Who's the afro?" one of them asked Sipho.

Sipho, who looked scared to Max but didn't show an ounce of fear to them, answered. "No one, he's just a friend."

"He's not from around here," said the second one, in Zulu. The third one simply watched.

"You know we don't like outsiders," said the first one.

"He was just visiting," said Sipho.

The conversation continued in the same passive-aggressive tone, with Max realizing that they didn't know he understood every word that they said. Max was intrigued by their motivation for this confrontation as it was clear that it wasn't because of the colour of his skin that they were making a fuss but because he wasn't from around the neighbourhood. From what Max could gather, these three – like many in the neighbourhood – didn't like outsiders because they were afraid of what nonsense they would bring. Their neighbourhood was low on crime because they looked after their own – having found no joy in getting the S.A.P.S. to do it.

Max was about to step in when the third man noticed the race car in the driveway. He tapped the first man who looked at it and everything changed. "Is that the *Tumbler*?" Sipho reluctantly acknowledged that it was with a nod. "Why didn't you say that Christina was back?"

It dawned on Max right then that they knew who Shade was. That was why Sipho hadn't bothered hiding the vehicle. *Did the whole neighbourhood know that Christina was Shade?* Max was amazed by this and suddenly saw the neighbourhood in a whole new light. Now he understood why these three were being so nosy. They really did look after their own.

"She's not back," said Sipho. He pointed at Max. "He was dropping it off for her."

For the first time, the first man looked at him. After a moment, it dawned on him who Max was. "Haibo. Maximum," said the man now smiling. "Yazi, I didn't see you."

Max realized that they were referring to *him* as 'Maximum'. "You guys know me?"

"We've seen you racing. Kaah-mon maan," he said if Max was supposed to just know this. The man then walked towards the *Tumbler*. "So, you know who Shade is, huh?" He continued when Max nodded. "Mmm, she must really trust you if she let you bring the *Tumbler* home."

"Home?" said Max, not realizing that Christina lived here as well. But he was corrected quickly.

"Yah," he continued. "This was where this car was born, ek se. We all helped Christina build it. Everyone played a part."

Intrigued to learn this, Max asked to hear more. He offered to share their drink and chips to which they accepted but not before the third man took a hike to the tuckshop to buy more chips along with a loaf of bread. They sat on the veranda as the man regaled Max on how Christina ended up needing almost the whole community to build the *Tumbler* as she needed odd parts from various people. The man went on to say that looking at it now, he could see that she eventually upgraded some things, but it was good for her as they still felt proud every time she won a race.

Max had eventually spent almost the whole afternoon on the veranda talking to the guys. Even Christina's grandmother had come out to greet them and shared a smile with them, remembering them from when they were small boys. When Max saw the sun starting to set, he said his goodbyes, with the guys wishing him luck for his race against Christina tomorrow as he was going to need it.

As Max made his way back to the city, heading out of Noresto, he couldn't help but smile. He couldn't believe that he once thought that staying on this island was going to be a bore. And even though he had barely judged the township of Noresto, he realized he'd still not given it the credit it deserved. While it wasn't without poverty and crime, there were definitely a lot of good people there. And, if anything, *they* were the shining example of what it meant to be an Azanian.

CHAPTER TWENTY
CHAMPIONSHIPS AND DEALERSHIPS

Moodswing never liked coming to the Dealership. It reminded him of the destiny he'd turned his back on. It was the legacy that his father had left for him and the one that he had yet to turn into his own as it wasn't what he wanted in his life right now. No, Moodswing wanted to create his own legacy.

Instead, it was Moodswing's older sister, Shaan, who had taken over the Dealership and steered the ship after their father had retired. The Moodley Honda/Hyundai Dealership was the biggest in the city. In fact, it was the biggest on Azania as there was no bigger dealership elsewhere on the Island Province.

Moodswing was currently at the Dealership because Shaan had asked to meet with him. She always did, but Moodswing always ignored her. But every once in a while, he would agree as he needed to come here to use the garage in the basement. As the owner's son, every mechanic who worked there attended to his every need and didn't bat an eye when he brought the *Dracula* in for a tune up. Of course, they relished the chance to work on an open wheel race car as it wasn't every day that they worked on one of those.

As Moodswing watched the mechanics do their work, a familiar face walked over to him. As part of their mentor/apprentice deal, Moodswing had given Stevie access to all his resources which included bringing the *Candyfloss* to the Dealership's garage. It was a win-win scenario really. The mechanics now had two vehicles they got to work on and Moodswing got to sink his hooks into Stevie deeper.

"So how is it looking?" asked Moodswing.

"They're almost done, actually," she said. "Hey, thanks again for letting me come down here. It would have been a nightmare servicing the *Candyfloss* without your help."

"Oh, I'm sure you would have managed," said Moodswing, smiling.

"I doubt it. I'm not exactly flush for cash, you know."

Moodswing scoffed, dismissing her words with a wave of the hand. "Argh, it's easy. Just a race or two for some stakes and then it would have just been a matter of finding a mechanic who was willing to work on your car on the down low."

"You make it sound so easy."

"I've been doing this racing thing for some time. I've seen how things get done on the scene. It's quite innovative." It was true. While it was relatively simple back in the days of his rich friends, the second generation showed how thinking outside the box could keep the scene going. It helped that seeing two desperate drivers squaring off in order to make up the money they needed for the car service was highly entertaining. At least it was for him.

"Well I'm still glad for your help."

Moodswing saw that something was troubling the teenager. "What's wrong?"

Stevie hesitated before answering. "It's just," he took a breath, "why did you tell Max and Lisa that we were on a date?"

"I didn't. If you recall I simply said—"

"You suggested it, Moodswing. I don't need these guys thinking I'm prostituting myself or something for some kind of advantage on the scene."

"Whoa, whoa, whoa. That's not what's happening here. And it doesn't matter what those guys *think*."

"It does when they tell my brother these things."

So that was what was bothering her. "Did Tar shout at you again?"

"He didn't have to. He's just judging me silently. Which is so much worse."

Moodswing wanted to smile but he refrained. "Stevie, we weren't on a date," he said as a matter of fact.

Stevie scoffed. "Tell that to my brother."

"I'm not telling Tar anything. I don't have to explain myself to your brother," he said harshly. Upon seeing her startled look, he added more gently, "and neither do you. The only thing you have to worry about is becoming the fastest thing on open wheels in Southern Africa."

Stevie nodded. This wasn't the first time that Moodswing had to keep her in line. It was reasons like this that he could never date Stevie. She was too young, and he didn't mean age. It was her maturity, or lack thereof, that put Moodswing off. She was too timid, or easily manipulated. Moodswing's taste in women had him looking for someone more aggressive, his intellectual equal.

The funny thing was, the reason he'd never date Stevie was the same reason that she was the ideal person for his plan, which was working perfectly. Unfortunately, Stevie had a habit of trying to throw his plans off track albeit inadvertently, as she tried to do now.

"So, I was thinking, wouldn't it be a good idea if I defend my title tonight? Show that I'm a fighting champion, like you."

"No," said Moodswing quickly.

This threw Stevie. "Why not?"

Moodswing looked at her. "Stevie, tonight is not about you. So, stop trying to make it about you." Upon seeing Stevie's guilty look, Moodswing continued. "Tonight, *I'm* defending my title. And the reason I'm doing that is because I want McKay and Shade to see it. Now if they're paying even a little attention to you then their minds won't be on how dominant I am when I wipe the floor with my opponent."

"I thought you said your race tonight was just a tune up race."

"Oh, wake up, Stevie. *Every* race that I race in is a show stealer, even if I'm racing a nobody like I am tonight. Every race counts towards something. There's always an angle."

Stevie went silent for a moment and Moodswing believed it was sinking in until she went on. "But I don't see why that means I can't race tonight."

"How about because I say you can't." Moodswing had given her a hard look and that had been enough. She'd shut up and shut up for good. Not wanting to hear anymore from her, Moodswing left the garage and went upstairs to the dealership showroom. The double volume area was brightly lit due to the front wall being ceiling to floor windows, doubling as doors for the demo cars to get in and out when the occasion called for it.

Across from the front doors was a line of desks and men and women sitting at those desks attending to customers. He looked one storey up to see another row of ceiling to floor window running across the length of the showroom, overlooking it from the first floor. One of the rooms was a rather large boardroom and the other, perfectly wedged in the corner was a large office where Moodswing's sister was currently working.

Moodswing went upstairs and entered the office without knocking, dropping himself in the guest seat before smiling at his sister. "Hello Shaan."

Shaan barely glanced at him before looking back at the papers on her desk. "I thought we agreed to have this meeting at four."

"I was busy."

"Doing what? Not having a job?"

Moodswing rolled his eyes. *Here we go. Here comes the pitch.* This was the reason that Moodswing hated coming here. Shaan was forever nagging him about the same thing. Even before it was Shaan, Moodswing still hated this office because it belonged to their father who practically did the same thing.

"When are you going to get out of that basement and come back to the family?"

"I'll have you know that it's not the basement. We're on the second floor."

"Of a parking garage, Terrance."

"You make it sound like *that's* where we race. We race on the streets."

"That is not any better."

"I'm not trying to prove anything to you."

"Perhaps you should. I mean, Terrance, look at how you dress."

Moodswing looked at himself, dressed in his black and red riding leathers which shared a colour scheme with his racing suit. He currently had the front of his jacket open so that his white v-neck t-shirt was visible. Moodswing then looked at her: impeccably dressed as always with a shiny silver silk blouse that was clearly tailored to her body which he knew she was wearing with a black pencil skirt that he was glad was hidden under the desk. While he understood exactly what she was trying to say, Moodswing remained defiant and shrugged.

Shaan simply shook her head disapprovingly. "So uncivilized."

"Well you didn't call me all the way to your office to talk about how I'm dressed."

"And you didn't come all the way up here to my office to come see me. I know that you were downstairs putting my mechanics to work on that monstrosity of yours."

"Hey," said Moodswing, playfully. "Don't hate on the *Dracula*."

"You should throw that thing away like the junk that it is."

This time Moodswing was serious. "Seriously, Shaan. Don't hate on the *Dracula*."

"That thing is destined to get you killed, Terrance."

"You underestimate my abilities."

"No," she said simply. "Just your intelligence."

"Ouch," said Moodswing, playfully.

"Terrance. Listen to me. You can't keep doing this. You can't keep racing on the streets, hanging out in parking garages. You do have a name to maintain."

"Argh," said Moodswing, standing up. "Not this again. You can't force me to work here, Shaan. Dad already forced me to go to university, you—"

"I love how you somehow think that *that* was a punishment."

"Well this sure as hell feels like a punishment." Moodswing had moved to the window overlooking the showroom floor and leaned on it. He looked down at the busy floor where cars were being sold by men in business suits. He didn't belong there. He didn't belong in a business suit. He belonged in a racing suit. Why couldn't Shaan understand that?

As if reading Moodswing's mind, Shaan looked at her brother and asked him the most critical question in the world. "Why do you do this, Terrance? Why do you spend your nights weaving between cars, dodging Metro cops and topping speeds over two hundred kays?"

"You wouldn't understand," he said, sounding almost sad.

"Oh, but I think I do." Moodswing turned to his sister and she continued. "You think speed is the answer to the world's dark obsession of sex and violence."

337

Moodswing blinked, almost too shocked by Shaan's answer to even laugh. Lucky for her she continued because he honestly didn't know what to say.

"It's hard to do anything truly bad around here, isn't it? They call this place the paradise that knows no colour. Well a paradise it is, right down to the low crime toll. With a void in the hearts of those thirsting for a thrill, what do you do? Well as it turns out, you drive. Really fast."

After she'd finished, Moodswing just stared at her. He then smiled, so eager to laugh it was killing him. "Wwwooooow." Moodswing moved off the window and slowly walked to her desk, leaned on it – leaned over her – and looked at her. "I have never seen a person be so wrong in my *life*." Now Moodswing laughed, falling back in the chair, chortling. "And you call me unintelligent."

However, Shaan, ever the classy woman, didn't lose her composure at being laughed at. Instead, she simply smiled, leaned back and watched her brother get it out of his system before speaking. "Okay then, Terrance, pray tell. Why do you do it?"

Terrance thought for a moment about how to answer and then smiled. "I do it because it's what I'm good at and I want to be known as the best. You want to know why I do it, Shaan, well that's it. That's my passion: winning. That's what drives me, what *fuels* me."

Shaan raised her eyebrows as if she'd just been enlightened to a puzzling mystery. "So that's it huh? You value," she thought of the word, "championships over dealerships? Even if the championship you have comes from an illegal underground racing league?"

Moodswing shrugged. "What can I say? I'm a Moodley. I love shiny things." Moodswing got up to leave, having said his peace, for the hundredth time. But before he could leave, Shaan had one last thing to say.

"Moodswing." It was rare for Shaan to use his nickname. But there was something about her use of it now that gave a ring of finality. Perhaps it was because she finally understood that there was no winning him over. "Just remember one thing. The racing scene: it was supposed to be fun. It was designed that way from the start. That's always what it was supposed to be."

Moodswing decided to grant her the last word and left. He wasn't going to bother to correct her. He wasn't going to bother to tell her that things had changed down there. They had changed a long time ago. Long gone were the days where fun was the priority. Now it was competition for them. Now it was sport to them. Now it was war! And he was going to make sure he won that war.

CHAPTER TWENTY-ONE
THE NUMBER ONE CONTENDER

With no race that night, Max took his time picking up *Baby Cradle* before heading down to the scene. Even though he didn't have a race until the following night, he'd become used to having the *Cradle* next to him while they loitered in the lot. The other racers were the same as it was very rare to have all of them race yet every night, without fail, the first and second floors were occupied with all the racers' XF vehicles.

As he met up with Thompson, he realized that tensions were high on the scene. And why wouldn't they be? Just two nights ago, the cops had interfered with their race. Thompson told him that due to the new cop presence, a new route had been picked that had them starting on the main road facing the opposite direction.

It was amazing that there was always something new to learn every time that he came to the scene. In fact, it was one of the newest things he'd learnt just the other night that he questioned Thompson about as they waited for the races to begin: the escape route.

"Why didn't anyone tell me that there was a predetermined escape route in case the cops show up?"

Thompson shrugged. "Well it's because cops haven't shown up in a while. Not since the rich kids were still around. They were the ones that created the route."

Max remembered Shade telling him that. "Well perhaps someone around here should run a refresher course or something."

Thompson laughed. He then made a face. "You know, something is bothering me. Why did the cops show up?"

"Well we are illegal street racers, Thompson."

"I know that. But what happened on Tuesday; that was orchestrated. I mean, them setting up roadblocks like that. It's like they knew something."

Max thought about that but then shook his head. "No. If they knew something, then they would have done a better job of stopping us. Hell, they would have raided this lot rather than put up roadblocks, and so far down the route."

Thompson was about to respond when something caught his attention. "What the hell is he doing here?"

Max followed his eyeline and tensed when he saw him. It was Tar. However, instead of walking in wearing a hoodie, looking suspicious, Tar was dressed in a denim jacket and matching jeans over a black v-neck t-shirt. He was accompanied by Touch and Canon Kelly.

When he reached them, he put his hands up, as if surrendering. "I promise to behave myself this time."

Thompson asked the question anyway. "Tar, what the hell are you doing here?"

"I used to race here, remember." As Tar spoke, Touch walked up to the other racers who were beginning to whisper, explaining that he was cool and that he wasn't here to hit anyone. "So, what's going on," he said to Max, "you're not racing tonight?"

Max shook his head. "Tomorrow."

"That's good. It gives you time to prepare," he said, ever the mentor. "Why don't you challenge someone, have a tune up race. I'm sure Shade's going to do the same."

"I doubt it." Max fought off gritting his teeth again. He was not supposed to know anything that Shade was up to. Max continued quickly, before anyone picked up on it. "But a tune up race is not a bad idea."

"Fat chance of that happening." It was Stevie who spoke the words, having walked over from the *Candyfloss* and joined them. Before they could ask her anything, Stevie looked at her brother. "Tar, what are you doing here?"

Tar put up a hand. "Relax, I'm not here to give you any grief, okay. I came to support Max."

Stevie shook her head. "I'm not asking because of me. I'm asking because of what happened the last time you were here. Tar, if you came back to beat up—"

"Your boyfriend?"

"He is *not* my boyfriend, dammit! I told you, that wasn't a date!" Stevie had tried not to raise her voice but was loud all the same.

"It sure looked like a date," said Max. It had been him that told Tar that night after seeing her and Moodswing at the movies. Since he knew he had no business telling Stevie what to do, he passed the information to her brother and left it at that.

She pointed hesitantly to Max. "You, don't start." She still found it hard to hate Max. She turned to Tar. "Seriously, you need to go."

"Would you relax," said Tar, reacting as if she'd just blown a gasket. "I'm not here to hit anybody, okay."

Not wanting this argument to go on any longer, feeling Tar had made his point, Max picked up on something that Stevie had said a moment ago. "Hey, did you say that there was a fat chance of a tune up race happening tonight?"

"Because Moodswing wants everything tonight to be about him," she said.

While Thompson scoffed at the sound of this, saying it was typical of Moodswing, Max and Tar had shared a look having noted the tone in Stevie's voice. Like Tar, Max realized that for the first time, Stevie had said something negative about Moodswing. Was she finally seeing the light? Unfortunately, before either of them could try and pull her fully into that light, the man himself, the man of the hour arrived. And this time, he had Mook and Goone in tow.

"You here to finish what you started, Tar!? Oh, wait, you didn't actually get to start anything, *did you*!?"

Tar looked at him as if he didn't know who he was at all. "Why are you speaking so loudly?"

"You're not welcome here, Tar." said Moodswing.

"You don't get to decide that, Moodswing."

"Oh, really? After what you tried to do to me last time, I don't get to decide that? Who the hell are you to tell me I don't get to decide that?"

Tar smiled. "You don't." Tar then lifted his arms, gesturing to the now gathered crowd. "*They* get to decide that. They get to decide whether I look like a man who wants to use violence to get to you or if I look perfectly happy to watch your ass get owned on the blacktop."

Moodswing saw the crowd murmur and realized that he'd lost them. There was no way that he was going to get Tar thrown out tonight. So, he switched gears. "You come here to spectate? Well tough. Only racers and their teams are allowed here. You want to watch the race, go to the website, download the app, and stream it like everyone else."

The two were now almost nose to nose. Everyone watched anxiously to see if Tar was going to be true to his word and *not* start a fight. "Listen to you. You think just because you're King, you get to call the shots around here."

Fearing for where this might go, Max raised his hand, calling attention to himself. "Actually, Tar is part of *my* team."

They all looked at him including Moodswing who gave a smirk of disbelief. "Oh really? And what is he doing on your team? Cheerleading?"

Max didn't miss a beat. "Isn't it obvious? He's here to check the oil." Max's quip got a chuckle from the gathered crowd. But from the little that Max knew, the job that Max had suggested Tar was here to do was enough to keep him around. In fact, as long as Tar did *something* to the car, he was allowed to stay.

However, Moodswing shook his head. "McKay, you're not even racing tonight."

"That's because some jackass, who will not be named," said Max before pointing dramatically at Moodswing, "wants everything to be about him tonight." The crowd reacted to Max's insult. "It's not my fault that you can't handle a threat to that precious spotlight of yours."

Moodswing clearly wanted to say something else but refrained. Instead, he recomposed himself. "Okay, whatever. Stay here. Watch the action," he said to Tar before turning to Max. "But Mckay, keep your eyes peeled. Because what I do tonight is going to be a preview of forthcoming events." He then turned around and started to leave. "I'll be back to discuss tomorrow night's race card."

While Moodswing had been laying down the law, doing his best to look like he was running the place, Max had been stealing glances at Stevie. He'd noticed that Stevie had been feeling uneasy with almost everything that she'd said. It was becoming more and more clear that pulling her away from Moodswing would not be the feat that they thought it would be.

*

The race was a thrilling affair. Max didn't know if it was because of the new route or because he was finally seeing Moodswing with his game face on, but he was entranced. The man was good when he wasn't showing off. It was crazy how well he could corner at high speeds.

349

The King was currently defending his title against some guy named Trapper Junction. No one had any idea why he'd named himself that. Naturally his vehicle's name was the *Blockader*. Max wondered if there was something he was missing with this guy. Did Moodswing pick him simply because of his name to somehow allude to Tuesday night? Why? What the hell was the point of that?

The more Max thought about it, the more he was convinced that Moodswing only chose him because of his name. Moodswing had created such a gap that this was a clear thrashing. The only thing worth watching about the race was Moodswing tearing the route apart with technical proficiency and the reveal of the new route as the race went along.

The new route was something to behold. Watching it come to life during this race made Max wonder if it was in the pipeline the whole time. Was it something they wanted to bring into the fold but needed the excuse they got on Tuesday night to do it? Max didn't know. What he did know was that he needed to study it because this was what was in his immediate future.

The route, now kicking off facing west, travelled down the main road, passing the offramp from the M1 and continued along the coastline before taking a dramatic left into the Ngelosi river! More specifically, it was onto the concrete flood control channel of the river, which was a concrete base, the width of the Ngelosi River which was almost bone dry at the moment. Max realized that this was the same river that he and Shade had crossed at the dam and if it wasn't *for* that dam, Moodswing and Trapper Junction would be driving under water.

With the river basically running alongside the M1, it now formed the straight stretch of the race and the two racers continued before exiting somewhere in the downtown industrial area. After crossing at a railway crossing, they made a left onto a familiar road that Max later realized was the main road further on which was confirmed as the home stretch began after they zoomed under the M3 and all the way back to where they began.

351

Moodswing had naturally won the race but celebrated like he'd just beaten Apollo Creed. While his performance was something to behold, the fact that he beat a nobody didn't really mean anything to someone like Max. But Max didn't have to think about that much longer as someone made their way up the rampway and rode right onto the first floor. There were gasps from the others and Max immediately realized why. There, sitting on a black Suzuki Hayabusa was Shade.

Dressed in black from head to toe as always, Shade kicked out the stand for her bike, switched off the engine and folded her arms. *Dammit Max, don't call her 'her' when you open your mouth!* As Max reserved himself to not making that mistake, he took note of how careful Christina was of hiding that she was a girl by simply not making any big moves. She just sat there. Naturally, the others on the first floor were restless. How could they not be? This was a first for them: Shade being *anywhere* in the building except the roof was bound to be an event. But there was a reason she was here. It was time to find out about the number one contender's race tomorrow.

352

*

Moodswing had been serious when he said that they were going to discuss tomorrow's race card when he got back. But there was only one race that was the topic of discussion: the feature race for the next night: the number one contender's race. Everyone had formed a circle around Max, Shade, Moodswing and Admin with Thompson and Tar standing close behind. With Shade, ever the badass, not moving an inch from where she stood leaning on her bike, the circle had been formed around her.

"Okay," said Moodswing, "so, the deal seems simple enough: Shade versus McKay on the new route. Any questions?" Moodswing had directed the question at Max and Shade but it was Tar who responded.

"Yeah, I gotta question." Tar stepped forward so he was now next to Max, centre of attention as well. "Why don't you let Admin do his job? He's the one who should be conducting things, am I wrong?"

There was a murmur from the crowd who looked to agree with him. Moodswing ignored Tar. "You two," he said pointing at Max and Shade, "any questions? No? Good."

"Nothing's good here, Moodswing," continued Tar. "Because, you see, the way I see it: there's no need to have another number one contender's race. Because they already had one."

Moodswing rubbed his eye, clearly tired of Tar's interference. "Clearly you didn't see what happened because then you would know that a *cop chase* busted up the race and any way of determining a number one contender from that night."

"Funny," said Tar, "I remember there being only one way for a race to end in disqualification." Tar was referring to intentional collisions. "And I think there is a way of determining who won. Or don't you guys have replays anymore?" The crowd began to murmur again. "What do you say, Admin?"

Admin looked to Moodswing who gave him a scowl before turning away and thinking, for himself. "Well perhaps," he said, struggling to speak with Moodswing staring daggers at him, "perhaps, we can determine the number one contender by seeing who was closest to the finish line?" The crowd cheered in agreement, but Admin looked to Max and Shade who both nodded. Moodswing was the only one who didn't like this.

However, Tar didn't care and raised his arms again. "Like I said," he said directly at Moodswing, "*they* decide."

A minute later, Admin had a tablet in his hand and was reviewing the recording of Tuesday night's race. After replaying it a couple of times, he smiled sheepishly. "You're not going to believe this. But it's a draw." The crowd got restless, some even taking out their own devices to see for themselves. Max saw Thompson do the same with his tablet and leaned over him to see as Admin explained his findings. "While Shade was leading the race, he stopped about three metres from the roadblock. He then turned around at which point Max reached the same mark, three metres from the roadblock, and turned around as well. It's a draw."

Max thought back to that night and realized that Admin was right. He remembered turning around and how he hadn't gotten any closer to the roadblock than Shade. Which meant, technically, they had both ended the race the same distance from the finish line much, much further away. What the hell were the chances of that? Moodswing was thinking the same thing but he looked to take advantage of the situation.

"Well there you go, Tar. You see? No contest. That means rematch."

"Or," said Tar, truly testing Moodsiwng's patience.

"Or what? Or *what!?*"

"What about a triangle match race." The crowd came alive at Tar's words, the excitement building now.

Moodswing screwed his face in disgust. "A three-way race? No, no way."

"C'mon, Moodswing," continued Tar. "You, the King, defend your title against Max," he said putting a hand on Max's shoulder, "and Shade." he said extending his arm to Shade who hadn't moved an inch. The crowd began to cheer at the sound of it. It was a unanimous agreement.

Unfortunately, Moodswing remained resolute, not interested at all in this farce. "No. It's not happening. It's not happening." He looked at the Admin. "You, set a rematch race between Shade and McKay. *That's* your feature race for tomorrow." But, for the first time since Max had been here, Admin seemed unsure with Moodswing's 'order'. But before Moodswing could say anything else to Admin, Tar spoke again.

"How about we sweeten the pot for our poor old King," said Tar, now teasing Moodswing. "What if we say that last place leaves town?" The crowd cheered once again, and Tar made his now patterned 'they decide' hand gesture. While Tar hadn't discussed it with Max, Max was behind the decision one hundred percent.

Moodswing looked around and saw that he had lost this one. Tar had done the same thing that Moodswing had done the last time he had been here: he'd used the crowd to get his way. Moodswing knew that there was nothing he could do or say to talk his way out of this one. But Moodswing would be damned if he didn't get something out of this sham.

357

"Fine, but only if, as King, I choose the route." Moodswing spoke again quickly, as if to prevent Tar from refusing. "Take it or leave it."

Max couldn't help but feel Moodswing's last words were his vain attempt to make it look like this was somehow his plan all along. It clearly wasn't. "I'm in," said Max.

The crowd cheered at the sound of that. Max looked at Shade as if the rest relied on her also saying she was in. Shade, who had stood absolutely still, arms crossed, leaning on her bike, finally moved. She spun around, got on her bike and kick-started it to life before making one final gesture: she nodded her helmeted head. Then, not a second later, the crowd parted out of her way as she revved her motorcycle loudly before spinning it around and taking off down the rampway much in the same way she did in the *Tumbler*.

"Then the race is set," said Admin. "Tomorrow night's feature race will be King Moodswing versus Max McKay versus Shade." The crowd became unglued with cheers. It was clear from the sound of their jubilation that this was the race that they had been waiting for. It was the culmination of weeks of animosity, if not months when one considered the rivalry between Moodswing and Shade. It was one for the ages. But with stipulations like this, Moodswing and Max both looked to be on the same page about one thing: whatever happened, they could not finish last!

CHAPTER TWENTY-TWO
BLUE, WHITE AND RED-HANDED

Moodswing could not believe that he was once again back at Harbour High, waiting in the parking lot as he'd done almost two weeks ago. This was the last place he wanted to be. But he had no choice, what with his plan going down the toilet and fast. Now he needed a contingency.

As he waited for Stevie to arrive at school, Moodswing couldn't stop shaking his head. He guessed that it was a step up from swearing non-stop, which was pretty much what his night consisted of after leaving the scene. He'd hoped to wake up in better spirits, perhaps realize that the situation wasn't as bad as it was. But he hadn't. He'd woken feeling just as lousy as he had gone to sleep.

Nowhere in the plan did it say that he was going to be involved in a three-way race with his crown on the line. His plan, had in fact, been quite simple: destroy Tar's world. Destroy Tar's world by using Stevie to take down McKay. Moodswing had planned to get Stevie and McKay to face off with very high stakes causing McKay to get stuck between a rock and a hard place: chose between winning and destroying his friendship with Tar and taking Stevie down. Or losing and finding himself taken down.

At that point, Moodswing would turn on Stevie, who would now be all by her lonesome on the scene, leaving Tar to either watch her taken down or *finally* get back in a vehicle and face off with him once and for all. At that point, his plan would be complete and his revenge would have been fulfilled leaving *him* the dominant force on the scene.

It was a plan that required patience. Patience to build animosity between McKay and Stevie. Patience to teach Stevie how to attack the weak points in a relationship:

trust. And patience in building Stevie's ego so that she'd be willing to bet big.

It was a plan that required cunning. As much as Moodswing had invested in Stevie, it was still necessary for him to be able to turn on her when the time came. Of course, that wouldn't be enough. He'd also have to be willing to turn her into mincemeat in a high stakes race and end her career at the scene.

It was a plan that only he could accomplish. And now it was up in flames. With a dangerous driver like Shade and the fastest rising wild card in McKay, Moodswing's title was in serious jeopardy. The idea was to humiliate Tar and show that he had no clout on the scene. But after last night, not only did Tar increase his clout, but he was well on the way to humiliating *him*.

When Stevie finally did arrive, he honked his hooter and called her over. The confused Stevie hesitated before coming over. "What are you doing here?"

"Can't your mentor pay you a visit?" said Moodswing trying to be as conversational as possible.

"That depends," she said being playful, "you're not going to ride off with me again, are you? Because I think the sch—"

"Listen Stevie," said Moodswing, not having time to banter with her, "I came because I need something from you, and I can't wait until after school ends at three—"

"It ends at two."

"Whatev—" said Moodswing, now too frustrated to complete his words. "That's not the point, Stevie!"

"Then what is the point, Moodswing? Why did you come here to my school? What do you want from me that can't wait?"

"The *point* is that I'm King!"

"I suppose this is the point where I'm supposed to cite Tywin Lannister to you, but I can see you're not in the mood."

Moodswing sighed dramatically. "When did you become such a pain in the ass?"

"I've pretty much always been this way," said Stevie nodding.

"No, you haven't. Up until now, I haven't heard you make one joke."

"What do you want me to say? I get this way when certain people don't let me race my car."

"Oh, so is that what all this attitude is about? If it means so much to you, you can race your damned car. But not tonight, there's too much at stake."

"Isn't that the truth," said Stevie mostly to herself.

Moodswing sighed. He needed to get to the point. "The reason that I'm here is because I need a favour."

"Okay," said Stevie a little too quickly.

"Don't you want to hear what the favour is, first?"

"You have a point. Okay, shoot."

Moodswing sighed again. *Bloody children.* "Tonight, during the race, there's something that I need you to do for me."

"During the race? What could you possibly want me to do *during* the race?"

"Listen carefully. At exactly five minutes after the moment that the race begins, I want you to call the Metro Police."

It took a while for the request to register with Stevie. But the moment it did, her eyes went wide. "You want me to what?"

"Dial the number for the Metro Police and tell them of the race. Tell me where we are and then hang up before they ask for your name."

Once again, Stevie took a while to respond. "But Moodswing, that's cheating."

This time, it was Moodswing who didn't answer right away. "No. For you, that's doing your civic duty. For me," Moodswing felt the venom of his own words as he spoke, "that's winning at any cost."

"No, I can't do this. It will put everything in jeopardy. They could find the parking lot."

"They won't find it if you hang up in time."

"But after what happened last time, why would you *want*..." Suddenly, something dawned on Stevie and Moodswing realized that perhaps, he hadn't given Stevie enough credit. "Wait, wait, wait. You didn't..." Stevie was struggling to even form the sentence. "You didn't call the cops last time, right? That's not why they showed? It wasn't because you called them?"

Moodswing opened his mouth to say something but then closed it again when he realized that he didn't know what to say. He didn't know whether to deny it or explain it. He didn't know which he needed in order to manipulate her right now. So, he just looked at her.

"Holy crap, you did. Why the hell did you do that? Max, Shade, they could have gotten arrested?"

Moodswing scoffed. "I doubt the cops would have caught them both. Just one of them. And that would have rid me of one problem." It was true. Moodswing had anticipated Shade winning the race so he had hoped that he would be the one that ran straight into the cops' hands while McKay made the getaway. After all, he had plans for Max McKay.

366

"No, no, no," said Stevie, backing away from Moodswing. "I can't be hearing this. I can't be *hearing* this."

"Hey. Come back here. Stevie!" But she was turning her back on him... literally and figuratively. So, he fired one of his silver bullets. "If you value your racing career, you'll come back here."

Stevie turned around slowly. "What did you just say?"

"I said: if you want to keep racing in an XF race car, then you'll come back here and listen to what I tell you."

Stevie hesitated, shaking her head. "No, you can't do that. You can't do anything to me. They're rules."

Moodswing scoffed again. "Stevie, I was there when they made those rules. So, I know how to loophole my way around them. And here's the tip: it only takes one race. One race and you lose your vehicle and then," Moodswing chuckled, "you don't even have to be exiled after that. What are you going to do without a vehicle?"

"Yeah but," said Stevie, now back in the conversation, "you can't make me bet my car. You can't make me put it on the line in a race."

"I won't have to. Popular opinion rules. You saw it first-hand yourself, last night. I mean, up until then, I believed that *no one* could make me defend my title against two opponents. And yet. So, go ahead and walk away. I assure you; your car will be mine again by the end of next week." When Moodswing saw her swallow hard, he knew he had her.

"So, what do I have to do to keep my car?"

"Exactly as I said. And to not. Tell. Anyone." Moodswing put his helmet on and started his bike. He then looked at Stevie and extended his hand, palm up, indicating the five minutes they talked about with his digits.

Moodswing was not a happy man as he rode away. He hadn't wanted to fire that silver bullet because it meant that the jig was up. There was no way that Stevie didn't know that she had been manipulated from minute one. While he could still get what he wanted out of her, now that she was going to be doing things that she didn't want to do, there was going to be resistance that wasn't there before. But this was tomorrow's problem.

Today, Moodswing had to worry about McKay. He had to worry about Shade. They were the threats he faced tonight. But if Stevie did her part, then he'd stand a chance of winning. All he'd have to do was be far enough ahead when the cops arrived.

CHAPTER TWENTY-THREE
TRIPLE THREAT SHOWDOWN

Being nervous wasn't something that Max had a lot of experience with but right now, he was nervous as hell. He was currently sitting inside *Baby Cradle,* holding the steering wheel anxiously as he awaited his opponents. They were playing mind games with him and he knew it. Moodswing was the first to show up, driving up to the line slowly, keeping the revs of the *Dracula* low, which gave it this popping sound as he took his place next to him. A few seconds later, he heard an engine revving very loudly back at the parking lot.

Max looked up to the roof just in time to see the *Tumbler* spin its wheel and begin its screeching descent

370

down the rampway and come speeding out of the lot and come to a screeching stop on Max's other side. Their mind games had been very different, but they had worked just the same: they put his nerves at an all-time high.

Looking over at Shade, he wondered what Christina's expression was under that black helmet. Did she have that nerves-of-steel expression he'd imagined Shade had before Max found out it was her; the one he'd imagined she'd had when she'd dared to touch his wheels in their last race? Or was she as nervous as he was but just playing at being calm?

He'd wanted to speak to her at school earlier today, but he hadn't managed to find her. He imagined that she'd intentionally made herself unavailable to him so that she wouldn't let him into her headspace. But the funny thing was all he wanted to ask was where she'd gotten that motorcycle. As a motorcycle guy himself, it had been downright awesome to see her straddle that thing. In fact, it had been hard to imagine her as Christina last night because seeing her on that motorcycle was pure Shade. He didn't need to deduce which side of her she was channelling that time.

As Max stood at the start line, another thing that made him nervous was the route that Moodswing had chosen as they were currently facing *east* on the main road: the same way as their old route. In fact, the first leg of the route took them on very much the same path as the old route: up onto the M3, off onto the M1 and right past where the roadblock had been. It only changed after the offramp onto the main road as, instead of heading back towards the lot, finishing once they hit the main road, they turned away from it and took the new route which had them turn onto the Ngelosi river.

From there, it was the straight stretch which went all the way to the dam. And when they came out of the river, instead of doubling back towards the city, they would take the escape route and cross the river. After that, they went in the opposite direction that Max and Shade had taken that day, heading back west, down alongside the river but on the south side before hitting the M3 and travelling south back towards the city. That would form their home stretch as from there, it was merely offramping onto the main road and crossing the finish line.

It was a crazy route to say the least as Max wondered why in the *hell* Moodswing would have them go to the *exact* same place where Shade and him almost got arrested? But Max didn't have time to question it. He wasn't even *allowed* to question it as they had agreed that Moodswing got to choose any route he wanted for the race. Thompson and Tar, who were both in the lot, streaming the race as his tech support, had told him why Moodswing had chosen the route. It was because his vehicle was the one that could handle the long distance as it was known that his vehicle was the best maintained and serviced.

Max tried to throw all of that out of mind as he closed his eyes and spoke to the *Cradle*. "Okay baby, you've gotten me this far. Now, it's time that you get me to that Crown. It's just this one last race and that's it."

"Who are you talking to?" asked Tar. Max had forgotten that Tar and Thompson were listening in. But he didn't care. It was *his* pre-race ritual, not theirs.

"He's talking to the car," said Thompson, having caught Max doing this before. "Or more like, praying to it or something. It doesn't matter. He's got this."

Thompson was right. He did have this. And that was just what he needed to be thinking as the young woman stepped in front of them with the red cloth in her hand. Max watched with a determined look on his face as the cloth was dropped. In that instant, all three racers screeched their tires on the start line and took off.

Moodswing led the race as they sped down the main road. On Max's left, Shade was once again driving dangerously close to him. He realized that she was crowding him as he'd once done three nights ago when he'd adopted a more aggressive driving style. Now Max imagined that Christina was smiling inside that helmet.

Just as Max wondered why Shade was fighting with him and not going after Moodswing, they bent around the corner and Shade accelerated, aiming to catch up to Moodswing on the onramp onto the M3. The three ended up entering the freeway in a single file as Max drafted

Shade who in turn, drafted Moodswing. Once on the freeway, the fight was back on.

This time, all three of them stuck to the right-hand side of the road. As Moodswing did as he always did and used the emergency lane, Shade attacked from the left, using the fast lane to keep close to Moodswing. Not one to be outdone, Max came up to Shade's left, although he had to swerve out of the way of two cars before he could do any attacking. Once free, Max came up so close to Shade that their wheels were almost touching.

"How do you like them apples, Shade?"

"Max, what the hell are you doing?" asked Thompson.

"Showing that turnabout is fair play."

"That's all well and good," Thompson continued, "but you know how this works. You only win here if you're willing to sacrifice yourself. It's a bluff."

"Then watch me bluff."

"Back off, Max," said Tar. "You don't want to cause a wreck."

Max felt inclined to do what Tar was telling him to do. After what he'd told him about Jeremiah, surely, he knew what he was talking about. But then Max saw Shade looking at him from inside the *Tumbler*. And while Max couldn't tell with her helmet on, he sensed that she was nervous about this situation. That's when he decided to ignore Tar and follow his own gut instinct.

"Max, did you hear what I said? I said back off."

Max ignored him. After all, he was still being ruled by fear. After seeing his best friend get into an accident that paralysed him, how could he not? But Max didn't need to be ruled by fear right now. No, he needed to instil fear right now. He watched as Shade's helmet turned from him to Moodswing and back to him. Realizing the dangerous position she was in, Shade did the only thing she could – the responsible thing – and pulled back so that she was now behind both Moodswing and Max.

Max smiled. "Now your turn, you bastard," said Max as he turned his attention to Moodswing.

"Argh Max," complained Tar, "c'mon." Fortunately for the disapproving Tar, Max ran out of time to attack

Moodswing as the offramp to the M1 came about and Moodswing and Max turned onto it followed closely by Shade.

Max had expected Shade to follow them closely right through to the M1 so, he was surprised when Shade crossed to the other side of the freeway – the correct side of the road –between a gap in the safety barrier.

"What the hell is," *crap, almost said 'she'*, "he doing?" said Max. He wondered if she was chickening out of a fight.

Tar was the one that answered. "I'll tell you what he's doing. He's being smart. Remember, when you come off the Mike One, you're turning *left*. Meaning, now that he's on that side, *he* will be closer to the front. It's genius."

Max swore. Tar was right. It was genius. Now when they got to the main road, him and Moodswing would be behind. But that was a problem for later as right now, Max needed to at least try and beat Moodswing while they were still on the M1. Max gunned his engine, looking for any opportunity to pass Moodswing.

They were neck and neck when the offramp – or onramp rather – came about. Remembering how well Moodswing could take a corner at high speed, Max widened the space between them just enough and when the time to turn came, made sure to maintain his grip on the steering wheel as he navigated the turn just as well as Moodswing. They swooped under the bridge where the M3 continued over top and continued neck and neck while Shade pushed on now up ahead.

Max managed to gain a few inches of headway as they continued down the main road away from the finish line so that when the turn onto the river entrance came about, he turned right into second position. When all three of them were now on the concrete channel, it was Shade leading, with Max in second place and Moodswing behind. If the race finished this way, Moodswing would be forced to leave the scene and city for good. But Max wasn't going to count his chickens before they hatched. He wasn't going to settle for second place either. He aimed to win.

Having managed to close the gap on Shade, Max was now directly behind her, drafting her. "Good, that's good." said Tar. "You're in Shade's slip stream and there's plenty of straight road ahead of you. Which means when you go for the overtake, you should be able to pass right past him."

Max smiled. "Preaching to the choir there, Tar."

"My man," said Thompson. "You see, he's got this."

Knowing that the exit from the river was on the left, Max prepared himself to overtake on the left. As soon as he saw the ramp to the exit, he escaped the slip stream and was taken aback by the boost he got when he sped right past Shade, onto the ramp and went flying through the air! Knowing that he might only get this one shot at being in front of Shade, Max didn't hit the brakes but accelerated so that when his vehicle hit the ground, there was a screech as he lurched forward.

"Holy hell," he exclaimed.

"You alright, there," said Tar clearly feeling the excitement of the moment.

379

"Yeah, I'm good. I'm good. It was just..." Max was still feeling the goose bumps. "What a rush."

"Oh yeah. You, uh, got the whole world cheering your name down here, man."

Thompson whistled. "The likes are spiking online, man. And people are loving yyyyooouuu in the comments, man."

"That's great guys but which way again?"

"Take the next right," said Thompson quickly.

While Max knew he should know the way, he admittedly had no idea how he was going to navigate the escape route through the old section of the hydro plant. Having only been there once at night, driving behind Shade, he wasn't sure which way to go. It was a maze in here. But then again, that was the point, was it not? So that even if the cops dared to follow, they wouldn't know which way they went.

Unfortunately for Max, this proved to be a pain, as he found himself struggling to navigate the plant. When she saw Shade coming at him from behind, he relented and let her pass. It was a strategy on his part as the way he saw it, at least if he was following her through the place, then he wouldn't hit some kind of dead end.

Indeed, they came out the other side with Shade in the lead and Max right on her tail. As they travelled down the old backwater road now heading back down alongside the river in the same general direction they came in, Max wondered how long they had been driving for. While it felt like ten minutes, he knew that due to how fast the cars were, it was probably closer to five minutes.

While it was harder, due to the road not being completely straight, Max tried to draft Shade but to no avail as she kept shifting to the left and then to the right, preventing him from entering her slipstream. As Max continued to try and find an angle, he glanced at the city's skyline and marvelled at how beautiful it looked from here. And with their engines echoing into the night, the atmosphere was unreal. But that's when he heard it: a very different sound. And a very familiar sound, wailing far in the distance.

Max knew that sound anywhere. It was the sound of police sirens and they were getting louder by the second. On instinct alone, Max pressed down on the throttle. He'd been here before only so many times except this time he wasn't in a car... he was in a XF race car.

As Max's heart rate increased, he began to sweat inside his helmet. The sirens were getting closer but for the life of him his thoughts weren't on the Metro cops at all. Despite the clear and present danger, all Max could wonder was whether Shade was feeling the same way as him. Ahead of him, the *Tumbler* raced on, showing no signs of even noticing the sirens. It was almost easy to forget that they were in a race to decide their fate.

"You've got to be kidding me!"

"What's wrong, Max?" said Thompson.

"The cops are coming, *again!*"

"You're kidding," he said. "How far away are they?"

"It doesn't matter because we're heading straight for them."

Max had expected to find a roadblock up ahead but there wasn't one. Instead, they on-ramped right onto the M3 before they saw any cops. But when they did see them, it was like they were everywhere. It wasn't just the three behind them but the three ahead of them too. They were Metro cops too, as if they didn't have enough problems. They were driving VW Golf GTIs and they were driving them expertly.

All of a sudden Max and Shade were no longer fighting with each other but rather fighting to outmanoeuvre the cops. That's when Moodswing seemed to come the hell out of nowhere and regained the lead in the race. Shade and Max shared a look and realized that Moodswing planned to use the cops to try and win the race.

"Guys. I think you need to get everyone the hell out of there because Moodswing is dead set on crossing that line first. And that line is right outside your front doorstep."

"Way ahead of you, man." said Thompson. "Everyone is already packing up."

"Yeah," added Tar. "Everyone can see Moodswing's madness, live. I mean, c'mon, he's supposed to lead the cops away from the scene when they show up, not straight to it."

"Well after what happened last night with the replays," added Thompson, "I'm sure he thinks whoever is closest to the finish line will be considered the winner."

"Well great," said Tar, "congratulations to him for winning the race. I'm sure he'll enjoy celebrating when we're all in jail."

"Guys," said Max, moving between all the cop cars, "trying to concentrate here."

A moment passed. "Sorry," they said in unison.

With Moodswing up front, the cops split their focus from just Max and Shade to all three of them which gave the two trailing XF racers the opportunity they needed to get back in the race. They managed to lose half their pursuers when the racing trio ducked onto the offramp, losing one more when they navigated the left-hand turn at so high a speed that when one of the three still-pursuing cop cars tried it too, they ended up rolling their car.

With only two more cop cars left and the finish line half a kilometre ahead of them, the most exciting thirty seconds of their lives began. Somehow, after coming off the M3, the three of them managed to be side by side by side and almost neck and neck as they barrelled down the home stretch. Max floored it but watched anxiously as Moodswing began to pull ahead. However, when another XF race car came speeding towards them, obviously escaping from the parking lot, Moodswing made the mistake of dropping his speed while Shade had *increased* hers.

The end of the race was a spectacle in and of itself as Shade just managed to cross the line first as Moodswing crossed it a split second later and Max a split second after that. Max didn't even have time to think about the fact that not only had he lost the race, but he was now going to leave the scene. He still had to worry about the two cop cars following.

However, when Max looked in his rear-view mirror, he saw that it was only one cop car now as the other one had tipped over too. Max realized that it must have happened when the other XF racer sped past him so fast, that the force of it passing, threw the car onto its side, not helped by the cop car swerving hard at the exact same time.

Max thought about how to lose this last guy when he smiled. He made a sharp left turn onto a concrete road before making another one before the cop could see where he went. He then quickly ducked into a familiar venue and found a corner to park the car. He was at the old plant on the Empiko side of the main road and he remembered that there were so many places to hide there that there was no way that the cop would find him.

As Max sat there trying to keep dead quiet, he contemplated his future. It was over. Racing on the scene; that was now in the past. He could not believe that he'd lost that race. Parked similarly to how he and Thompson had parked back when they were just spying, Max looked across the way at the parking lot which was now vacant. He couldn't help but be saddened by the metaphor.

The only good news about tonight was the fact that Moodswing was no longer King. No. That title now belonged to Shade. It now belonged to Christina. He had to remember to congratulate her tomorrow. And Lisa for doing such a good job with the *Tumbler*. She'd be happy that her work led to Shade winning a big-time race. He wondered how she would feel about him no longer racing. Would she be happy? Would that mean that they stood a chance together now? There was so much to think about. But for now, Max just focused on being still and finally trying to calm his nerves.

CHAPTER TWENTY-FOUR
CROWNING AT THE BEACH

Lisa wasn't sure if what she was doing was such a good idea. But she had made up her mind. She was going to tell him how she felt. She was going to tell him that she didn't care if he was an XF racer, she wanted to be with him. After that kiss, it was a strange sensation trying to ignore her attraction to him. That's when she realized that she couldn't. She wanted him any way she could get him.

Finding his house hadn't been that hard. It was the last house on Scully Road. When she got to it, she found that the door was open with a box on the veranda. When she knocked on the door and stepped inside, she saw him, topless with his hair still wet. He had clearly just had a shower.

Max wore a surprised look on his face. "Lisa, what are you doing here?" But Max found out immediately when Lisa crossed the room and pressed her lips to his.

The kiss was epic. Lisa couldn't help but think that he tasted even sweeter when he was fresh out of the shower. Their lips folded together like lovers who had known each other for years. Their passion was overflowing as the kiss went on for what seemed like years. When it finally ended, Lisa could hardly breathe. But she could feel his breath on her. *So sweet.*

He spoke first. "So, I take it you heard about last night, then?"

Lisa was lost for words. What had happened last night? "No."

Max let out a breath. This time it was a sad breath, clearly disappointed about what happened. "There was a race and I lost."

Lisa contemplated this. "Shade beat you?"

"Shade," he said. "And Moodswing." Upon seeing her confusion, he continued. "It was a three-way race and Moodswing's title was on the line. Shade won."

Lisa smiled. *So Moodswing wasn't King anymore.* "Well that's good to hear."

"But his title wasn't the only thing on the line." He'd walked over to the window and looked out of it like a person contemplating their future. "The person who came in last would have to leave town."

What!? "Oh c'mon, that's ridiculous."

"No. It's the rule we agreed to."

Lisa looked at him and realized that he was serious. "Max, they can't make you leave Ngelosi!"

"No, just *North Ngelosi*." Max explained that she was right, it would be ridiculous to chase someone out of the city as there was no way of policing such a thing. But leaving the borough was a different matter completely. He was no longer allowed to be seen in North Ngelosi.

"But Max, you live here. You go to school here."

"Then I guess I'm dropping out."

Lisa could not believe what she was hearing. "Max, you cannot be serious."

"Lisa, this is serious."

Lisa sounded hopeless when she spoke. "Dammit, the racing scene is supposed to be fun, not," she was beginning to get upset, "not *this*."

Max looked at her, tears on the horizon. He went up to her and took her hand. "Lisa, I was skipping so much school anyway that I was destined to get kicked out. Lord knows how far behind I am now."

While Lisa wanted to cry, there was a determination inside her that wasn't going to just take this lying down. She wanted him to be her man. Which meant she needed to protect her man. Even if it was from his own ambition – or lack of ambition in this case.

"That's not the point, Max. School is important. Education, it lasts. The fun: that will eventually come to an end. You need to think about your future. You need to start building it. And you need to start now."

Max looked at her as if only truly seeing her for the first time. Then he smiled that irresistible smile of his. "So, is *that* why you're building the *Yellow Prancer*?" He lost her for a moment. "It's a metaphor. You building that engine is you building your future."

Wow, he figured it out. If he was smart enough to figure that out, why wasn't he smart enough to figure a way around these horrible rules and keep himself at school? Why were boys so weird? Couldn't he see that wanting him to stay at school wasn't just about education? It was also about keeping him near her? Couldn't he *see* that?

Lisa looked at him with soft eyes. "The *Yellow Prancer* is a metaphor for the hope of my future." She then pulled him close. "Do you want to be in it?"

Max nodded and then pulled her in for another kiss. It was hard for her to stay upright with her pressed to his bare chest like this. It was hard for her to even think. But the little she could think of, she thought of them and she hoped that this kiss meant that he would stay.

*

392

Ever the romantic, Max had asked her out on a date right there on the spot. He then proceeded to tell her that the date was tonight and that she should go get her bathing suit because he was taking her to the Crowning party which was on the beach. He explained that he was determined to wipe the memory of their last proper date away once and for all.

When they got to The Dive, they saw that the beach behind it was 'lit' as they saw what looked like the whole Harbour High student body there. With music booming the night air and dancing everywhere, there was joy all the way around. When Lisa looked at Max to see what he thought, he saw that Max was looking at her.

"What?" she said playfully.

"You look beautiful. In case I haven't told you already."

Wow. And that was without any makeup on. But before Lisa could say anything, they were joined by Angela who immediately took one look at Lisa and exclaimed, "damn girl, you look hot." Lisa rolled her eyes. While Max's praise had been a compliment, Angela had been looking at Lisa's red bikini – particularly how revealing it was – and was probably overjoyed that she was finally rubbing off on her.

When a few cute boys walked past, Lisa was surprised that Angela's eyes didn't bother to follow. "Don't you have hotties to chase down or something? Hey, what happened with the Mister Price guy? Why didn't you invite him?"

Angela made a face. "Naah, I'm over boys right now. I mean, none of them know how to treat a lady. All they want is," she made a disgusted face, "the physical stuff, kissing and..." she shook her head.

"And here I thought you were into all that."

"Then you read me all wrong, my friend. What I want is romance. What I want is a gentleman. What I want is," she pointed at Lisa and Max's interlocked hands, "*that*."

Lisa reassured her friend that she'd find what she was looking for. When Angela asked where she found someone like Max, Lisa joked that there was no one like Max which in turn convinced Angela that she definitely needed to quit boys. Lisa chuckled, knowing very well that her friend would be back on the prowl by the time they started Matric next year.

As Angela left them to have some alone time, they walked into The Dive only to be greeted by Thompson. *So much for some alone time.* But what could Lisa expect when they literally came to party?

"Hey man. About last night, I'm so sorry about what happened."

"It's not a problem."

"Not a problem? You've just been banished from town and you're saying that that's not a problem!?"

"Well I wouldn't worry about it," said Tar from behind the bar, having overheard everything. "You forgot the most important thing I told you about the scene: majority rules."

When Thompson saw Max give Tar a confused expression, he tapped him. "It's like wrestling, man. You can retire more than once, and a loser leaves the show match only means you go on a very long hiatus."

As Max pondered this, Lisa pondered something else. *Why the hell didn't you tell him that last night!? You had my boyfriend walking around, going to bed ashamed last night and now you tell him the stipulation won't stick!?*"

However, Max surprised all three of them by shaking his head and saying, "no. Let's not bend the rules this time, guys. I'm not Moodswing. I'll play by the rules. I lost so I'm outta here. Or at least," he said putting an arm around Lisa, "outta the scene."

However, before Lisa could say anything again, someone else spoke, and very loudly. "You should be out of here right *now*!" They all turned around to see Moodswing, once again dressed in his biker leathers.

"Does this guy sleep in those clothes?" said Max, earning a smile from Lisa.

"You know the rules, McKay. You need to leave town, *now*!"

Max feigned confusion. "What, like right *now*? But I just ordered a hamburger. I love hamburgers," he said, now sporting an earnest expression.

Looking to join in, Lisa added, "it's true. He really loves his hamburgers," she said in an as-a-matter-of-fact tone.

"Oh, you guys think this is funny?"

"Oh, relax Moodswing," said Max. "I'm just here for the crowning. I'll be gone by sun-up, tomorrow."

While Moodswing seemed satisfied with that, he decided he wasn't done playing the sore loser. "Huh, crowning. That's cute. How can we have a crowning when the new *King* isn't even here."

As Lisa thought about that, she caught Max glancing up and she followed his eyeline to see Stevie sitting in a booth with Christina, upstairs. *What's Christina doing here? I didn't think she went anywhere that wasn't a classroom.* But looking at Stevie, she realized why Max was probably looking at her. He must have realized just how badly he'd failed her.

"Yeah," said Max, "we could talk about that: the guy who kicked your ass. Or we could talk about how funny it was that cops raided our race two nights in a row." Max had closed the gap between them so that they were having more of a private conversation.

"Watch it, McKay. Watch what you're insinuating."

"Wait," said Tar, "Max, what are you saying? That Moodswing called the cops last night." Max's silence spoke volumes. "C'mon, that's ludicrous."

Max continued. "I thought so myself until I saw it. And I think Shade saw it too. When the cops showed up, Moodswing here immediately took advantage and took the lead back. It was almost as if he knew that they would be there."

Moodswing shook his head. "You can't be ser—" he said, getting angry. "Look, don't blame me because I'm a good enough driver to anticipate everything."

"I don't think you anticipated everything. I think you anticipated just *one* thing: the cops being on that freeway."

"You're wrong, McKay."

"Am I? Because I think you did it back on Tuesday night as well. I mean, you even had the arrogance to race a guy with the name Trapper Junction."

"So what?"

"*Blockader*?" said Max, as if that put all the puzzle pieces into place.

"I was *making fun* of you, McKay. Can't you take a joke?"

"Not anymore. I have to leave town because of you."

Moodswing's expression beamed as if he just realized something. "So *that's* what this is all about. You're a sore loser."

"Not at all. But *you* are a cheat."

"Look at you. You make all these allegations and you can't prove a *thing*!"

"But I can." Everyone looked up to see Stevie. She stood up from Christina's booth and started down the stairs. "I can prove it," she said in case anyone had not heard her.

"Stevie," said Tar, "what the hell are you talking about?"

Before Stevie said another word, Moodswing moved in close to her to say something Lisa barely caught. "Stevie, remember you owe me." Moodswing stared a hole through her as Lisa wondered just what the hell this man had on a fifteen-year-old girl!?

Stevie ignored him much to Lisa's sheer satisfaction. "*I* was the one who called the cops because *he* made me do it." There was a gasp from everyone in earshot. Lisa wondered if everyone who was listening to this was in on the scene because if they weren't then this certainly wasn't going to help with the whole 'secret' thing.

Instead of blowing a gasket, Moodswing stood up straight with a proud expression on his face. "There. She admitted it. She was the one who called the cops, *not me!*"

"Only because you made her do it," spat Max. Then everything happened at once.

Max tried to make a move to hit Moodswing only for Thompson to hold him back. Moodswing had looked like he was ducking behind Stevie but Lisa couldn't be sure from where she was standing. But she was sure standing in perfect view when she saw Tar leap over the bar counter and land a flying haymaker on Moodswing which knocked him out.

Everything went quiet for a moment before Tar stood up and spoke. "Solo, Canon. I don't suppose you could help me get this piece of trash out of my business?"

Solo Magubane and Canon Kelly smiled as if to say, "with pleasure" and did as was requested of them. As they did, there was cheering from the crowd and suddenly the world seemed to be an okay place. Stevie hugged her brother; Thompson got a beer and Lisa kissed her man. Just for that moment, all was right with the world.

CHAPTER TWENTY-FIVE
THE LAST STRAW

Max didn't know why he was being called into Mrs. Turner's office again. He hadn't missed a day of school since he last saw the Grade 11 H.O.D. so he didn't know why he was being summoned. But, alas, here he was walking down the corridors alone on Monday morning. Lisa had offered to go with him, but he'd declined. He didn't want her to see him getting disciplined, even from outside in the hallway.

It was a bummer that one of the most amazing weekends he'd ever had was going to be followed by whatever the hell Mrs. Turner had in store for him. Lisa and Max had enjoyed the party more than they'd both thought they would. Moodswing getting handed his ass helped with that. But then, the following night had them finally go see Stand/Off. And Max had to admit, for a movie almost completely taking place in one location, it was one hell of a thriller. But now... this.

When Max walked through the door that still hadn't been changed from Mr. Pillay, he had expected to see Mrs. Turner sitting at her desk. Instead she was standing by the window, talking to an older Indian gentleman. When Mrs. Turner saw Max, she cleared her throat.

"Ah, Max, thank you for being so prompt."

Max ignored the jab at his punctuality. "You asked to see me, ma'am?"

"We both did, son," said the man. "Now sit down." Max didn't take his eyes off the gentleman as he took his seat. The man had a hard expression on his face although it didn't seem to be because of anything he was angry about but rather because he'd seen his fair share of discipline cases and now his face was pretty much set like this. He wore a full-blown suit, tie and everything making all of this seem that much more serious. "My name is

Mister Pillay." When he saw Max instinctively look at the name of the door, he went on. "I'm the Acting Principal of this school."

Acting, thought Max, *which most likely makes him the Deputy Principal in earnest. Either way, this wasn't good.* "Am I in trouble?"

"Well, Max," started Mrs. Turner, "I'll have you know—"

Mr. Pillay cut her off. "Yes, you are, Mister McKay. Yes, you are." Max noted the mispronunciation of surname.

"For what?" asked Max, gingerly.

"For what?" Mr. Pillay took a file off of Mrs. Turner's desk who didn't seem to want to be here at all. "Mister McKay, I seem to notice quite a few absences on your file."

"That was earlier in the month. I've been coming to school since Missus Turner called me to her office."

"Is that so?" Mister Pillay dismissed the improvement in his behaviour and went on. "Well, that would be all well and good except that all those absences took place within your first two weeks here. You see, to me that shows that you didn't have any interest in learning here at all."

"That's not true."

"Are you arguing with me, young man?" The look he gave Max was fierce.

Max didn't like this. "I was just trying to explain that—"

"Explain what? Why you missed your Control Test Assessment?"

"I've made up for that too."

"Oh, have you now." This wasn't a question on Mr. Pillay's part.

"Mister Pillay," said Mrs. Turner, jumping in. "If you look at Mister McKay's See-Tee-Ay results," she said pronouncing his surname perfectly, "I think you'll find that he's more than proven that his potential—"

"I don't care about potential, Missus Turner. I don't care that he's trying to improve *now* after he's caused the damage that he has. I care about protecting the reputation of this school. I care about keeping children in line. So, that maybe, just maybe, they grow up to be decent human beings."

Max took in everything that transpired since he'd spoken. First of all, did Mrs. Turner just *support* him? It must have been because of the C.T.A. test. Which begged the question: was it *that* good? Wow. But now, this bugger, he was ignoring all that and seemed intent on punishing him. So, what now, was he going to go to detention for the rest of the year?

"Mister Pillay," said Mrs. Turner, "before you make any final decisions—"

"I've already made my final decision, Missus Turner." He turned to Max. "Mister McKay," he said clearly not caring to pronounce his surname properly, "you have been expelled from Harbour High. From this day forth, you are not to set foot in this school, do you understand?"

Max was stunned. That did not just happen. This had to be a mistake. But the look on his face was unmistakable. "Sir, can't I get a second chance?"

He shook his head before Max had even finished speaking. "I'm sorry, young man. But discipline cases like yours cannot be taken lightly. I'm sorry, but you're expelled." Since there was nothing more to say, Mr. Pillay turned for the door and started to leave before Mrs. Turner stood up to protest.

"Mister Pillay, I must protest." The Acting Principal stopped and turned to look at her. "This young man deserves a chance to prove himself."

Mr. Pillay sighed, as if he were tired of this life he was living. "Missus Turner, when I had your job," he said pointing at the old sign on the door, "my job was to make sure that the School Principal *didn't* come down here. *My job* was to make sure children stayed in line so that things like this *didn't* happen."

Mrs. Turner gave him a shocked look. "Are you saying that I didn't do my job?"

"While I'd prefer not to have this discussion in front of a boy, but since he is *no longer* a student; you keep persisting and I *don't* want to have any further discussion on the matter, I'll tell you the truth right now. You're not a bad teacher. You're not even a bad Head of Department. You're good at your job, sincerely. But you seem to have trouble looking after the school's wellbeing *alongside* those of the students. Expelling students gives me just as little joy as discipline cases like this one," he said pointing at Max. "Missus Turner, I need you looking at the whole picture, not just the one in front of you." Having said his peace, Mr. Pillay finally left.

Mrs. Turner eventually closed her mouth and sat down. While she had been getting a little discipline of her own, Max had been listening to every word. "That guy is such a—" But Max simply put a hand up to stop her. "Max, I'm so sorry."

Max was as calm as could be. "Don't be sorry, Missus Turner. I tried to turn things around, but it was too little too late."

"Too little, too late? Don't listen to him. He was being a—" This was clearly not Mrs. Turner's day as yet another sentence of hers was cut short, once again by Max's hand.

"I don't *want* to listen to him, ma'am but he's not wrong. And all I keep thinking is that if *I* had paid just as much attention to the big picture, then I wouldn't be where I am." Max wasn't just speaking words. While he had also wanted to call Mr. Pillay all the words that Mrs. Turner wanted to call him, Max realized that Mr. Pillay wasn't a bad guy. He'd seen bad guys, like Moodswing: people who truly didn't care about other people. Mr. Pillay was different. Yes, his demeanour was aggressive, but where he was coming from, was a righteous place. He wanted to make society better, not worse.

Something occurred to Max that hadn't occurred to him before. "What about my mother? Surely you guys need to tell her that I'm being expelled." *Yes*, thought Max, *exactly! You can't just expel me without informing my parent. Surely, she had a right to know.*

Mrs. Turner confirmed this. "You're right, Max." But before Max could get on the horn to the cavalry, Mrs.

Turner continued. "When a child is expelled, the parents or parent not only need to be informed but have a right to motivate why they should stay. In normal circumstances, your C.T.A. marks alone would have given your mother a leg to stand on and overrule the expulsion."

"*Normal* circumstances? What's not normal about *these* circumstances?"

Mrs. Turner took a deep breath before answering. "Your mother agreed with Mister Pillay to expel you."

*

While Max had been surprisingly Zen about his expulsion, hearing that his mother was in on it had crippled him. When he came out of Mrs. Turner's office, he found Lisa waiting for him. She saw the sadness in his eyes and asked what was wrong at which point, Max told her everything that had transpired. Max had never been so happy for someone to *not* do what he wanted them to do. He was glad Lisa was here.

As they made their way through school on their way out, they ran into Thompson who failed to immediately see that Max wasn't in the mood. "Hey man, just the man I was looking for. I've come up with a plan for your comeback."

This was the last thing that Max needed to hear. All it did was remind him of how everything good about the weekend had suddenly come crashing down on him. The weekend had been good for more reasons than just spending it with Lisa. Tar had done him a solid and used his clout to adjust his banishing from 'town' to just 'the scene'. But Max knew that, deep down, Tar had every expectation to see him racing again. But that didn't matter. None of it mattered. But Thompson didn't know that yet.

"So, here's what I was thinking. So, what if you lay low for a couple of months. Say, until the end of the year. And then, early next year, you make a return and immediately challenge Moodswing with the stipulation being the overturning of your banishing versus *him* being banished? It's a good one, huh?"

It was Lisa who answered, first with a face. "Argh, so juvenile." She then explained what happened and didn't leave out the part about his mother.

411

"Your own mom did that? Jeez, that's hectic."

"Yeah it is," agreed Max. "Look, I'm not thinking about the scene right now because I need to go and talk to her. I need to go and see her, and I need to find out what the hell is going in my life right now." Thompson nodded.

"I'll go with you," said Lisa. And with that, they were off, with Max perhaps leaving the school for the last time.

CHAPTER TWENTY-SIX
HOUSE MCKAY

When Lisa said that she'd go with Max to see his mother, it had been on a whim. She'd said it because she wanted to support her boyfriend. She wanted to be there for him. But now that they were there in the sitting room of Max's house, waiting for his mother to come home, she didn't know if this was the place for her.

Knowing that his mother tended to come home late at night, Max had specifically called her and asked her to come home early. The conversation had been quick. Max told Lisa that his mother said that she was already on her way and that he suspected that she knew exactly what he wanted to speak to her about.

As they waited, Lisa looked at her man, worried about him. She'd never seen him look like this. His eyes were puffy like he'd been crying even though she hadn't seen a single tear. His voice was nasally like his nose was blocked, again, symptoms of someone who had been crying. Yet, no tears. He must have been very upset but fighting tooth and nail not to show it. But part of her wished that he would, just so he could get it out of his system.

When Mrs. McKay showed up, there had been an awkward moment as Mrs. McKay sized up this stranger in her house. She clearly didn't know that Max had a girlfriend. She recovered quickly and extended a hand, introducing herself while giving her son an evil eye for not doing the introductions himself.

"Lisa, could you excuse us. I need to talk to my son."

Lisa graciously excused herself and went to the veranda and closed the door behind her, leaving Max and his Mom in something of a stand-off as they were both standing there looking at each other. She had no idea that she would be able to hear their whole conversation through the door. She didn't intend to, but she needed to know what terrible fate waited for Max. So, she put her ear to the door and listened.

"So why, Ma? Why did you do it?"

Mrs. McKay didn't answer immediately. From her next words, Lisa deduced that she had given him a hard look. "Careful of your tone, Maximillian." Lisa wanted to smile at hearing Max's full name but not when it was said like that.

"Ma, you got me kicked out of school and you're worried about my tone?" Lisa found herself proud of Max. Despite being really upset, he was managing to keep from letting his emotions explode out on his mother. She hated people who disrespected their parents – particularly their mothers – by shouting at them.

"First of all, *I* didn't get you kicked out of school. You did that all by yourself. Second of all, you have the nerve to accuse me of anything when you basically disobeyed me from day *one!?*"

"What are you talking about?"

What was she talking about?

"I'm talking about you street racing, Max. You weren't here one week and already you were off in the middle of the night participating in illegal activities."

Lisa had to cover her mouth to keep from making a sound. She couldn't believe it. She couldn't believe that Max's mother found out about him racing.

However, Max denied it, lying straight to his mother's face. "I don't know what you're talking about."

"Hayi uyayisa maan," said Mrs. McKay. Lisa rolled her eyes. While she understood her country's vernacular languages – as did most Caucasians, Indians and Coloureds on Azania island, admittedly her Zulu wasn't up to scratch. But she understood it better than she spoke it. Mrs. McKay continued in Zulu. "Well you might not know anything about it, but the police do."

"Bathini amaphoyisa?" said Max asking what the police were saying. While Max's Zulu was good, she could detect that his fluency had taken a knock possibly during his time in Australia.

"They're suspecting you of illegal street racing. What else?"

"So, all this over something there isn't even proof of?" Lisa could imagine Max putting his arms in the air out of frustration.

Mrs. McKay broke back into English. "They don't need proof, Max. They just need to suspect you." Max must have looked as confused as Lisa because Mrs. McKay went on. "Max, you're already suspected of street racing in Australia. You may not have a record, but these things build up."

"And what does this have to do with school?"

"The school agreed to investigate alongside the police so when they said the alternative was expulsion, I took it. Because while the police would be hard-pressed to find any evidence; with the school watching you like a hawk, possibly doing who knows what to hear what you say to your friends, they were bound to find something out."

Max must have been stuck because he didn't say anything for a while. Lisa heard the faint sound of the couch squeaking and assumed that Max had moved back to it. When it squeaked again, she knew that Mrs. McKay must have joined him. When they spoke again, they were back to Zulu.

"Max, I care about you. I always have. I was never going to let you get arrested that's why I got you out of there." She sighed. "Max, I'm sending you off the island, somewhere where the police are not as efficient as these Metro Police." Lisa had to cover her mouth again, this time tears welling in her eyes as well.

Max sounded so sad when he answered. "You're sending me away again? Like you did when you sent me to live with Dad?"

"I'm not sending you back to Australia. You'd face the same problem there. I'm sending you to the mainland. There's a school, a boarding school in the middle of Kay-Zed-En where you won't get into so much trouble." She tried to ease the tension by chuckling. "You should be honoured for the acceptance. It was your See-Tee-Ay marks that did most of the talking."

Now Max was crying. "But Ma, I like it here. I have friends, here."

"I know you do son but now you have to leave them behind." Max must have shaken his head. "Max, Max, listen to me. Listen to me. You have to leave if you're going to have a future."

"No." But Lisa had heard enough. She opened the door and saw Max with his head on his mother's chest, eyes red, cheeks wet. "Lisa," he said.

"Max, I don—"

"Lisa, I don't want to leave you."

"I don't want you to go either," said Lisa who looked at his mother who in turn, eyed her suspiciously. But Lisa continued. "But I think you should go."

Mrs. McKay, who went from giving her a hard look for listening in on their conversation to being relieved for her support, spoke softly to her son. "Listen to your girlfriend. It looks like you picked a smart one." They shared a smile.

Max had had more of a cry before finally relenting and giving in to the consensus. It had been a long tearful goodbye for Max and his mother, but they had decided that it would be best if he left that night. Lisa had told Max that she would go with him to the airport. When the maxi taxi that his mother had called arrived, Max smiled when he saw the driver.

"Hello my friend."

"Hello Joseph Sibusiso." Max explained how he knew the driver as he put his bag in the boot and they climbed in the back seat.

"I know what you are thinking, my friend," said Joseph Sibusiso as they started their journey. "What are the chances? Well when I heard this address on the dispatch, I had to come I..." Joseph Sibusiso had continued to talk, clearly a talkative driver. It helped as it seemed to distract Max better than Lisa had managed to.

Max had only taken one bag – apparently exactly the same amount of clothes that he had brought with him. He joked that it ended up being some kind foreshadowing as he'd stayed just long enough to only need the amount of clothes he'd brought. When they got to the airport, Lisa walked him all the way to the edge of the terminal and suddenly it was time to say goodbye.

"I'm not sure what to say, Max."

"Well I think we've been through so much that words won't encompass everything we want to say to each other right now."

"Yeah," said Lisa, chuckling. "We really have been through the most, haven't we?" They laughed. "Will you send me a postcard?"

"A postcard?" He scoffed. "I'm going to visit you as soon as I can."

Lisa wanted to tell him that it would be too dangerous, but she resisted and simply smiled. "I'd like that." Lisa looked at the board and saw that it was past time for him to board and surely his plane had started boarding already. "Any last words?"

"Yeah. Don't be afraid to do what you really want to do, Lisa. Ignite the passion that fuels you."

Lisa lifted her eyebrows one last time. "Colourful words."

"Meaningful words." He smiled that smile she loved. "Goodbye Lisa."

Tears welled in her eyes. "Goodbye Max." Their lips then met one last time before it all came to an end. Then he was gone. She knew right then as she watched him leave that nothing would be the same again. He hadn't just etched a part of himself in her soul... he'd etched a part of himself in the soul of this city.

ABOUT THE AUTHOR

Bernard Bayede was born Sphu T. Kubheka in the city of Durban in the beautiful province of Kwa-Zulu Natal, South Africa. Born to Thabo and Nompumelelo, Bayede enjoys spending time with family that includes his fiancé, Juliet Mentoor as well as his younger sister, Naledi as well as watching motorsport. He also has an undying love for karate and construction.

Learn more about the author at: kubhekastories.co.za

ALSO BY THE AUTHOR

If you enjoyed *Ignighted*, then you should also try out
Bernard Bayede's debut book: *The Bowman's Apprentice
and Other Stories*. As a collection of short stories from

very different genres, Bayede gives you something for everyone.

Tales

of the

Planet of the

Rings

Volume 1

Planet of the Rings Vol. 1 is a gothic fantasy story that blends Bernard Bayede's growing mastery over the art of the short story with the epic nature of the fantasy genre. Taking place in a world far from ours, this story follows multiple characters as they go on individual journeys that brings them all face to face with supernatural forces and certain death!

www.ingramcontent.com/pod-product-compliance
Lightning Source LLC
Chambersburg PA
CBHW051540250626
47157CB00001B/119